D1130363

The Green Room

Also by Deborah Turrell Atkinson
Primitive Secrets

The Green Room

Mai Huli 'Oe I Kōkua O Ke Kai
Respect the Ocean

Deborah Turrell Atkinson

Poisoned Pen Press

Library of Congress Catalog Card Number: 2005925399

ISBN: 1-59058-198-9   Hardcover

Poisoned Pen Press
6962 E. First Ave., Ste. 103
Scottsdale, AZ 85251
www.poisonedpenpress.com
info@poisonedpenpress.com

Printed in the United States of America

This book is dedicated to Rob, Egen, and Andrew with my love.

Acknowledgments

Sitting in front of the blank computer screen may be a solitary activity, but seeking accuracy in a mystery requires a lot of help. I'd like to thank my friends and colleagues for their expertise. Attorneys Claudia Turrell and Patty NaPier helped Storm with her budding law career. Kellen Chong and Andrew Atkinson helped me find the North Shore neighborhoods where guys like Marty Barstow and Steve O'Reilly might live while they organized their contest. (We also checked out a few good surf breaks.) Austin Yeargan, M.D., and Burt Moritz, M.D., shared their North Shore surfing experiences, including stories of the feared caves, though I made up the one Storm discovers. Many thanks go to Karen Huffman, Michael Chapman, Michelle Calabro Hubbard, Lisa Pavel Cohen, and Honey Pavel for their assistance with the developing manuscript. Mahalo to the kind and erudite Dr. Kekuni Blaisdell for his help with the Hawaiian expression in the front of the book.

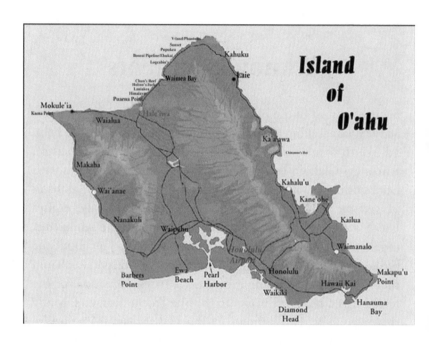

Island
of
O'ahu

V-land/Phantums
Sunset
Pupukea
Bonzai Pipeline/Ehukai
Log cabin's
Kahuku
Chun's Reef
Haleiwa's/Jocko
Laniakea
Himalayas
Waimea Bay
Laie
Puaena Point
Mokule'ia
Hale'iwa
Kaena Point
Waialua
Ka'a'awa
Chinaman's Hat
Makaha
Kahalu'u
Wai'anae
Kane'ohe
Kailua
Nanakuli
Waipahu
Waimanalo
Honolulu Airport
Barbers
Point
Ewa
Beach
Pearl
Harbor
Honolulu
Makapu'u
Point
Hawaii Kai
Waikiki
Diamond
Head
Hanauma
Bay

Chapter One

Storm Kayama rearranged books on the newly varnished shelves. The place was looking good. Welcoming. Cozy, even. Now all she needed was a client or ten, preferably before the rent was due next month.

Just last week, she and Ian Hamlin opened an office together in a small converted house, only about a mile from Miles Hamasaki's former high-rise, high-rent law firm in downtown Honolulu. Though Hamlin had been fairly well established before Miles Hamasaki's death, Storm had been a mere law clerk for her beloved Uncle Miles. He'd died before she had a chance to tell him she'd passed the bar.

Storm had never imagined she'd be setting up her own offices without her mentor's guidance. Hamlin had told her he'd handle the big expenses until she had a steady income, but she wanted to avoid that situation. It was kind of him, but Storm was already testing new waters in their relationship, which was built on love, lust, and a common profession—in ever-shifting priorities.

She was on her own, which was how she preferred to work. But her thirtieth birthday loomed, her income was inconsistent at best, and most of her friends had regular salaries and growing families.

She tried to shove financial concerns to the back of her fretting mind. It's a Friday in mid-January, she told herself, people are recovering from the holidays. Of course the phone wasn't ringing. Who wants to start the New Year considering legal problems?

She pushed a wiry lock of mahogany hair back into her French braid, went back to the rosewood desk she'd inherited from Hamasaki, and picked up the call list for the Public Defender's office, to which she'd recently added her name. According to a handful of people who should know, the PD's office would start sending clients. And Honolulu, despite a population of around 300,000 people, was a small town where the coconut wireless operated faster than certified news sources. A person's reputation was built by word of mouth, and Storm's friends, Hamlin especially, assured her that with her family network and heritage, she'd be turning away clients before too long. Storm sighed. She could also starve before too long.

If only Uncle Miles were here, to share stories about how he set up his practice, which had been one of the most successful in the state. She missed him deeply.

Storm shook off her dark thoughts and turned up the Bose Wave radio, an office-warming gift from the Hamasaki family. "High surf advisory for the North and West shores of O'ahu, Maui, and the Big Island. Semi-finals for the second of three pearls in the crown of one of the ASP's most important contests has been postponed until Sunday, due to services for surfer Ken Matsumoto, who died of head injuries last week at Pipeline. Top-ranked competitor on the world pro-surfing circuit, Matsumoto's loss is a real tragedy for the Association of Surfing Professionals."

The loud ring of the phone startled her. It was Grace Nishiki, Storm's and Hamlin's shared secretary. "You've got a call on line two. It's a client, kiddo, someone who knows your cousin." Her excited voice dropped in volume, though they were on Storm's private line. "Is he anything like his name?"

Nahoa, the daring one. Wow, a blast from the past. It had been eighteen years since she'd seen him.

"I suppose so," Storm said. "I heard he's a professional surfer now."

Grace disconnected and Storm took a deep breath before she picked up the outside line. "Storm Kayama speaking."

"My name is Stephanie Barstow. Could we come see you? I—I need some advice about my husband."

"How's tomorrow at nine?" Storm said.

"Do you have any time this afternoon? We're driving back to the North Shore tonight."

"Uh, yes, I could do that." Her mind raced. She could tear home, shower off the smell of furniture polish, perspiration, and dust, put on a suit, and tame her unruly hair in an hour. "How about—"

"We'll be there in fifteen minutes," Stephanie Barstow said.

Storm looked down at the faded and spotty T-shirt she wore over a baggy old pair of board shorts. "Okay." She spoke to a dial tone.

Grace poked her head through the office door about a minute later. And Storm could only surmise that it was the expression on her face that caused Grace to plant her hands on her wide hips and shake her head from side to side. It couldn't have been the hole in her Eddie Aikau Big Wave Invitational T-shirt, could it?

"Good thing it's only your cousin coming," Grace said.

"It's a friend of his. Some woman who needs a divorce."

"Oh dear." Grace wagged her head again.

"I was cleaning." Storm planted her chin in her hand and eyed Grace's voluminous muʻumuʻu. No way. That yellow would make her look like a candidate for a liver transplant. It didn't do much for Grace, either, except set off the huge yellow double hibiscus she wore in her hair.

Hamlin, on his way down the corridor to his office, passed by the door. He wore a pressed blue dress shirt, with the long sleeves rolled to just above his wrists, and creased wool gabardine slacks. Woven leather loafers, no socks. Storm eyed him; she knew how she could get his clothes off. It would take five minutes. Well, to do it right, it would take twenty.

Grace stood, hands on hips, in the hallway. One eyebrow was climbing. "What's so funny?"

Storm met Grace's narrowing eyes with wide-eyed innocence. "Oh, nothing. Stephanie Barstow is going to have to accept her lawyer in cleaning clothes."

"Did I miss a joke?" Hamlin came back to Storm's office door. Grace rolled her eyes and wandered off.

"Uh, no. Looks like I've got a client," Storm said.

"Hey, that's good."

"But I'm in grubs. I cleaned cupboards today."

Hamlin shrugged. "This a referral from the PD's office? Most crackheads don't do wardrobe critiques."

"No, it's someone who knows my cousin."

"He's family, right? He'll understand."

He sauntered down the corridor to his office, missing the exasperated look Storm gave him. She shut the door, and slid her bare feet into the rubber slippers that were positioned on the pretty, but fake, Chinese rug. Costco had had a whole bin of them on sale and she'd just laid it on the newly-finished hardwood floor. At least her office looked decent.

She dashed into the bathroom that adjoined her office, lathered her face from a bottle of Dial antiseptic Softsoap, and promised her skin she'd treat it gently tonight. Sometimes she knew she was lucky to have the olive-toned, forgiving skin of her Hawaiian mother and Japanese father.

Storm found a hairbrush in the bottom of her backpack and redid the French braid that kept her wavy hair under control. She had applied mascara to the eyelashes of one eye when someone knocked on the door. It was a sober tap, definitely not Grace or Hamlin, who wouldn't have bothered knocking.

Storm opened the door. "Come in." She opened her mouth to explain her appearance, but stopped.

Stephanie Barstow looked too preoccupied to care. Storm's first impression was that Stephanie's concerns probably weren't financial. She was dressed casually, but with good taste, in Capri slacks and expensive, strappy sandals, and Storm was pretty sure the Kate Spade handbag she carried wasn't a Seoul knockoff.

Stephanie appeared to be in her late thirties, and had a mixture of Asian and Hawaiian blood similar to Storm's own. Except for the worry lines etched between and around her eyes, she was drop-dead gorgeous.

A very tan young man, around nineteen or twenty, took Stephanie's elbow and guided her to one of the two chairs facing Storm's desk. Storm could see his mother's features in his face, but he had the rounder eyes and longer, narrower nose of a Caucasian.

Stephanie gave the boy's arm a gentle pat. "This is my son, Ben. We moved back to Hawai'i about a year ago."

"You're from here?"

Stephanie nodded and twisted her fingers together. "Yes, and it's good to be home."

"Is your husband here in the islands?"

Ben glanced at his mother, who kept her eyes on Storm. "No," Stephanie said, and she allowed relief to show in her voice.

"But he will be soon," Ben added. Stephanie chewed on her lower lip, but didn't look his way. "He will, Mom."

She ignored her son's comment. "Marty and I separated about a year and a half ago, and he doesn't want a divorce." Her eyes flicked to her son, who slumped in his chair and picked at a callous on his thumb.

Storm let a few moments pass. Miles had taught her that people try to fill silent gaps. Stephanie, however, dug in her purse, extracted a tissue, and blotted her lipstick.

"And how can I help you?" Storm asked.

Stephanie sighed deeply. "I need to finalize things. It's not a marriage any more."

Storm looked at Ben, who let his gaze slip past hers before sliding down further in his seat. "Is he going to be angry about this?"

"Yes," Stephanie said softly. "He's going to fight it."

"He knows where you are, right?"

"He knows we're in Hawai'i," Stephanie said.

"What does your husband do, Mrs. Barstow?"

"Call me Stephanie, okay? He's a commercial real estate developer in California." She sighed. "For years, we worked together in the family business. I helped him get it started."

"What was your role?" Storm knew that Barstow's version of her involvement in the business could be the polar opposite of what she heard now. Uncle Miles had hated divorce cases. He'd refused to do them because he claimed everyone lost. Someday, when she could afford rent and groceries, she would, too.

"I ran the office side of things. Made follow-up phone calls, set appointments, collected bills. Sometimes, when Marty had to be two places at once, I'd do some of the negotiations." Stephanie looked at her hands. "I stopped a little over two years ago."

"What happened?"

"He got moody and secretive. It got worse and worse."

"Are you afraid of him physically?" Storm asked.

Stephanie shot another glance toward her son. "I…well, he's not here." She took a shaky breath and tore little pieces off the tissue she'd twisted in her fingers.

Storm turned to Ben. "Are you over eighteen?"

"I'm nineteen. I was seventeen when we moved out, and Dad was pretty upset."

Storm turned to Stephanie. "He's paying support now?"

"No, I've been managing a restaurant in Haleiwa." Her eyes darkened with emotion. "Marty told me if I divorced him, I'd never get a penny."

"How long did you work with him?" Storm asked.

"Almost twenty years. We set up Barstow Developments in the mid-eighties, and we did pretty good." She sighed. "But a couple of years ago, Marty stopped telling me things, what investments he made, what people he was doing business with. About three years ago, I found a bank statement for an account I didn't know about. It was for more than four hundred thousand dollars." Stephanie squeezed one hand in the other until her knuckles were white. "When I asked about it, he screamed at me to stay out of his business. And after that, he…he got worse."

Storm had heard other lawyers rant about difficulties evaluating a spouse's financial worth, and hoped Stephanie's case wasn't going to be one of these. "Have you been signing tax returns?" Storm asked.

"Yes."

"Do you think he's correctly reporting his income?"

Stephanie shook her head and kept her eyes on her hands.

Storm winced, though she'd expected as much. "The IRS hates it when that happens. I'll need your past tax returns, and any current information about his business you can find. Get me the names of clients, partners, people on the payroll, and jobs he's done in the past five years."

Stephanie chewed on her lower lip. "I'll try. I know some people I can call, but some of them might tell him I asked questions."

"I'll call the ones you're worried about. Just get me the names," Storm said. "Since you've been here for a year, we'll file in Hawai'i, though California divorce laws are similar to ours. Unless the spouses agree otherwise, property is usually divided fairly equally." Storm went over the personal information she required, what steps she would take on their behalf, and explained her rates.

"Um, Ms. Kayama? Can you protect my bank accounts here in the islands?"

"Is his name on them? Are they joint accounts?"

"No. But he might want to find out what I've saved." Stephanie tore the tissue into smaller pieces. She didn't notice the little scraps fall to the carpet.

Why would a wealthy developer want to investigate a North Shore restaurant manager's bank accounts, Storm wondered. Unless the guy was a total power freak.

"If his name isn't on them, he shouldn't have any access to them. You might want to alert your bank to the possibility of unauthorized inquiries, though. Have them contact you—and me—if someone attempts to get information about the accounts."

There was a chance the guy was so controlling that he couldn't stand the idea his wife was making a living independent of him.

Then again, the restaurant managers Storm knew, and she had a friend who ran a local Zippy's, didn't have the Neiman Marcus wardrobe Stephanie wore. She didn't look like she'd just dressed up for this appointment, either. Something to keep in mind, Storm told herself.

"Thank you, Ms. Kayama. I'll work on getting what you need," Stephanie said, and stood up.

"Call me Storm. It's easier." She offered her hand first to Stephanie, then to Ben.

They headed toward the door, and Ben turned back. "Do you surf?"

"Just small waves. Not anything like Nahoa. How about you?" Storm didn't need to ask the question, she could tell by the light in his eyes.

"I grew up surfing in California. But it's not the same as here. Were you there?" If his eyes hadn't dropped to her shirt front, she wouldn't have known what he was talking about.

"No, a friend gave this to me. His cousin was in one of the meets."

"The Eddie Aikau Big Wave Invitational? You know somebody who did that? Is he still around?"

"Sure, he runs a dive shop on Maui."

"Cool." Ben paused. "Hey, I'm going to be in a meet this weekend with Nahoa. You wanna come out?"

"You're in the Sunset Triple Pro? I just heard about it on the radio." Storm did a quick reevaluation of Ben. This guy was more than a wannabe. The Sunset Triple Pro was by invitation only. "Are you seeded?"

Ben shrugged. "Fourth or fifth, since Ken died." His shoulders sagged a little.

"You knew him?"

"Not well. He was older than I am, better established. Makes you think."

"Yeah, I'll bet. Sure, I'd love to see the meet."

Stephanie's expression had become even more worried during this exchange. "Call me if you come out," Ben said.

"I will," Storm promised, and saw them out of her office.

No wonder Stephanie looked troubled. She had a nasty ex and her only son wanted to compete in the waves that had killed his competitor.

Storm remembered the forecast for rising surf. Hadn't the announcer mentioned waves in the twelve to fifteen foot range? In the Asian-Polynesian tradition of downplaying grandness, waves in Hawai'i are measured from the back. Consequently, when the weather service reports that waves are "breaking three to five," experienced islanders know that the face of the wave approaches twice that.

Twelve to fifteen foot waves would be monsters, but still not the biggest of the big-time waves. Certain surf meets weren't even held until the waves were in the twenty to twenty-five foot range. Storm knew that surfers at Pe'ahi, on Maui, had to use jet skis to get past the break zone, then catch the liquid mountains that Mother Nature devised with her winter storms. The Eddie Aikau Big Wave Invitational not only didn't take place until the waves were at least twenty feet, the contest required surfers to paddle themselves.

She never, ever wanted to be in waves that big. But it would be awesome to watch: just to feel the ground tremble under the crashing force of those rushing walls of water would be a thrill. Big wave surfers like Nahoa would be flocking to Haleiwa in droves, as if the weather report were a party invitation instead of a warning. There are a handful of places on earth where the ocean's huge waves curl in a form perfect enough to hurtle a steel-nerved athlete on the ride of a lifetime. From November to February, the north shores of the Hawaiian Islands beckon to surfers the way Everest calls to climbers.

She'd see if Hamlin would go with her. Maybe her best friend Leila and her eleven-year-old son, Robbie, would come along, too. It would be a weekend they'd talk about for months.

Chapter Two

Steve O'Reilly squinted against the oblique rays of the rising sun and hoisted his board shorts over his skinny ass to his growing waistline. The sun was just peeking over the horizon, filtering through the briny mists that blew in from the surf a few hundred yards off shore. Six forty-five and "dawn patrol" was already out, catching the glassy waves before the wind kicked up. These were the local men and women—schoolteachers, firemen, shop owners, and waiters who wanted to catch some rides before they had to be at their jobs. They probably also wanted to avoid the more aggressive crowd that rose later, who at this hour were still replenishing the energy depleted by their late partying. These were the characters of legend, the glittering barracuda that lived on the edge, both day and night.

And these were the people O'Reilly sought. In their so-low trunks, tattoos, and tiny thong bikinis, they were the photogenic icons that reminded him of the days when he was a sports announcer for a prestigious San Diego TV station. Before he had the thing with Alicia, that is. The producer tolerated a lot, including an indulgence in raves and Ecstasy. But not an affair with his younger wife.

That was seven years ago, when O'Reilly was a mere thirty-five, and he'd been on a slow but steady slide ever since. Going the same direction as his gut and thinning hair: down, down.

But life was going to change with this gig. This sport was hot, daring, and glamorous like no other professional sport. It was just coming into its own with a growing media response. Sponsors were beginning to offer huge money, and were fresh with altruism, social and environmental platitudes. Plus, his old fraternity buddy, Marty Barstow, had been a lifeguard and semi-famous surfer here some years ago. Marty still had contacts, still knew whose palms to cross for the permits and "help" required for surf contests. This was going to be big, and he wasn't just talking wave size. There were millions to be made, and compared to sports that took place in arenas, not as expensive to pull off.

O'Reilly checked his watch. In about a half hour, the aspiring pros would be rolling out of bed and into the water. Of course, the media representative he was meeting was late, even when O'Reilly had carefully explained to the doofus how to find Himalayas.

Gordon never had been known for punctuality, and he was supposed to be here at seven. It was hard to know which break was named what, and Mainlanders seemed to only remember Pipeline or Sunset. Still, O'Reilly had explained all this, told him where to park and the whole deal.

Maybe a little of what was bugging O'Reilly this morning was that Barstow had called yesterday from California, when he was supposed to be on a flight here. Marty said he was hot to make this happen, but he maintained he couldn't come until this afternoon. O'Reilly brooded on this transgression. One of Barstow's jobs was to line up sponsors, and it was a critical role.

So what if he had some big shopping center contract to sign off on, he's still gotta show me this deal is important to him. O'Reilly hadn't seen much of Marty in the last ten years, but had heard his old friend was doing well and had all kinds of contacts on the West Coast and Hawai'i. And he was certain Barstow's competitive nature wouldn't have changed, but he wondered if he should have spent some time with the guy before asking him to come on board. Just to make sure they still saw eye to eye.

It didn't help O'Reilly's mood that the number one seeded kid for the Sunset Triple Pro, Nahoa some-weird-Hawaiian-last-name, didn't show up for their quasi-appointment last night, either. O'Reilly had planned to invite him to the meeting this morning, have him meet Gordon, but Nahoa obviously couldn't be bothered. What was on these people's minds, anyway? The surfer, who was built like a Roman god, would make quite an impression on TV. O'Reilly planned to use him as a liaison to the surfer community—the Hawaiian "voice," so to speak. He knew the kid could talk, deal with the media. He'd seen him do it.

But the goof was apparently too provincial to realize how this would help him get endorsements. Big ones, like the credit card and cell phone companies, who could offer seven figures.

To make matters worse, the Hawaiian's girlfriend, a six-foot blonde with a Frappuccino tan and eyes the deep blue of Hanauma Bay, wouldn't even give O'Reilly a hint as to where her squeeze was. Or a smile to go with the hint. That hurt.

O'Reilly took a deep breath and tried to concentrate on the positive. Here he was, on one of the most beautiful beaches in the world, and a big swell was on the way. It was January, when winter storms pounded Hawai'i's North Shore and ushered in waves that approached fifty, sometimes sixty feet. It was pretty damn hard to measure walls of water the size of a condominium, traveling at the speed of an F-16. Perfect for the Tow-In Contest he and Barstow had planned.

Even better, surfer Ken Matsumoto's death had amped up the media attention for these events. It was crazy how more people than ever clamored for places in the lineups for the big meets. Yup, the money was increasing, the surf was rising, he had the media contract in hand, and that dweeb from KZXM TV was finally stumbling down the beach in his Ferragamos.

Chapter Three

"Congratulations on your client." Hamlin held up his glass of cabernet.

Storm touched his glass with hers. "It's a divorce situation, maybe even a hostile one, but I'll take it."

"What's your read on it?"

"I can't tell if the mom and son are trying to protect each other, or if they're at odds, but I know they're not telling me the whole story yet."

"You'll figure it out."

"I hope so." Storm grinned at him. "I've got a plan that will help me get to know them better. Ben is in that surf meet this Sunday, the Sunset Triple Pro. He invited us to watch."

Hamlin's eyebrows rose with interest. "That would be fun. What time would we need to leave?"

"Maybe tomorrow around ten? I asked Leila and Robbie to come, too. Brian has to work." Leila's boyfriend Brian was a Honolulu police detective, and he was involved in a trying case that had been going on for a few weeks.

"Where would we stay?"

"Aunt Maile and Uncle Keone have friends with a cottage at Laniakea. They've offered to let us use it." Storm knew Hamlin thought she was related to half the population in the islands, which was a concept she didn't discourage. He enjoyed her aunt and uncle, who lived on the Big Island, and had raised Storm until she moved into Miles Hamasaki's household. Both she and Hamlin knew that the six degrees of separation people talked about on the Mainland shrank to one or two degrees in Hawai'i.

"Are your aunt and uncle coming?" Hamlin asked.

"No, they're going to a baby lu'au."

Hamlin took a sip of his wine and Storm knew he was mentally reviewing his obligations for the weekend. "I'd love to see one of those meets. What's the surf prediction?"

"Big and rising."

"Yeah?" he said, and Storm knew she had him. Hamlin wasn't a surfer, but he had been an All-American runner in college and was still a fan of most active sports, especially if he could see the event live.

Storm slipped off her shoe and ran her bare foot up his trousered leg. "Want to start our wild weekend at my place?"

His green eyes sparked candlelight from across the table and the corners of his mouth curled up beneath his bushy moustache.

⚬〰〰⚬ ⚬〰〰⚬ ⚬〰〰⚬

The girl's brown knuckles glowed white against the bucking gunnels of the *wa'a* and her short, wavy black hair flopped in time with her swooping stomach. Why had she volunteered to sit in the front, anyway, where she could see the prow climb vertically against the wall of blue, blue water, so angry she thought the canoe would be hurtled like a flimsy spear halfway to the center of the earth?

Weren't they too far from shore? It seemed like the wind, which whipped the crest of each wave into her face with the blast of a fire hose, was pushing them farther down the coastline. Why didn't Uncle Bert turn around now? They were certainly out far enough to catch some waves. That was the plan, wasn't it?

She could see right through the adults' efforts. What did they think, she was stupid? A year ago, she would have killed for this adventure, but now, with the whole neighborhood trying to console her, she would rather have slipped off alone to her secret spot in the sugar cane fields. She would puff stolen cigarettes and try to sort out her mother's death. Instead, she'd let her best friend Pua, who had seemed genuinely excited about the idea, talk her into canoe surfing.

The boat plowed through a wave, but the next crest was hidden behind the first, and the boat hit it head on, instead of on the quarter. Storm catapulted from her seat and banged her knees against the bow. Just as she scrambled back to her place, the boat rocketed down the face of another wave.

"Try bail!" shouted Uncle Bert. He dug with the paddle and gasped with exertion.

Storm grabbed the plastic bucket as it floated by at mid-calf level, though she knew it wouldn't help. Her arms and shoulders ached with the effort, but she couldn't keep up with the water coming over the gunwales. The canoe was foundering, no longer cutting through the water.

Pua looked back over her shoulder, her mouth a gaping chasm as she shouted, "Look out!"

"Jump!" Uncle Bert's voice was ragged and choked-sounding.

Storm didn't jump; she was launched. And this time, Hamlin woke her up.

"Storm, you're having a nightmare." He stroked her damp hair from her face. "You're safe. Was it the water one, again?"

"Yeah," Storm whispered.

He held her, and before long his breathing became deep and regular. But Storm was afraid to close her eyes, because she knew the next part of the dream lurked behind her lids, whether she was awake or asleep. Her lungs would burn just as they did that day when she was tumbled in the roiling water until she didn't know up from down, while the red hull of the overturned boat, with its broken and jagged *ama*, hovered ten feet above her head.

The dream was always the same, and her eyes burned with salt, or tears, in the effort to snatch a breath while she gasped and strained to find Pua and Bert in the white, churning surf.

Eighteen years later, she still couldn't tell anyone how she'd navigated the surging reefs from a half-mile out, except to say that she could see an animal pacing the beach. She was certain that it was *pua'a*, the pig, her *'aumakua*, and it appeared to paw and snort its distress as it kept vigil.

People still avoided mentioning the canoe accident; it was too painful for everyone involved. Storm had made her way through a channel in the shallowest and most treacherous reef, where the waves were so big that one of the rescue canoes capsized. None of the crowd lined up on the shore had seen a pig, or any animal, but few of the Hawaiians questioned her story. They were too busy comforting Bert's wife.

Chapter Four

The Tubin' Tanker, with its hand-painted sign and cool, cave-like interior, was a surf-enthusiast's Mecca. O'Reilly's eyes meandered over the vertically arrayed boards, which were arranged in no apparent order. Thrusters were interspersed with guns, and there was even a tanker or two in the mix. The place smelled of fiberglass resin and strong coffee. A guy could get a buzz off that blend if he wanted, O'Reilly mused.

He had some time to kill before he made the hour and a half drive to Honolulu Airport to pick up Marty. One of the young surfers he'd met this morning on the beach had told him to check out the Tubin' Tanker. The owner of the store, Mo'o Lanipuni, was a popular surfboard shaper. This was a respected profession in the islands and could be extremely competitive, especially if the shaper was working with competitive surfers. God forbid one shaper copy another's design. Blood could flow.

O'Reilly wanted to pick out a board for his own use, but not one of the guns used for the really big waves. He figured he needed a Malibu, something in the nine foot range. They were six hundred bucks and up, so he wanted to ask Mo'o's opinion before he shelled out the green.

The riches that would be coming in from the meet sponsors and media moguls weren't in the bank, yet. Still, he could afford to treat himself. He had to keep up the image, like with the rented house near Chun's Reef. These were the facts of business, after all. Big bucks begat big bucks.

There was a little coffee bar set up in the back of the store, and it looked to O'Reilly like Moʻo made espresso for customers he favored. Right now, two men, a husky guy with arms the size of O'Reilly's thighs and some wizened, dark-skinned dude, were involved in an argument that seemed to have been continued from an earlier time. They ignored everyone else in the store, which meant O'Reilly and a teenaged tourist couple who had been seared to a peeling pink.

"I tell ya, damn contests going make the situation worse," the skinny guy said.

"Not all bad, Buster," the stocky one said. He conjured a sweating carton of half and half from someplace under the counter and splashed dollops into the chipped ceramic mugs they both held. The big guy—O'Reilly thought he must be Moʻo because he sat behind the counter where the cream was kept—wore a ragged muscle shirt with the faded name of a surfboard on the front. He looked in his fifties, with thin gray hair pulled back into a ponytail. Though he was about five-five and two-fifty, the swell of muscle under his extra flesh was daunting.

O'Reilly guessed at his ethnicity, which was a game all islanders seemed to play with each other. Hawaiian, Caucasian, and one of the Asian races, probably. Wide face, high cheekbones, deeply tanned skin, and light gray eyes, which gave the guy a harder look than the dark-eyed wiry one, who was doing more of the complaining.

O'Reilly grabbed a couple pairs of board shorts and headed for the sheet-draped cubicle that served as a dressing room.

"Business going get bettah all over town. Wait and see," Moʻo said.

"Maybe bettah for you, cuz people buy surfboards an' stuff, but there's no more space to use 'em."

"You making too much of it. Restaurants, hotels, shops all going do good."

"You, you're shortsighted, you missing the big picture." Buster set his cup down with a thwack. "It's anti-Hawaiian. The old ones put value on giving and sharing, not ownership.

They wen' start the sport, and now it's all about money. Who gets the best beaches, the best breaks. Going get Lono all stirred up, you wait an' see."

"You think?" Mo'o's voice held a note of amusement. "Most words I hear you talk for long time."

"What you think, this guy Matsumoto die from accident?"

Mo'o's voice was no longer amused. "Matsumoto hit his head on his board, the reef, a cave, something. Can happen any time." O'Reilly heard him take a breath. "And you shouldn't be talking about the old legends." His voice had lowered to nearly a whisper. "You only going scare locals, not the ones you want to scare."

"Me? Hey, at least I take responsibility. I join O'ahu Surfing Alliance, already."

"Fuck that." Mo'o's voice was hard. "What you think those whiners going do? Talk to City & County?"

"Who else will do it? Everyone knows what the Blue Shorts do, but no one will stop it."

"What?" Mo'o hissed.

"You know."

O'Reilly stopped pulling on the board shorts mid-thigh. Blue Shorts? He'd heard that term somewhere before.

"You stupid bolo-head *pupule*, join some *haole* committee." Mo'o's voice was cold.

Buster sucked in his breath. "Not all *haole*." His voice was defensive.

"Most." Mo'o's tone held a sneer. "They're *malihini*, been here a year or two, think they fuckin' own the place."

"Not. Got surfers on it, too. Guys you know." A cup slammed to the countertop. "But I guess you already pick your side."

Mo'o chuckled softly, in what sounded to O'Reilly like a conciliatory attempt to reach his friend. "Not. Come on, Buster. We been friends a long time. What surfers you talking about?"

"Ask someone else." The door slammed.

"Shit," Mo'o muttered, and O'Reilly heard the coffee mugs clank together, as if Mo'o was clearing his countertop in a hurry.

Chapter Five

"Hi, Aunt Maile. We're here." Storm stood with her cell phone on the lanai of a newly-remodeled beach cottage overlooking Laniakea Beach. "Thank Cheryl and Joe for me, okay? They could rent this for a lot of money, it's so gorgeous. It's nice of them to let us use it."

Robbie shot by her, jumped down the steps to the sandy yard, and darted for the water, his feet shooting up plumes of fine white sand in his rush. Leila and Hamlin followed him. They toted beach chairs and towels, and Leila carried a canvas bag spilling over with novels, magazines, and sun block.

Storm hung up and made her way across the front yard, a sandy expanse shaded by ironwood trees, to the beach. It was around eleven Saturday morning, and she had called Ben from the road to tell him they were on the way. When she'd mentioned eleven-year-old Robbie, Ben had said he'd try to get a couple of surfing buddies to give lessons to the youngster.

The guys arrived soon after Storm had joined Hamlin and Leila in the shade of a cluster of palms. Ben was more cheerful than he'd been when he accompanied his mother to Storm's office.

"Storm, this is Goober Stevens."

Storm stood up and took the hand of the guy Ben had introduced. Goober grinned through slightly crooked teeth and tossed a mass of blond dreadlocks that reached his shoulders. "Hi."

When Goober turned to greet Robbie, Storm noticed the wide tattoo of a sea turtle across his lower back, just above board shorts slung so low Storm was afraid she'd get to see whether Goober was a natural blond. Another *honu*, tiny and in jade, hung on a leather thong around his neck.

A man, bigger and broader-shouldered than Goober or Ben, split off from chatting with a couple of surfers down the beach and jogged toward them.

"Hey, you finally get free?" Ben asked him with a grin, then turned to Storm. "You know Nahoa."

Nahoa threw his arms around her. "Storm, it's been like what, decades? And now you're a big-time lawyer."

Storm burst out laughing. "In my dreams. Last time I saw you was at Missy's wedding. You were making your mother crazy."

"Yeah, I was supposed to be an usher, wasn't I?" He laughed. "I never did stop making my mother crazy."

"Leila, Hamlin, this is Nahoa Pi'ilani, my second cousin."

Hamlin shook his hand warmly. "You won the Pipeline Masters last year, right?"

"Yeah, I was lucky. Got a good wave." Nahoa shrugged. "Right place at the right time, you know?"

He took Leila's hand. "Are you related, too?" He gazed at her strawberry blond hair and green eyes, still holding onto her hand.

Leila didn't seem to mind Nahoa's flirtation. Few women would.

"No, Storm and Hamlin let us tag along, get out of the city for the weekend," Leila said.

Robbie had moved next to his mother and stared up at Nahoa. The boy's eyes gleamed with wonder. "You're in the Sunset Triple Pro?" he asked.

"Yup, I made it so far," Nahoa grinned.

Storm watched him, too, and marveled at seeing him again. Years ago, she'd been very close to his family, but Nahoa's mother had taken her children and fled the Big Island when her husband died. Storm hadn't seen Nahoa since he was seven.

It amazed Storm that he'd tracked her down and recommended her to his friend. His face had the same fine planes, coffee-hued skin, and lively black eyes that she remembered, but she wouldn't have recognized him if she'd passed him on the street. She might have looked twice, though. At twenty-five, he was not only six-three, he was movie-star handsome, and looked like he knew it in a good-natured way.

Storm stifled a grin and wondered if Rochelle still worried about him like she used to. Probably. Nahoa had been seven and his sister twelve when their father died. Storm had heard that Rochelle Pi'ilani never remarried. Instead, she'd poured her energy into her children, especially her son, whom she adored and spoiled. The day he was supposed to be in Missy's wedding, he'd run off to go surfing with a handful of other grommets and showed up fifteen minutes late to the church—barefoot and with sand still in his hair. Rochelle often wrung her hands at her son's nature, which was irreverent from day one, but she was a "boys will be boys" kind of mom.

Robbie still gazed at Nahoa, and the young man smiled at him. "Wanna go out and help me practice?"

Leila's head swiveled to the shore break in front of them, where the waves crashed onto the sand and sent a foaming sheet of water up the beach. Her smile shrank.

"We'll go out and down a bit." Nahoa pointed to set of gentler, curving waves about a hundred yards to their left. "Storm and I won't let him out of our sight."

Storm's mouth dropped open and she promptly clamped it closed. She hadn't planned on this. She wasn't at all comfortable in big waves. Laniakea wasn't breaking big today, especially in terms of North Shore winter surf, but some of the waves were taller than she was, though she'd bet the surf report would place them at three to five feet. Still, if she showed Leila that she was frightened by the water, Leila wouldn't let Robbie go. And Robbie would be bummed. More accurately, judging by his worshipful expression, he'd be devastated.

"Me either," said Goober. "We all watch out for each other."

"I brought a tandem board," announced Nahoa. He turned to Ben. "I'll take Robbie and you can use my new Lanipuni."

"Is that the seven-footer Mo'o was bragging about?" Ben asked. "The thruster with his special skegs? Thanks, man."

Hamlin had sidled up to Storm and draped his arm over her shoulders. "You okay?" he asked softly.

Some of the tension in Storm's shoulders abated and she gave a tiny nod. The tandem board was good news. Robbie would share it with Nahoa, who would paddle out, catch the wave, and keep the boy out of the danger zone. And she'd stay as close to them on her own board as she safely could.

Robbie didn't allow any delays in getting into the water. He barely let Leila apply sunscreen to his face and shoulders. Storm stayed quiet and ignored Leila's questioning glances. It was all she could do to keep from revealing her nervousness when she picked up her board.

Trundling down the beach behind the frolicking Robbie and tall men, Storm took deep breaths and told herself that the waves at Laniakea weren't that much bigger than what she normally surfed. She hoped. When she leaned over to fasten her surfboard leash around her ankle, she noticed that her fingers trembled a bit.

"Hey, you're goofy footed," Nahoa said. "So am I."

Nahoa's gestured to his left leg, where he'd attached his own leash. "It's good luck." He grinned at her and Storm knew he'd seen her trepidation. Being goofy only meant that they surfed with their right foot forward, as opposed to their left, like the majority of surfers. It didn't really bring luck, but the comment made Storm feel better.

"We're just going out to play." He squinted out at the water. "And be part of the ocean and her power."

"That's what I like," Storm said. "Being in the water, feeling that clean purity."

Nahoa's dimples deepened. "That's what it's all about."

With the first cooling splash, she began to relax. Soon her mind and body were occupied with the mechanics of paddling and watching the currents and waves, and much of the apprehension she'd felt washed away.

Nahoa and Robbie were about ten feet in front of her, while Ben and Goober flanked the little group. Getting out past the breaking water wasn't difficult, in large part because the experienced surfers knew where the shoulder of the wave would be easiest to swim over. Plus, they were patient with her and didn't make her feel as if she couldn't keep up. That was a relief, especially on the North Shore, where catching and riding waves can be aggressive and competitive.

"Hey, Nahoa. That how you're surfing Sunday?" someone yelled from the water.

"I'll still beat you," Nahoa shouted back.

The surfer swam over and gave Nahoa the local handshake, butting fists together before clasping. He then did it to Robbie.

"This is Robbie, a friend of mine," Nahoa said. He looked over his shoulder. "And my cousin, Storm."

Storm caught up and the man gave her a nod. He looked part Hawaiian, part *haole*, with maybe an Asian ancestor in the mix somewhere. His skin was tanned to a deep chestnut, and his short, bleached hair had dark roots. Wide tattoos of tribal designs encircled his biceps, wrists, and ankles.

"I'm Gabe," he said, and ran his eyes first down her, then her board.

"Hey," she said.

"Keep your eye on Gabe. He can teach you a thing or two," Nahoa said.

She noticed that Ben and Goober had gone past them and joined the lineup for the next set of waves. "I will."

Gabe gave her another nod. "See you around, dude," he said to Nahoa, and paddled off.

Nahoa waited a minute, then spoke in a low voice. "Watch out for him. Some people get *huhū*, you don't get out of the way or wait your turn in the lineup. Not only does he do that, he'll snake you. You know, drop in on the wave. It's dangerous."

Storm watched Gabe's broad back paddling away. She knew some of the unwritten etiquette of surfing, but what she didn't know worried her. This was a different scene than the mellower South Shore breaks. She'd had the feeling that Gabe hadn't come over just to razz Nahoa, but also to check out who was with him. "Are people territorial out here?"

Nahoa made a snorting noise. "Yeah."

An understatement. "No sharing a wave then, eh?"

"You can with Ben or me."

There was a lull in the sets, so it was a good time to get through the break zone, where the next waves would curl. Nahoa struck out for the outside of the break. Robbie lay in front of him and grinned back at Storm from time to time.

Goober appeared beside Storm, and Ben sat on his board about twenty feet away. They didn't want to get too close to one another, because banging into one another's fiberglass boards was not only one of those bad etiquette mistakes, it was dangerous to both people and equipment.

Goober sat up on his board and narrowed his eyes as he assessed the oncoming waves. "When a set comes in, don't catch the first wave. A lot of the regulars will be going for it."

Storm saw Ben nod in agreement, though his eyes never left the horizon. Goober's didn't, either. Storm looked out to sea, too, and remembered the warning every child in Hawai'i grows up with: Never turn your back on the sea. She knew the warning was even more critical out here.

"I usually find the second or third wave is better. Maybe bigger, with better form," Ben said. "Find a couple of points on the shore and make sure you stay within them. There's often a pretty good rip current out here and you don't know you're in it until you're farther out than you meant to be."

Goober lay down on his board and paddled a few strokes to the right. "Set coming in." He turned back to Storm. "Stay on the shoulder, you'll have less of a drop."

Drop? She didn't do drops—that took too big of a wave. She could see the water building now, and she dug in to get off to the side. She'd follow Goober's advice, wait and see how this one went. It was probably the first in a set of four or five.

The swell reached the surfers quickly. A number of them paddled to catch the wave, vying for the best place in the lineup. Storm watched Nahoa, probably a hundred yards in front of her and facing the rising wave, move toward the outside, and she followed his direction. She flew over the top and down the other side with a swoop that made her stomach soar. God, this was fun. And God, it was scary.

Nahoa and Robbie were both sitting on the big tandem board now, and she could see Nahoa rotating it to face shore. They were going for the next wave. Nahoa kept the board perpendicular to the line of the rising line of water, out on the shoulder. He shouted something to Robbie, then gave two or three strong strokes and got to his feet as easily as if he'd been lying on the living room floor. Robbie got to his knees and stayed there, his arms out like a tightrope walker. The two of them soared by. Robbie's eyes were as round as quarters and his mouth stretched, with delight edging out the fear. When they plummeted with the rush of cascading water behind them, Storm heard Robbie's squeal of exhilaration. She dropped down the ocean side of the wave, out of sight, but she heard them both laugh out loud.

Ben paddled up to within about ten feet of her. "Next one's ours. You're in the right position, on the outside. It's going to break right, so anticipate that and go with it. I'll be nearby, just relax and have fun." He looked over his shoulder, then back at her.

"Start paddling."

Storm's stomach felt like it had risen to her throat. She dug into the water, hands stiff, shoulders and triceps flexing with effort. She felt like she wasn't moving. Instead, the ocean seemed to suck her back into a rising wall of water. The roar drowned out all other sound, any concept of anyone near her; it eradicated any thought in her mind but how to keep from tumbling down the face of the wave.

If she fell now, she'd go over the falls. And then she'd be in the washing machine, with no idea which way was up. If that happened, all she could do would be to hold her breath and hope that the greater density of salt water would push her to the surface before her air ran out.

She wanted to turn back, but it was too late. Instead, she plunged down the face of the wave, still lying down, afraid to rise, terrified she'd fall and be engulfed in that liquid green wall. Somewhere off to her left, she heard Ben shout. "Stand up!"

And she did. She scrambled up, knowing as she did that she had to, or she'd bury the nose of the board and be launched like a cannonball, held to the razor-finned slab of fiberglass by the rubber leash around her ankle, only to land in the exact spot where the leading edge of the curl would crash to the ocean. She'd have as much free will as a piece of driftwood.

On her feet, she found that her petrified brain started to function once again. She was up. In this position, she had control. She could shift her weight back on the board to avoid pearling, or she could move forward and adjust for a lull in the water's force. And once in control, she was no longer as frightened.

The ride was perfect. She sailed past Nahoa and Robbie, who shouted and gave her a thumbs-up. Twenty yards beyond them, the wave petered out, and Storm let herself fall, laughing, into the ocean.

"Way to go." Ben had appeared nearby, and calmly sat on his board as if he'd driven up and parked.

"That was great." Storm was breathless with exertion and a roaring adrenaline buzz.

"Wanna do it again?"

"Yeah."

◌⟳◌ ◌⟳◌ ◌⟳◌

A couple of hours later, the surfers traipsed back to where Leila and Hamlin had set down beach chairs. They'd had a hard time staying in them, though, and met the wet and sandy group halfway down the beach.

"That looks really fun," Hamlin said.

"You could do it," Storm assured him. "Let's start on smaller waves, though."

"They look pretty big," Leila said. "Lots of white water."

Robbie was carrying the tandem board with Ben. "It was so fun, Mom. I want to do it again."

Leila had laid an old bedspread in the sand next to the beach chairs. Robbie and Storm sat down on it, but the guys insisted on sitting in the sand. "We're going back out again pretty soon," Goober said.

"Speak for yourself," Ben said. "I've got to get some work done."

"Gotta check in with your mom, you mean?"

Ben glared at Goober. "Maybe. So what?"

Nahoa interrupted them. "Waves will be better later this afternoon, when the wind dies down."

Goober shrugged. "Whatever."

Storm was seated on the blanket so that she faced the arguers. Consequently, she gazed down the beach in an effort to ignore the friction. Nahoa reacted as if he'd heard the sniping before, and he turned to Leila to discuss Brian's work as a police officer.

A small group of surfers walked along the beach, boards under their arms. One of them pointed toward Storm, Hamlin, and their little group. A sunburned, tow-headed kid of nine or ten in a brand-new Matsumoto Shave Ice T-shirt ran up to them. Someone had coated his peeling nose with zinc oxide.

"Some guy asked me to give you this." The boy handed Nahoa a package, wrapped in brown paper and twine. He then dug in his pocket and pulled out a Subway napkin, complete with calorie counts and a couple of oily spots. "Can I have your autograph, too?" He handed the napkin to Nahoa. "I heard you're gonna win the surf contest tomorrow."

"We'll see," Nahoa said. "Anyone got a pen?"

Leila dug around in her beach tote and came up with an old ballpoint, which Nahoa used to sign the napkin.

"What's in the package?" he asked.

"I dunno." The kid stood on one foot in the hot sand, then the other. "You prob'ly should open it."

"Okay." Nahoa untied the twine and peeled back the layers of paper. For a moment, he didn't move.

"Who gave this to you?"

"A man." The boy pointed down the beach in the direction he'd come.

Everyone looked toward the layers of brown paper. All that was visible was a heavy dark, carved wood handle. By the size and heft of the package, Storm guessed the item was about eighteen inches long and weighed several pounds.

The skin had tightened around Nahoa's eyes and she could see that he was pale beneath his tan. The handle sparked an image from her childhood, reinforced by Nahoa's reaction.

Nahoa spoke, his voice dead calm. "What did the guy look like?"

The boy looked around as if he might see the guy. "He was tall. Um, he had a blue shirt with a surfer on it."

"What did he say to you?"

The kid had picked up on Nahoa's gravity. Nervous and off-balance, his foot knocked the edge of the wrapping. The item poked out so that Storm saw the other end, which was a flattened, heavy oval, its perimeter embedded with shark's teeth.

A jolt of revulsion went through Storm. Aunt Maile was a *kahuna lā'au lapa'au*, or traditional Hawaiian healer, and Storm had learned a great deal of their ancestors' history and tradition under her watchful eye. The rest of the group looked perplexed, but the frown on Hamlin's face told her that his mind was on the same track as hers. Hamlin was a voracious reader of Hawaiian history.

The package held a *lei o manō*, or shark's tooth club, used in *lua*, an ancient form of Hawaiian warfare.

The boy perceived the tool's malevolence; it was hard not to. "He gave me a twenty dollar bill." The boy's voice shook. "I'm sorry, I guess it's not a nice gift."

"You didn't know." Nahoa's voice sounded resigned. "Somebody's just trying to scare me."

"Yeah, that's it," the boy said. "Hey, I'm really sorry." He scampered off, anxious to get away. For a few moments, no one spoke.

Goober was the first one to break the uncomfortable silence. "Hey man, you'll be okay. Isn't your *'aumakua* the shark?"

Nahoa attempted a laugh. "No, it's *pueo*, the owl."

A chill puckered the flesh on Storm's forearms. That was her mother's *'aumakua*, which wasn't surprising because these deified ancestors, who took the shape of animals, were passed within families. But Storm's mother had suffered from depression and committed suicide by taking an overdose of sleeping pills when Storm was twelve.

Storm had never been able to understand what drove her mother to take her life, and throughout her teen years, she'd been tormented with the idea that the illness everyone whispered about would be passed down to her daughter. Nor had she been able to stop wondering whether she could have done something—anything—to prevent her mother's gradual slide toward death. The *pueo* hadn't helped her mother, so Storm chose Aunt Maile's *'aumakua*, from her grandfather's side of the family.

"*Pueo* is a good, powerful totem," Ben said. "Anyway, like you said, someone's just trying to rattle you."

"Yeah, like that asshole Gabe," Goober said. "He wants to win the meet tomorrow."

Nahoa squinted at the water, which glared in the hot afternoon sun. "It's not a big deal." He picked up the package. "Maybe I'll intimidate a few people with it. You know, hang it from my rear-view mirror or something."

It was a weak joke, but everyone in the group attempted to smile. He stood up. "I've got to get going. See you tomorrow at the meet?" He directed this comment to Storm, Hamlin, Leila, and Robbie.

Storm stood and gave him a hug. "Wouldn't miss it."

She sat back down and watched the back of his muscled shoulders head down the beach. He nodded a greeting to a group of surfers as he passed. She could see by their gestures that they wished him luck in the upcoming contest. He exchanged a few words and kept walking. She admired his equanimity in the face of the threat he'd just received.

Meanwhile, she fought the impulse to wish Nahoa had a stronger *'aumakua*. Anything but that of her mother. Stop it, she told herself. You're a modern woman, for crying out loud. And Nahoa, unlike her mother, was tough and strong.

Chapter Six

Barstow awakened O'Reilly at six a.m. by showing up inside the colorful but thorny bougainvillea-covered fence surrounding the beach house and banging on the sliding glass doors of the master bedroom. O'Reilly had the heavy drapes drawn and thought it was still the middle of the night, but the girl he'd brought home last night sat up with a little yelp and said her girlfriends were going to be really worried about her, especially since she had borrowed their car. She ran by Barstow on her way to the Mustang convertible she'd left, roof down, in the driveway. It was raining and in the mid-sixties, a typical winter morning in the isles.

Barstow hadn't changed much. He even looked the same, about five-eight and wiry as a jockey. O'Reilly had forgotten the guy barely reached his shoulder. He'd forgotten how impatient Barstow was, too. Definite Type A.

Barstow made a beeline for the espresso machine that the posh beach house supplied with other high-end kitchen equipment, and had two frothed and sweetened bowl-sized cups prepared by the time O'Reilly was out of the shower.

Fifteen minutes later, they stood side by side in the sand and watched the rising sun scatter fuchsia and flame sequins across the ocean. O'Reilly shivered in the damp morning air and wished he had another cup. With a little Irish whiskey in it.

"Hey, when did you get that tattoo?" O'Reilly asked.

"You like? It's my *'aumakua*, the shark." Barstow picked up his leg to give O'Reilly a better view of the design that encircled his ankle. "I can get you an appointment with the guy who does it. All the locals use him."

"Nice." O'Reilly liked it, but it wasn't really his style. He looked out at the ocean. "You know anyone out there?"

"Yeah. See that tube action? If that guy can keep it up, he can beat the Hawaiian." Barstow pointed to a short, muscular man with bands of tribal tattoos on his arms and legs.

"Who is he?" O'Reilly asked.

Barstow consulted a pad of paper. "Gabe Watson. He's seeded second, right behind Nahoa Pi'ilani."

"Hey, isn't Ben in this?" O'Reilly asked.

"Yeah," Barstow said.

"So what's his rank?"

"Hell, he's got to grow up."

"C'mon, you can brag to an old friend. If I had a son in this, I'd blab it all over the place." O'Reilly clapped the shorter Barstow on the shoulder. "He's in this thing, he's gotta be good."

Barstow grinned. "Yeah, he's okay. He's still in the lineup for tomorrow."

"All right." O'Reilly nodded appreciatively. "That means he's made it through four rounds. He's within striking distance of a trophy. It's a good purse, too."

Barstow shrugged. "We'll see. You never know till you're out there, getting your wave. Anything can happen in the water."

"I'll bet." O'Reilly nodded. He followed Barstow's gaze as three surfers headed out. "Isn't that Ben?"

"And Nahoa Pi'ilani. I don't know the other kid." Barstow squinted into the light, which was intensifying by the moment. He took an expensive pair of mirrored, wrap-around sunglasses out of his shirt pocket and put them on.

"Don't you want to go talk to him?"

Barstow shook his head. "Not yet. I don't want to break his focus."

O'Reilly knew Barstow's wife had taken off over a year ago with the kid, though the way Barstow talked about Ben, he was sure the father stayed in touch with his son. He wasn't sure of the details, though. A hardness had settled on Barstow's face when he implied he'd wait to talk to his son.

"Hey, you ever heard of the Blue Shorts?" O'Reilly asked, to change the subject.

Barstow looked at him sharply. "Yeah, they used to be a tough North Shore gang." He shoved his foot into the sand. "Where'd you hear about them?"

"I was talking to some surfer-types." O'Reilly could see the reflection of clouds drifting across the mirrors of Barstow's sunglasses. The glasses gave the man the expressionless demeanor of a magnified insect.

"They were bullies." Barstow's soft growl belied the impression the glasses left. There was an angry sneer in it, like that of an outcast disparaging a high school clique. "A lot of 'em were lifeguards, supposedly working to protect swimmers and surfers."

"They wore blue shorts?"

"Yeah, the lifeguards had these blue shorts with red piping and a slash of red and white print."

"Were you ever a lifeguard?" O'Reilly knew he'd hit a nerve the second the words were out of his mouth.

"Fuck, no. Me? A California boy?" Barstow's upper lip curled. "I was the type they were trying to get rid of."

O'Reilly grinned at Barstow. "Hell, I guess you showed 'em, didn't you? You were a finalist in the '86 Gerry Lopez Pipeline Masters."

Barstow let a smile lift one side of his mouth. "I guess so."

"And married a local girl, too."

"Yeah," Barstow said. "But that was a long time ago. Things have changed, people are different."

O'Reilly let that comment go. He didn't know whether Barstow was referring to his marriage or the local culture.

Chapter Seven

Robbie was the first one up, which didn't happen very often. "C'mon, it starts at eight."

"It's seven," Leila yawned. "And it's the only day I get to sleep in."

Leila owned a very popular bakery, and most weekdays she was in the shop at four a.m. so that succulent-smelling goodies were ready for the downtown professionals when they arrived at their offices. By eight a.m., Leila's place was standing room only, and that's what people did. They stood, talked story, and had a sticky bun or warm malassada or two with their lattes. She loved sleeping in on the weekends.

Storm poured coffee into mugs while Hamlin got the milk and sugar out.

"Uh oh, ants in the sugar," he said, and poked at the open box. He leaned against the countertop in a way that told Storm his leg bothered him again. He'd hate it if she said anything about it, though.

"Slam it on the counter a few times and they'll run away," Storm said. "Then transfer it to a jar with a lid. Ants are always in beach houses."

Leila poured cereal into a bowl and handed it to Robbie. "Mister, you don't go anywhere until you eat breakfast."

"Don't worry," Storm reassured him. "You've got time. What heat are Nahoa and Ben surfing?"

"Nahoa's in the last heat, but Goober's in the first," Robbie said. "Ben's in the next-to-last heat. We've got to hurry—it's already the semi-finals."

"Four guys in a heat, right?" Hamlin asked.

"Yeah," Robbie said. "The first and second guys in the heats are the only ones to make the finals." He gulped his cereal down.

"Has anyone checked the surf report?" Storm asked. They could all hear the ocean breaking a hundred yards from the front door, and it sounded louder than it had yesterday. It had wakened Storm a couple of times during the night, though she hadn't had the dream. Maybe the surf session yesterday had helped alleviate her fear of helplessness in the water.

Sunset Beach wasn't a long drive, but Kamehameha Highway moved like the Ala Moana Shopping Center parking lot on Christmas Eve. It not only took almost an hour to drive about eight miles, they had to park the car a half-mile from the meet. By the time they got to Sunset Beach, it was the middle of the third heat and Robbie was desperate to see how his new surf buddies were doing.

"There's Goober." The unusual turtle tattoo made him easy to pick out in the crowd. He stood a hundred yards away, holding binoculars on the four surfers nearly a half-mile out in the water.

"If you'll take Robbie to find out what's happening, I'll find a spot in the shade," Leila said, "or we're going to be charbroiled by the end of the day." She was wearing a wide-brimmed hat, but freckles were already popping out across the bridge of her nose and cheeks.

"I'll stay with Leila. You guys can give us a report," Hamlin said.

"We'll be back as soon as we know what's happening." Storm and Robbie made their way through the spectators toward Goober, but Storm looked back when she thought Hamlin wouldn't notice. Yes, he was limping more than he had been yesterday. He'd curtailed his physical therapy three weeks earlier than his doctors had recommended, and Storm worried because he pushed himself harder than the physical therapists had. He'd already increased his daily walks from one mile to three.

A too-familiar surge of regret flushed through Storm. She and Hamlin had been the lucky ones in the incident that brought down the once-austere law firm of Hamasaki, Cunningham, Wang, and Wo. Miles Hamasaki, her guardian and mentor, had been murdered, another of his partners died, one went to jail, and one retired in alcoholic shame. Months later, Hamlin struggled to recover from the assault that nearly killed Storm and him.

Robbie's shout to Goober lifted Storm from her unhappy recollection. Robbie had his hand in the air, waving, but Goober looked over his shoulder at them and walked away.

Robbie stopped dead in the sand and frowned at Storm. "Why'd he do that?"

"He's being a jerk," said a voluptuous young woman, who had lowered her binoculars to observe Goober's reaction. She was small and stood between two tall, athletic women.

"No kidding," said one of the taller women, a brunette, in a wry tone. "He needs to grow up."

"Aw, Dede, you're being hard on him," a tall blonde said.

Dede rolled her eyes. "Everyone loses sometime, Sunny. You know that. It's how you handle it."

"No one's taught Goober that yet."

"You want to?" Sunny asked with a grin. The sunlight glinted off the half-dozen earrings she wore, from colored stones to tiny hoops.

"No thanks," the dark-haired girl said with a chuckle, and the three women sauntered away.

Robbie watched them go. The brunette who'd criticized Goober wore a thong bikini, the kind Storm and Leila called anal floss. Storm grabbed Robbie's arm before he walked into the back of the person in front of him.

"Let's see if there's a scoreboard."

They wove their way to some umbrellas and a phalanx of cameras that showed above the observers' heads.

Robbie squinted at the tiny figures in the water. "Can you tell who's who?"

"We should have brought binoculars."

"Ben had on yellow flowered board shorts yesterday. Someone's wearing yellow out there."

A spectator turned to them. "Yeah, that's Ben Barstow. He and Gabe Watson are only three points apart."

"Who's ahead?" Robbie asked.

"Right now, Gabe is. But Ben's—yeah! Did you see that aerial cutback? What a ride!"

Robbie and Storm watched the figures, spellbound by their maneuvers. Fifteen minutes later, Ben's teeth flashed white against his tan as he walked up the sand. He tossed water out of his hair and reached out a hand to a fellow surfer waiting on the beach. The young man clasped Ben in a hug.

"He's made the finals, no sweat," the spectator said to Robbie. "Look at that grin. He and Gabe are neck and neck."

"What about Nahoa?" Robbie asked.

"He's going out now. It's the last heat." The fellow squinted into the sun. "Here, want to use my glasses?"

He handed Robbie a set of binoculars, which Robbie stared through for a few moments, then handed to Storm. The four men in the final heat were lining up.

"Nahoa's top seed for this meet, isn't he?" Storm asked, and handed the glasses back to the spectator.

"Yeah, you know him?"

"He's her cousin," Robbie said.

"Cool." The guy stared through the binocs for several minutes. "He's a real athlete. Has a reputation for doing what he needs to do to get his points."

Robbie looked at Storm, who shrugged. The comment sounded like a compliment, but she wasn't sure.

"Here, take a look. Each surfer is allowed ten rides per heat, so he'll be out there soon." The guy handed the binoculars to Robbie again.

"How're the heats judged?" Storm asked.

"Kind of like diving or gymnastics. Each wave a surfer rides is scored from zero to ten, then the highest and lowest scores are eliminated so the judges get an arithmetic mean."

"You know a lot about this."

The young man smiled. "I'm working on it. I compete, but I really want to be a judge."

Robbie jerked the binoculars a few inches to his left, which attracted both Storm's and the commentator's attention. He watched several moments without even appearing to blink. One of the surfers, in black shorts and a black rash guard, finished a nice backhand cutback and headed for the leading curl of the wave.

"Is Nahoa wearing the red and white shorts?" she asked Robbie.

"Yeah, you can tell it's Nahoa because he's goofy, remember? His right foot is forward."

Their new friend looked over at Robbie. "Hey, you're right. This is a right-hand break, though, which puts him at a slight disadvantage."

Robbie looked at him with concern, then back through the binoculars. "He hasn't gone yet. I think he's waiting for the guy on the wave." Robbie pointed without bothering to lower the glasses, then gasped.

Storm could see what happened without the binoculars. The black-clad surfer had misjudged the leading edge of the fourteen foot wave, and the curl slapped him from his board as if he were a mosquito. The guy bounced twice before the wave closed out on him and swallowed him in its salty spume.

Spectators murmured nervously and stood on tiptoe to catch sight of a tiny person on the vast plain of foam. Storm held her breath. "You see him yet?"

Robbie kept the glasses to his eyes and merely gave his head a quick shake.

"Lemme take a look, okay?" The spectator reached for his glasses. Storm's hands were balled so tightly that her nails dug into her palms. It seemed like minutes before the young man said, "There he is. Probably in the green room for a while."

He handed the binocs back to Robbie. "There, it looks like Nahoa Pi'ilani is taking off."

Storm swallowed hard and unclenched her fists. The green room. That's what people called the underwater space where either a wave shoved a surfer or where she dived to escape the crush of tons of churning water. Storm had been there; she'd been buffeted in the tumult like a dead fish, disoriented to the point that she couldn't tell up from down. Even with her eyes open, there was no sensation of direction. Everything was green.

A roar from the crowd brought Storm's awareness back to the surfer on his rocketing board. The wave was huge, and its thunder dwarfed the excited hum of the spectators. Red and white shorts plunged into a steep takeoff, hung for a moment in a gravity-defying stall, then cut back up the face of the wave. Nahoa launched himself into an aerial and the crowd gasped again in mute admiration, then broke into a throaty cheer. Nahoa landed in a deep crouch and plummeted down the face, leaned way out, and spun his board in a one-eighty. Lifting his body in a move worthy of a ballet dancer, he shot back to the top of the wave and faced the rising curl of the monster. There, he hovered for a breathtaking second, and crouched.

The crowd hushed. This was the move that the last surfer had blown. Fifteen feet above him, opalescent blue water curved in a fat wall. With a purpose that Storm would have sworn bordered on suicidal lunacy, Nahoa headed into a tunnel that moved with the velocity and mass of a freight train.

Seconds passed, and no one moved. For Storm, time stood still. Her lungs burned and her eyes teared with the effort of searching for a tiny speck of a person, either against a wall of water or in the acres of white foam on the heaving horizon. She recalled Ken Matsumoto, the surfer who had recently died, and for whom this meet had been postponed.

Suddenly, a tiny figure in red and white shorts squirted from under a blue curtain on the shoulder of the wave. The spectators went crazy. Storm and Robbie threw their arms around each other, and it was a few moments before they realized that their friend with the binoculars was hugging them, too.

"What'd I tell ya? He does what he has to," the young man shouted. "He's the best."

Storm wanted to sit down in relief. Her legs were weak, and she looked over her shoulder to see if she could find Hamlin and Leila in the surge of people. It was a comfort to see Hamlin standing only about six feet behind her.

He looked around at the surging tumult of surf enthusiasts, who cheered with the elation of watching a fellow human cheat a haughty and all-powerful Mother Nature of possible death. "Was that an amazing ride or what?"

"Totally," Robbie said.

"Absolutely," Storm said, and her voice shook a little.

"Leila and I found a spot down the beach a bit, but we have a pretty good view," Hamlin said. "We weren't sure you'd find us in this crowd, so I came after you."

He led them back by walking parallel to the water, near the clusters of camera operators and media announcers. A fellow with hair that didn't move in the breeze, though his expensive silk aloha shirt billowed around him, smiled into a camera.

"Nahoa Pi'ilani leads the finalists!" The reporter's voice was filled with the jubilation of an announcer at a football game after a touchdown. "A combination of innovative and radical maneuvers in the most critical sections of the rides Pi'ilani selected showed the style, power, and speed this surfer is known for. Ben Barstow and Gabe Watson are neck and neck, though they are probably competing for second place. It's doubtful that anyone can overtake Pi'ilani, though up-and-comer Kimo Hitashi, in third place, could still upset Barstow or Watson for the second spot."

The announcer's face glistened in the sun, and he held up his hand to stop the camera, then waved over a young woman in very tight, very low white jeans and a tube top that showed a wide expanse of brown midriff and a slew of belly-button rings. She dusted him with a big, puffy makeup brush. Two seconds later, he gave the cameraman a nod and continued with the commentary.

"The rising tide is changing the shape of the waves, so be with us at eight o'clock tomorrow morning, when some of the best surfers in the world face off at one of the toughest breaks on the planet."

He broke off and turned to a couple of casually dressed men who hung in the background. They each pumped his hand.

Storm watched the three interact for a moment, as the two talking to the announcer were certainly VIPs, maybe the meet directors. They looked like aging beach boys, though one was tall and had a paunch while the other was short and wiry and wore wrap-around mirrored shades. The tall one shook the announcer's hand again, and gave off an aura of relief.

Hamlin led them away from the media groupies, back into the shade of trees that lined the beach. The roofs of expensive beachfront homes peeked above the palms, and people drifted from the hot sand to the shelter of the exclusive refuges.

Leila waved from under a cluster of ironwood trees. "Too bad we can't stay for the finals. Nahoa was terrific, wasn't he?"

"Ben, too," Robbie said. "Can't we stay, Mom, please?"

"No, dear. Tomorrow's Monday. You've got school and I've got work."

"I've got an eight o'clock deposition," Hamlin said.

"And I've got…well, I've got to see what I've got," Storm said.

"You have a client and you've only been open a week," Hamlin said. "That's not bad."

"More people will be coming in this week," Leila said.

"I need to look into some things for Stephanie Barstow," Storm said. "It'll give me a great excuse to call her tomorrow and find out how Ben and Nahoa did in the finals."

Hamlin drove back into town, and all four spent the hour and a half talking about whether Ben or Gabe Watson would come in second and claim the $13,000 purse. They were certain that Nahoa had the $25,000 first place in his pocket, and Storm sat back and contemplated how happy Rochelle must be for her adventuresome son. It came with a price, though. She'd seen the worry on Stephanie's face.

Chapter Eight

"Your TV guy says we need a hundred fifty thousand purse," Barstow said. He drained the bottle of Beck's, burped, and put his feet up on the deck rail.

"He doesn't have a clue," O'Reilly answered. He got up, went into the kitchen, and came out with a couple more beers. "He figures if the purse is six figures, his pay will be, too. Fat chance."

"Whaddya pay these guys, anyway?"

"It's gone up since I was in the business, but not a hundred G's, I guarantee." He burped, too, longer and louder than Barstow's.

Gordon will always try for the big bucks, O'Reilly thought. He'd known him for years, and he knew when Gordon was trolling. Hell, he was campaigning.

"Maybe twenty grand. For a few hours' work, that's pretty damn good." He took another swallow. "But we'll offer him twelve to start. He wants this job. He'll get a lot of exposure."

"What'd he make today?" Barstow asked.

O'Reilly shrugged. "The meet promoters were a bit evasive about that, but I'd guess around six or eight. Maybe less. Ours is gonna be more spectacular. A tow-in, with minimum twenty foot surf."

"The Eddie Aikau looks for the same conditions. We don't want to compete with those guys—they're legendary." Barstow's eyes slid over to O'Reilly. "Have they started their holding period?"

"Not yet." O'Reilly took a long swallow. "That's why I need you to talk to the guys that make these things happen. I've had feelers out for months, but it's nothing like talking to the local people."

"Yeah, especially around here, where who you know is the bottom line. We've got to make sure we don't step on any toes."

O'Reilly made a rumbling noise in his chest that might have been a chuckle. "At least not the toes that matter."

"We better sprinkle some gin on *ti* leaves, too. For good fortune." Barstow smiled. "Stephanie always did it when there was some kind of event. She went nuts for our wedding."

O'Reilly looked at Barstow out of the corner of his eyes. He didn't know yet how much to tell him about the steps he'd already taken. The man's gaze was out to sea, where stars were beginning to appear in the night sky. Barstow had always been intense, but he seemed touchier than he used to be. Probably because of his marriage problems. As far as O'Reilly could tell, he'd only talked with his son for about two minutes after he'd done so well in the contest this morning, and this was the first mention he'd made of his wife in a long time.

O'Reilly knew that he, too, was different than he'd been during their college days, and he wasn't any more willing than Barstow to talk about it. One thing he knew for sure was that he needed this surf contest to be successful. Barstow, however, didn't look like he needed the money. He just wanted to be part of the surf scene again.

He wondered if he should tell Barstow that after they left the meet this afternoon, he'd gone back to the Tubin' Tanker. After all, Barstow's *kuleana* (O'Reilly had learned this term from Mo'o Lanipuni just today) was the surfing. He was supposed to use his contacts to get sponsors and to make sure that the local, uninvited surfers didn't get their noses so far out of joint they made trouble.

O'Reilly's business was getting the media contacts and the big names, so Barstow might get a little hinky if he knew O'Reilly was asking questions about the surf part of things. O'Reilly's visit had been a spur of the moment thing. He'd been driving by Moʻo's just as the shaper was opening up shop. He'd apparently closed during the semi-finals. Passing by at that moment had seemed like good timing, and the visit turned out to be productive. Moʻo had given him a few tips for getting beach and marine permits.

As he left, O'Reilly asked if there was anyone he should talk to about which jet skis to use for the tow-in contest, and whether any of the manufacturers would donate machines to the event. Moʻo had spent a few moments putting tubes of sunscreen in a display case before he answered. "Try see Gabe Watson," he said.

O'Reilly, of course, recognized the name as that of one of the morning's finalists, but something kept him from revealing this to Moʻo, mostly because he didn't want to appear like a know-it-all. O'Reilly remembered Moʻo's conversation with the skinny guy and knew that he might fit Moʻo's definition of a fuckin' *malihini* to a tee.

But he wasn't, not at all. He was asking locals' opinions about this deal. And he wasn't *malihini*, either. A long time ago, he'd spent two years in Hawaiʻi when his dad was in the Air Force.

O'Reilly popped open another Beck's. "Marty, you ever hear of Gabe Watson before this weekend's meet?"

He could sense, rather than see, Barstow's head turn toward him.

"Don't think so, why?"

"Cuz someone told me he knew about tow-in contests."

Barstow took his time finishing his beer. "Most of these guys have jobs other than surfing. They have to. You know where he works?"

"No."

"I'll ask around," Barstow said. "You still got media lined up for next few weeks?"

"The guy who owns the Tubin' Tanker gave me some contacts for the beach permits." O'Reilly watched Barstow for signs of annoyance, but Marty seemed to perk up a bit. "He said there's a big swell predicted, and he thinks we could get a holding period starting next week."

"As in Monday?" Barstow set his beer bottle down with thunk. "What's the surf prediction?"

"Big storm in Alaska. The NOAA buoys are pinging already. It could be huge by Thursday or Friday."

"Give me those names and I'll call tomorrow." Barstow picked up his beer again and leaned back in his chair with a smile. "It's really gonna happen, isn't it? I tell you, I've had my doubts."

"I know what you mean," O'Reilly said. It was a good thing, too. He couldn't afford this beach house much longer, and he certainly couldn't afford to go back to the mainland empty-handed.

He swung his feet down from the porch railing. "We've got a lot of work to do, though. Gordon's got to start doing TV spots for us in the next day or two. I've got four other networks coming in by the middle of the week. What's the response from the surfers we discussed on the phone?"

"So far, I've got eighteen out of the twenty teams you wanted. They've been waiting to see if the swell comes in. Some of the Australians and Europeans will leave in the next day or two if we give 'em a green light."

"You just made my week, man." In the light that filtered from the kitchen, O'Reilly could see Barstow return his grin.

"What's your time frame?" Barstow asked.

"If the surf's good, we could start the first round Thursday. Friday, we do two more. Surf prediction is for twenty-five foot faces and rising. Saturday, we'll have quarters and semis, and on Sunday, we'll do the finals. If we need, we can spill over to Monday."

He looked over at Barstow. "What sponsors you got so far?"

"It's lookin' good. Wait'll I show you. Not only equipment for the meets, but I've got some huge names—sports drinks, suntan lotion, clothing. Some of the surfers have their own sponsors, in addition." Barstow looked thoughtful. "What's the meet going to cost us to run?"

"About seven hundred fifty thou."

"Cheaper than football, I bet."

"No shit." O'Reilly chuckled.

"What will the winner's purse be?"

"I'm thinking of a hundred twenty thousand, which is bigger than any of the other contests. Plus, we've got sponsorship guarantees for the top three finalists that amount to multiples of that number. Right now, the winner could make up to two-fifty, three hundred with sponsorships. Minimum."

"Yeah?" Barstow squinted over his drink. "You've got something up your sleeve, don't you?"

"I was savin' it till I was sure, but one of the credit card companies is talking about a contract for the winner."

"You're makin' my day. How much we talking?"

"Seven figures. It's a first for a surfer."

Barstow nodded. He was looking happier by the minute, and O'Reilly felt good about that. If his old friend was going through a hard time on a personal level, it was nice O'Reilly could help out in a business sense.

"You haven't asked what we're going to clear." O'Reilly handed him a fresh beer.

"Okay, what are we gonna make?"

O'Reilly threw back his head and laughed. The ocean breezes ruffled his thinning hair. "Don't quote me yet, but we should each clear a half mil. And that's just for this year. This is the beginning of a wonderful new tradition."

Chapter Nine

Storm got two calls from the Public Defender's Office on Monday morning. One of her new clients came to the office in handcuffs with an HPD escort, and the other came in with her distraught mother, who insisted her daughter couldn't possibly have shoplifted the bathing suit she wore under her clothing when she left an exclusive teen boutique. Ink blots from the store sensor still spotted the kid's leg. It was eleven o'clock before Storm had a chance to call Stephanie Barstow.

"Hello," Stephanie shouted over a lot of background noise.

"Can you hear me? It's Storm."

"Barely." Her voice crackled with radio interference.

"How's Ben doing in the meet?"

"He came in second." Stephanie's voice broke, and Storm thought it was due to excitement, rather than the bad connection.

"All right," Storm shouted. "He beat out Gabe."

"Yeah, Gabe came in fourth." Stephanie laughed. "Couldn't happen to a nicer guy."

Storm had to grin. "What about Nahoa? And who came in third?"

"Nahoa won. The crowd loves him—I hope Ben is as strong when he's Nahoa's age. Kimo Hitashi came in third. It was a real upset, and Gabe was madder than a wet cat." Stephanie sounded downright gleeful. "Kimo dates Gabe's ex-girlfriend. They hate each other. Gabe wouldn't talk to reporters or anything."

"I'm thrilled for Ben. That's wonderful!" Storm said. "I also called about your case. I'd like to get together sometime this week. Will you be coming into town?"

"No, I've taken too much time off already. Any chance you'll be on the North Shore?"

"Um, I might be able to manage that." Storm knew that the two clients from the PD's office wouldn't need her until their arraignments, which would be at least a week away. She'd also had a call from one of Uncle Miles' former clients, an elderly woman who wanted to revise her will. Mrs. Shirome lived in Waialua, near Haleiwa. She would love the personal visit. It was the kind of thing Uncle Miles used to do.

"I'll pay for your driving time. I really need to talk to you," Stephanie said.

"No need. I have another client out that direction to visit, too." Storm reflected how good it felt to say that.

"Thanks, Storm." Stephanie sounded relieved, but Storm wasn't sure if it was because she'd said she'd come out or whether it was because she wouldn't bill her for the hour and a half drive.

"How's Wednesday, around lunchtime?" Storm asked. It would give her time to set court dates for the two people who'd visited this morning and catch up on some other office work.

"You mind coming to the restaurant where I work?"

"No problem. Congratulate Ben for me, okay?"

Storm got a few more phone calls from potential clients, transferred by Grace, who whooped enthusiastically before she connected them to Storm's line. Storm began to feel as if she might be able to make a living in her own law practice.

By Tuesday afternoon, though, she was rearranging her storage closet, which was pretty damned desperate, as her home closets were all a cluttered mess. Another of Uncle Miles' former clients called with questions about his estate, but Storm found that she still had plenty of time on her hands. She even went home early to do two days' worth of dirty dishes and feed Fang, the one-time skinny stray cat who now weighed fifteen pounds.

Fang purred like a lawnmower and did figure-eights against Storm's legs to show her appreciation.

"Don't get too excited. I'm meeting Hamlin for dinner. You'll have to entertain yourself tonight."

About an hour later, Storm sat on the lanai of a notable Hawai'i Kai restaurant, one of Hamlin's and her favorites. The live entertainment, a trio Storm enjoyed, was about to begin, when Hamlin called to tell her he was going to be fifteen minutes late. He'd had a crucial phone call just as he was leaving the office and now he was stuck in rush hour traffic on Kalanianaole Highway.

Storm didn't mind, though. She ordered a glass of merlot and some of the restaurant's special seared *ahi* sashimi and sat back in her chair. The guitarists were tuning, the sun was setting in a cranberry glow over the ocean, and a breeze ruffled her hair. She thought about the strange delivery Nahoa had received last Saturday. If someone had hoped to rattle him enough to affect his performance at the meet, they'd accomplished the opposite. No one had come near his final score.

The restaurant wasn't busy yet, and no one sat near her. She looked around and decided she could slip behind a potted bougainvillea to use her cell phone.

Aunt Maile answered cheerfully, sounding as close as next door, instead of 300 miles away on the Big Island. In the background, Keali'i Reichel sang from his album *Lei Hali'a*. Storm pictured her aunt, playing Reichel's soothing music and preparing supper, and she felt a pang of *hali'a* for the simpler, less confusing days of childhood. Back then, people were either good guys or bad guys, and jealousy was painful, but rarely life-threatening, though she hadn't realized it then.

"How are you, Aunt Maile?"

"Keone and I are fine, love. But you sound troubled. Is Ian all right?" Aunt Maile never referred to him by his last name, unlike Storm and the rest of Hamlin's friends.

"He's fine. His limp is getting better and his practice is booming. I'm waiting now to meet him for dinner."

"At a nice, romantic spot?"

Storm grinned. Aunt Maile and Uncle Keone loved Hamlin. Funny, because she might have expected them to want her to meet a nice Hawaiian man. But she should have known they'd see past culture and skin tone straight to his soul.

"Very. I'll bring you both here next time you're on O'ahu."

Aunt Maile laughed. "I can't wait. Now tell me why you called."

Storm hated to bring the subject up, but Aunt Maile had always been able to sense people's true motives. "I saw Nahoa Pi'ilani last weekend. He lives near Pupukea, and he's a really good surfer. He took Robbie and me out with some friends of his."

"That's wonderful." Maile's voice became thoughtful. "I wonder how Rochelle is after all these years."

"Me too, though she hated me after the accident."

"Not your fault. She was a troubled woman before she lost her husband."

"Nahoa seemed happy to see me, though, and he sent a friend to me for legal advice. He's a handsome guy, and by the way he looked at Leila, I think he knows it."

Aunt Maile chuckled. "Why am I not surprised?"

"But Aunt Maile, some kid brought him this package. Inside was a *lei o manō*."

"*Auwē.*" All the merriment went out of Maile's voice as she voiced the oath. There was a pause while she turned down the music in the background. "Did he know the boy?"

"No, he was just an innocent kid. He even asked for an autograph."

"What did Nahoa say when he saw the weapon?"

"He asked the boy where he got it. I got the feeling the kid felt bad when he saw our reaction. He said some guy had paid him."

"Sending a *lei o manō* used to be a challenge to battle. But when the old Hawaiian chiefs did it, they made sure the recipient knew where it came from," Maile said. "What was Nahoa's reaction?"

"He said someone was trying to scare him and we all assumed he was referring to the big surf meet this weekend."

"How did he do?"

"He won." Storm was proud of him. "In fact, he was great."

"Then we have to hope he answered the challenge and it's over." But there was a note in Aunt Maile's voice that told Storm she was worried.

"When one chief challenged another, what would happen?"

"They fought to the death, and the winner would dislocate the loser's joints and break all his bones. The victor wanted to make sure his enemy wouldn't return in another powerful form, like a shark or a boar. Sometimes he would even consume part of his victim to gain his *mana*, or power."

"Ugh."

"But only a coward would send a warning or threat in secret." Aunt Maile sounded grim. "It was probably a tasteless joke."

"Yeah," Storm said. She caught sight of Hamlin making his way through the tables. "Hamlin's here. I'll get back to you later."

"Be careful, love," Maile said, and they disconnected.

Hamlin bent over and kissed her. "Sorry I'm late. A client?"

"No, Aunt Maile. I called her about the package."

"Good idea. What did she say?"

"It's a threat," Storm said. "But you knew that, didn't you?"

"I read about it somewhere. Those old Hawaiians were brutal."

"You think it was meant to threaten Nahoa?"

"Sure, someone was trying to intimidate him. Nasty way to do it, too, if you know Hawaiian legend." A waitress stopped by the table and Hamlin looked up at her. "I'll have a glass of what she's having," he pointed his thumb toward Storm's half-empty wine glass, "and a couple of menus."

Storm shoved the plate of seared ahi toward Hamlin. "I saved some sashimi for you."

Hamlin picked up a set of chopsticks, dredged a piece of fish through the special wasabi sauce, and popped it into his mouth. "I'm starved."

"I was."

"You're worried." He pushed a wayward lock of hair from her forehead. "But Nahoa's okay. The threat didn't work, did it?"

Storm smiled at him and shook her head.

"So, do I need to distract you?" He ran one finger gently around the curve of her ear.

Storm gave a little shiver and edged closer to him. "You'll have to work harder than that." She grinned. "But I do have my appetite back."

"That's what I like to hear."

In a couple of hours, Storm's concerns about the parcel had faded to a lurking unease. The menu was filled with tempting dishes and neither she nor Hamlin had been able to make up their minds, so they ordered different entrees and shared. The restaurant was so accustomed to people doing this that waiters brought extra plates. She had *shutome,* or swordfish, which came with a red Thai curry basil peanut sauce. Hamlin ordered coriander-seared *ono,* or wahoo, and mussels with Kalua pork, taro hash, and Polynesian coconut crab. They took their time, and when they finally pushed away empty plates, Storm sighed with contentment.

"Want to share dessert?" Hamlin asked.

"You're going to go for a long walk tomorrow, while I'm going to be sitting on my derriere in the car. I've got to drive out to Haleiwa."

"You do?"

"I forgot to tell you. I want to talk to Stephanie about her case and she can't get any more time off work."

"Wish I could go." Hamlin ran his eye down the menu. "Did we have to order the melting hot chocolate soufflé ahead of time?"

"Yes, thank God. I love it, but the most I could eat now is a few bites of sorbet."

The waiter showed up as if he operated by telepathy.

"We'll have a scoop each of haupia and lilikoi sorbet, to share."

Storm sighed happily. "My favorites."

"I know."

"You're going to make me fat."

"No way," Hamlin said, and slid his eyes over to hers.

"You're bad," Storm said, and he just smiled.

Chapter Ten

Storm didn't even think about checking the messages on her cell phone until the next morning, when she went home to grab a bite of breakfast and feed Fang. The cat had already let herself in the kitchen pet door. She was sitting in front of the refrigerator when Storm walked through the front door, and she made scolding noises to let Storm know she'd been waiting.

Storm rooted through the refrigerator, sniffed at a carton of milk, which still smelled okay, and dumped the remainder of some fishy stuff in Fang's dish. She ground coffee beans, started a pot of coffee, and checked her answering machine while she waited for the coffee to finish brewing. There was a message from Ben Barstow, and when Storm called the number he'd left, she got his voice mail. She left her cell number and figured she'd catch up to him later.

By the time she sat down, dug into her cereal, and started the crossword puzzle in the morning paper, Fang had finished her fish and jumped into Storm's lap. This not only obliterated Storm's view of the paper, the cat's feet dug into her thighs. Storm got up and dumped the remainder of her breakfast into the cat's dish.

"This is why you're huge," she told Fang, and washed out her dishes.

Storm kept a bathing suit and beach towel in the trunk of her '72 Volkswagen Beetle, and she decided to take her board, which fit if she put the top down. This meant that she would only take the freeway from her Kahala cottage as far as the Likelike Highway to Kaneohe. There, she'd get on Kahekili Highway to Kamehameha and wind along the coast through Ka'a'awa, Hau'ula, and Lā'ie, where the Brigham Young University-Hawaii campus was located. It was her favorite route, more scenic than the faster-moving H-2 freeway up through the center of the island.

As an afterthought, Storm threw some toiletries and a change of clothes in a duffle, and added dry cat food to Fang's bowl. The cat looked up at her with round yellow eyes.

"Don't eat it all at once, or you're going to have to catch mice."

Fang kept looking at her, and Storm reached down and stroked her. "If I spend the night, I'll call Robbie to come over and play with you." The cat made a satisfied murrrp noise, and rubbed against Storm's legs.

∽ ∽ ∽

Storm's phone rang as she was negotiating a sharp curve through Kahulu'u. She downshifted the Beetle, followed the car in front of her around the heavily shaded bend in the road, shifted into third, and picked up her phone.

"Storm," Ben's voice said. "Can you talk?"

"Briefly, I'm driving."

"Okay. It's probably not a big deal, but I thought I'd tell you that your cousin didn't come home Monday night after surfing. His girlfriend is a friend of mine. She asked me Tuesday morning if I'd seen him. They were supposed to get together."

"She called you?"

"No, I went out to Chun's Reef for dawn patrol. She was there with a couple of friends."

"What about last night?"

"I don't know. I went to Chun's again this morning, but didn't see her. I heard she was at Outside Himalayas, though. That was some big surf," he added, "and people are talking about a new tow-in contest."

"Doesn't sound like she's too upset. What do you think?"

"She was probably looking for him. She's not the type to let on she's worried." Ben paused. "Um, he kind of has a reputation."

Surprise, surprise, Storm thought.

"But he's been seeing Sunny for a couple months now. I mean, without messing around. That's why I thought I'd see if you knew anything." Ben paused. "People talk and she may have heard, but I didn't want to bring it up."

"You probably know more about his friends than I do," Storm said. "Look, I'm on my way out to Haleiwa to see your mom, so I'll give you a call this afternoon."

Storm ended the call and gripped the steering wheel. Ben had seemed more concerned that Nahoa's girlfriend would find out Nahoa was cheating than he was about his disappearance. And the girlfriend was out surfing, but then again, that's where she figured she might see him.

His friends might not be losing sleep, but Storm felt a niggling anxiety. Few of the people who'd seen the *lei o manō* on Saturday knew what it meant in terms of Hawaiian legend. They looked at it merely as an artifact. At the most, a challenge. But the person who sent it knew it was a threat.

And a threat is still a threat—maybe a worse one—if the person on the receiving end doesn't recognize it as such. Storm wondered about surfer Ken Matsumoto's death. As a Japanese national, would he or any of his friends know if he'd received a threat by way of an artifact? A half mile down the road, Storm pulled into Ka'a'awa Beach Park and dialed the Honolulu Police Department.

"Detective Brian Chang, please," she said to the receptionist.

She considered it a stroke of luck that Brian, Leila's boyfriend, picked up his line.

"Hey, Storm. Wish I could have been with you this weekend. Robbie's talked of nothing else. What's up?"

"I wish you could have been, too." Storm could hear the rattle of papers in the background, as if someone were giving him forms to sign. "Brian, did Leila tell you about that package my cousin received?"

"Robbie did. A club with shark's teeth. One of those Hawaiian warrior things, I gather. Robbie said it was cool."

"Nahoa handled it pretty well, and he didn't let on that it could be a threat."

"A threat?" The background paper shuffling ceased.

Storm took a deep breath. "Do you know if Ken Matsumoto got any packages before he died?"

"I don't think so. It would be in the report, which I've read, but I'll check with the officers who handled it."

"Could you tell me about Ken Matsumoto's injuries?"

"What do you want to know? It was classified an accidental death."

"Did he drown because a series of waves held him under water too long?"

"As I remember, he had a head injury, but let me get back to you. One of the officers on the scene plays rugby with me and I have to talk to him about practice, anyway."

Storm's phone rang about fifteen minutes later and she turned into the huge parking lot at the Polynesian Cultural Center in Lāʻie. Brian Chang had talked to his colleague about Matsumoto's injuries.

"No packages." Brian sounded relieved. "He had extensive head injuries, consistent with the material in the reef where he'd been surfing, and a V-shaped contusion, probably from his surfboard. His family is devastated, but satisfied with that explanation."

"So he drowned?"

"Right, there are caves and shallow coral beds out there." She heard Brian get up and close the door. "The ME reported that the contusion probably would have killed him if his lungs hadn't filled with water first."

Storm could hear a note of something, dissatisfaction perhaps, in his voice. She waited him out, and he continued.

"He had other injuries, too." Brian's chair creaked, as if he leaned back in it. "Both femurs were broken, all three major arm bones. One knee and one hip were dislocated, plus—and this is what bugs me—he'd had two back molars pulled. His gums were still bloody."

Despite the hot sun, a chill crept over Storm.

"He must have been one tough SOB. I'd have been home with an ice pack."

Storm doubted that, as she once saw Brian play a game of rugby with a cracked wrist, but she kept quiet, knowing that he hadn't finished.

"It's pretty unusual to see so many broken bones, though the surfers we talked to say it could have happened if he got pounded inside one of those caves. The washing machine effect, I guess."

"And the teeth?"

"We asked around and one of his friends reported that he'd been to the dentist that day."

"He had a lot of friends?"

"He moved here six months ago from Japan. He apparently was pretty cocky, but no one seemed to have any malice for him. He hadn't been around that long."

Brian sighed and his chair creaked again. "Storm, there's no evidence of foul play. The case is closed. In the last four days we've had an eleven-year-old girl disappear from her Kailua school yard and a tourist stabbed by a prostitute in Waikiki. We've got our hands full of ongoing crises."

"I see," Storm said, and she did. "Thanks, Brian."

"You bet. I'll see you soon."

Storm looked both ways when she pulled back onto the highway, but her thoughts were on Ken Matsumoto and Nahoa. Matsumoto's death was sad, but not particularly suspicious. Brian would have told her if he'd received a package like Nahoa's, or been threatened in some other way, but she wondered if he might not know about it.

She vowed to herself that right after her meetings with Mrs. Shirome and Stephanie, she'd talk to a few of Nahoa's friends and check on who his girlfriends might be. It would be a relief to find out Nahoa was shacked up with a cutie in Waianae.

Storm had to put her worries aside for a while. Mrs. Shirome was delighted to see Miles Hamasaki's niece and so grateful for the personal visit that she put out plates of mango bread, star fruit, coconut manju, and enough iced tea to float an armada. The frail, white-haired lady talked story for nearly a half hour and Storm had three of the flaky manju pastries and two big glasses of iced tea before she could convince Mrs. Shirome to get out the will. The older woman was changing the primary beneficiary of a trust from her daughter to her grandson, at her daughter's request. Both were worried about the boy's future, as he wanted to be a professional surfer.

Storm tried, with great tact, to advise an educational fund, but the old woman had made up her mind. Because Storm was leery of getting grease spots from the manju on the documents and she was having difficulty concentrating with Mrs. Shirome's ongoing chatter, she ended up slipping the papers into her brief case to read more carefully later. She told Mrs. Shirome she'd have them rewritten and sent to her for a signature.

The older woman was a pleasure, as long as Storm didn't let herself feel pressured by the fact she'd told Stephanie Barstow that she'd be in the restaurant around lunchtime. But they hadn't named a specific hour, and she needed to spend time with this client, too. When Mrs. Shirome wasn't refilling Storm's iced tea, she would tap Storm's arm with a shaking forefinger to tell her another anecdote about Uncle Miles, which amused Storm.

By the time she left Mrs. Shirome's, it was one-thirty. Upon her arrival at Damien's, the popular seafood restaurant where Stephanie worked, Storm crammed her car between a double-wheeled pickup and a Hummer, grateful that the old VW was small and already had plenty of door dings. The outside seating area was crowded with sunburned tourists huddled under Cinzano umbrellas, and Storm picked her way over and around beach bags and snorkeling equipment.

Stephanie was hovering inside the door. "Where have you been?" She twisted her hands together.

"What's wrong?"

"Let's sit down." Stephanie gestured to a table in a corner of the restaurant. The interior of the place was dark, especially compared to the glare outside, and delightfully cool.

She pulled out a chair. "Can I get you something to drink? A sandwich?"

"No thanks."

Stephanie dropped into the chair across from Storm, rearranged the silverware, and refolded the napkin. "Marty's in town."

"He's not threatening you, is he?"

"No, but he's seen Ben."

"Ben told you?"

"No, someone saw Marty at Food Town. When I confronted Ben, he finally admitted Marty had called."

"Ben didn't want to tell you about it? Wasn't he worried for you?"

Stephanie shrugged. "I don't think Marty's going to come beat me up. He's the manipulative type, and his threats are more psychological." She chewed on her lip. "He'll use them on Ben."

Her eyes flitted around the room. "Have you heard about the big tow-in surf meet?" She met Storm's gaze for the first time. Storm shrugged. She wasn't sure she wanted to reveal yet that she'd heard about it from Ben.

Stephanie plowed ahead. "Marty and this old friend of his are the promoters. They're putting the event together." Storm began to guess why stress was rolling off the woman in waves.

"You know what I mean by a tow-in, don't you?" she hissed. "The surf's so big they have to use jet skis to get the surfers out to the waves." Her voice got louder with her distress. "There's a huge swell predicted for this week, continuing through the weekend. Thirty to thirty-five, Hawaiian style. That means it could get as high as fifty foot faces." Stephanie's voice broke. "And the holding period started already."

"What's a holding period?"

Stephanie swallowed. "It's what the promoters do to make certain they have a specific break reserved for a surf meet, when they expect the surf to be the best. It's supposed to keep other surfers away."

"And Ben?" But Storm already knew the answer.

Stephanie opened her mouth, but no sound came out on the first try. "His dad offered him a spot in the lineup," she finally croaked.

Storm took a deep swallow from the water glass that sat on the table. "What did Ben say?"

She could understand Stephanie's fear; participating in a contest like this was to flirt with death. And here it was, being run by the boy's estranged father.

"Not much. He's afraid I'll have a fit." Her eyes filled with tears. "So he acted nonchalant, which is how I've always known he's hiding something. Then he told me about the sponsorships."

"Sponsorships?"

Stephanie nodded. "There are sponsors, big companies who want their products marketed by participants in the meet. The sponsorships can be worth hundreds of thousands of dollars. Plus, it's a way to make a name for himself." Her mouth twisted wryly. "He could quit bagging groceries."

"And get invitations to other big surf meets?"

Stephanie chewed a hangnail. Her manicured nails of three days ago were chipped and broken. "It's the answer to his dreams. His whole life, he listened to Marty talk about it."

Storm regarded the misery in Stephanie's eyes. "When did Marty get into town?"

"Last week, I guess. I'm not sure, but he saw Ben compete on Sunday." Stephanie's eyes were filling up again.

"What worries you most?" Storm asked softly.

"That Ben will get hurt." Stephanie heaved a sigh. "And of course, I hate it that Marty is able to offer an opportunity I can't. But I can't say no to him, either." She used the napkin to wipe away a tear.

Stephanie looked at Storm with red-rimmed eyes. "You see, Marty never stopped longing for the days when he was a competitive surfer. Those were his glory days, and he wished he'd accomplished more. I think he's still trying to prove he can be a champion. And I can't be the one to take that chance away from Ben. To crush his dreams."

"Has Ben always admired his dad?"

Stephanie shrugged. "What boy gives up on his dad? When we moved out two years ago, he resented Marty's threats and bullying." She took a drink of water. "But he also missed him. There are things he admires about Marty. As he should."

"Marty was a champion surfer?"

"He was a finalist in the '86 Gerry Lopez Pipeline Masters. Got beat out by an Australian."

"Why didn't he try again?"

Stephanie moved the silverware around on the table. "I was pregnant. He was twenty-one and surfing didn't pay much in those days." She laughed, without humor. "I didn't know how expensive this decision would be in the long run."

"You asked him to quit?"

"His parents did, too," she added quickly. "They didn't like his lifestyle, the drugs, the whole scene. They didn't like me much, either—the brown-skinned wife. But it was finally something we agreed on."

"What happened after Ben was born?"

"I tried to convince him to go back to surfing." She smiled sadly. "But he'd started the real estate business and developed his first, successful shopping center. He was making real money." Her hands dropped to the table. "You know the rest."

Storm reached out and touched one of Stephanie's hands. "Getting a divorce isn't going to stop Ben from entering this contest."

"I know." Both women sat without speaking, and Storm watched the emotions play across Stephanie's face.

After a few moments, Stephanie spoke quietly. "The divorce is for me. I've been living in limbo, and I can't go on this way. I'm sick and tired of it."

"How does Ben feel about the divorce?" Storm asked. She thought back to Ben's ambivalent behavior in her office, how much more subdued he'd been there than on the beach.

"He'll go along with it," Stephanie said.

Storm figured Stephanie knew best, but she also had the feeling that Stephanie was leaving out details of her relationship with Ben and his father. So be it, as long as they were personal, and not issues that would affect the divorce agreement.

Chapter Eleven

Stephanie's gaze followed a troupe of sandy beach-goers who had traipsed into the restaurant and stood blinking as their eyes adjusted to the cool, subdued dining room. "I've got to get back to work," she said. "My hostess is on lunch break."

"Okay," Storm said, and realized that during Stephanie's explanation of Marty's and Ben's relationship, she'd made a decision of her own. She was going to take advantage of the beach cottage again for at least tonight. That way, she could talk to Ben and track down Nahoa. She jotted the phone number on the back of a business card and handed it to Stephanie. "This is where I'll be if you need me tonight. You've got my cell number, too."

Outdoors, the mid-afternoon sun seemed even hotter than when Storm had entered the restaurant. The ocean breezes, when they wafted across the blacktopped main street, carried heat and the aromas of suntan oil and car exhaust. Suddenly, Storm wanted to get out of the congested little beach town and closer to the water. In the distance, she could see Waialua Bay through a scrim of crowded shops and dusty palm trees, beckoning like a silver platter.

The car seat was so hot that she yelped when the back of her legs hit the vinyl. Her damp cotton shift conducted the heat to her sweating back. Fortunately, no one had bothered her surf board, probably because it had some obvious fiberglass patches, but the wax had melted in the sun and dripped in greasy blobs onto the passenger seat. It was time to get out of town.

By the time Storm was on Kamehameha Highway, she'd decided she'd change into a bathing suit, re-wax her board, and head for the water. Even if she didn't find Ben or Nahoa at Laniakea, she'd reenergize so that she could track them down later. There would be other surfers in the water, and she could ask questions as to Nahoa's whereabouts. Maybe some gossip would give her the lowdown on his love life.

The key to the beach house was still where Storm had hidden it when they'd left on Sunday, and the first thing she did after opening the louvered windows to the trade winds was to call the owners and ask permission to stay a few more days. Aunt Maile's friends were delighted to have her "looking after the place." Storm thanked them for their hospitality and promised herself that she'd send a thank you note later in the week.

The next phone call Storm made was to Leila and Robbie, to ask them to look in on Fang. No problem there, either. In fact, to Robbie's delight, Leila said she'd pick up the cat that afternoon and bring her to stay with them for a few days. Hamlin wasn't in the office, but Grace told Storm she'd tell him to call her that evening, then teased Storm about recruiting clients from the surf crowd.

Storm dropped onto the sofa with a happy sigh and put her feet up on the coffee table. Grace might be onto something there.

Ten minutes later, Storm was paddling toward a cluster of surfers on modest waves just down the beach from the cottage. It looked so appealing she couldn't resist. The waves weren't scary, and the people on them looked even less experienced than she.

Once she got to the break, she found that the small cluster of surfers was actually a class made up of high school-aged students. Their conscientious and serious instructor was Goober, who waved a greeting at Storm, then went back to holding a big, wide board steady for a chunky, laughing kid.

Storm went out a little farther, so as not to distract Goober or his students, and stood up easily on the first wave she tried to catch. After a half hour or so of working on technique, she caught the second wave of an incoming set. Three of the students had caught the first wave, which was what she'd anticipated, and Goober sat on his board, watching their progress. When she went by, she attempted a cutback. Though she blew it and fell off, she was where she wanted to be and popped out of the water not far from Goober.

"I didn't know you taught surfing," she said.

He looked a bit sheepish and cast his eyes around to see if anyone was within hearing distance. "The guys hate it."

"Your surfing buddies? Why?"

"We tie up breaks, which pisses 'em off. Plus, no one in this group can turn, so they can be a little dangerous sometimes. Watch out, okay?"

"These waves are a bit small for your friends, aren't they?"

"Yeah, but there've been some clashes."

"Everyone's got to start sometime. And you're helping these kids have fun."

"Helps me pay the bills."

Goober waved his students over and Storm let herself drift to the other end of the break. Soon after, Goober led his students to the beach. Storm was the only person on the water, and she let herself take a few more risks. The waves were perfect for attempting to shift her weight from rail to rail of the board and for practicing turns on the face of the wave. After three or four short, experimental tries, she got a long ride on a perfect, glassy wave. When the wave closed out into white water, she was still standing on the board, and was within a hundred yards of shore. She knew she could hardly end on a better ride than that, and dropped to her stomach to paddle the rest of the way in.

Goober was collecting his fees and seeing the last of his students off.

"Wait up," Storm called to him.

He turned to her. "Yeah?"

"You going to meet your friends at a bigger break?"

He pushed sand around with his feet. "No, I've gotta meet some people."

"Have you seen Nahoa?" she asked.

Goober shook his head. "Ben was asking about him, too. Haven't seen him for a coupla days."

"He's got a girlfriend, now, doesn't he?"

She could see a dead tooth in Goober's sly half smile. "Which one?"

"Ben mentioned someone named Sunny. Who else is there?"

"How would I know?"

"Come on, my aunt wants me to find him. I don't care who he's seeing, and I won't tell anyone."

Goober exhaled noisily. "I don't know her name. Just some old squeeze who started calling him again."

"You know Sunny, right?"

"Everyone knows Sunny. She's a babe and a good surfer."

"Did you know Ken Matsumoto?"

Goober answered with deliberate nonchalance. "Enough to say hello." With a little smirk, he shrugged and walked away.

Storm watched him amble off. She'd hoped to find out if Matsumoto had received a package, but Goober wasn't giving up information, and whether the reason was social awkwardness or some other problem, she sensed that the young man had closed down to questions.

His figure grew smaller against the backdrop of trees. Although being in the ocean makes a person feel clean, purified even, Goober gave Storm the impression he hadn't used soap for a long time. Though he knew she still stood where he'd left her, he walked over the sand embankment toward the highway without looking back.

Chapter Twelve

Steve O'Reilly woke up Wednesday with a dagger of sunlight slashing through the gap in his bedroom drapes directly into his throbbing eyeballs. He rolled over with a groan, then sat up suddenly with an onslaught of beer-induced borborygmi that sent him scuttling to the toilet, glad he'd awakened alone.

By the time he got to Waimea Bay Beach Park, where he'd told Barstow he'd meet him and the two guys who wanted to discuss the permits for the upcoming meet, he was a half hour late. He found that Barstow had arrived an hour earlier than the meeting after jogging from his Sunset Beach cottage. Then, O'Reilly discovered, Barstow had borrowed someone's board and gone out to test the incoming swell. Asshole acted like he'd gone to bed with the birds.

O'Reilly burped a coffee-tinged, burning eruption. Of course, he'd stayed up for a few after Barstow had left. And this morning he'd used a couple lines he'd scored from one of the surfers to help him out the door. Now he felt like something the ocean would abandon on the sand when the tide went out.

O'Reilly looked around at the beach, which was pretty damned pristine, and felt a chill. No, the ocean didn't waste much. Uncle Whitey would take care of any drifting dead stuff, wouldn't he? Sometimes it wasn't even dead.

"Huh?" Barstow had been talking to him and O'Reilly hadn't heard a word.

"Steve, this is Garret Tasake and Bob Waterson. Garret works for the State of Hawaii Department of Land and Natural Resources. He'll get our permit for the use of the near-shore waters. Bob's with the Honolulu Department of Parks and Recreation, so he can guide us through the red tape for the beach permit."

"Hey." O'Reilly pumped both of their hands and ignored Barstow's second glance. "Thanks for helping us out."

Tasake spoke up. "You're okay with beach permits, but you know that any member of a tow-in team has to take a six-hour course at an accredited institution? And tow-in surfers are only allowed to go out when the National Weather Service has declared a high-surf day."

Barstow spoke up. "What are you saying? That means anyone not already accredited would have to be here a day before the contest begins."

"At least."

"Shit." Barstow hit one fist into his palm, then squinted at Tasake. "Okay, then. That'll only be a couple of people, but could I count on you to get them set up with the class they need?"

"I'll give you the name of the guy, and he'll tell you what the fee is," Tasake said.

"I figured. Hope he goes for a group rate."

Tasake shrugged. That part was out of his hands.

The two men left after setting up a couple more meetings, and Barstow turned to O'Reilly. "You awake yet?" The cords stood out in his neck and he bit off the words.

O'Reilly stood up straighter. "I heard 'em. Ten-thirty tomorrow morning, Sunset Elementary School." He looked down on Barstow and hoped the guy didn't piss him off. They were too far into this.

Barstow narrowed his eyes. "Good. I want this meet to happen without any fuck-ups."

"Hey, me too. But there are always fuck-ups, buddy. It's how we deal with them that counts."

Barstow looked at him out of the corner of his eye. "Right."

O'Reilly put his arm on Barstow's shoulder. "What's driving you in this?"

Barstow moved away, so that O'Reilly's arm dropped off. "What do you mean?"

"You know, your motivation. What's pushing you?" O'Reilly squinted at him. "You know my story. I need the money—hell, I need a job. It's public knowledge I got canned from KZXM. What about you?"

Barstow shrugged. "I'm going through a divorce."

"Yeah?" O'Reilly kept his eyes on the side of Barstow's face.

Finally Barstow spoke up. "It feels good to be back on the surf scene."

"Any chance you wanted to be near Ben?"

Barstow kept his eyes on the waves breaking at the mouth of the bay. "Swell's building."

O'Reilly didn't answer, and a few moments elapsed.

"Yeah, okay. I want to be near Ben. So?"

"It's normal, man. I'd want to be near my kid, too." O'Reilly nodded. "Just wanted to hear you say it."

Barstow turned to face O'Reilly. "I want Ben to be in the lineup for the Intrepid. If he wants to, that is."

Now they were getting down to it. People always had an agenda. O'Reilly rubbed the bridge of his nose. "I don't know, man. We got guys all over the world wanna be in this tow-in. And we've got room for fifteen teams, thirty people. How we gonna fit in another guy, especially a kid who hasn't won a major event yet?"

"He was second last week."

"True, and he's an up-and-coming competitor, for sure. But that was his first major meet."

Several long moments elapsed.

"Fine," Barstow said. "Just don't close your mind to the idea. You know some of the guys we invited will miss their planes or get injured. We'll have a couple of last minute holes to fill."

"Okay. I'll keep an open mind." O'Reilly knew it was time to change the subject. "You had a chance to touch base with that guy Gabe Watson about getting the guys we need to help out with the logistics of a tow-in?"

"Yeah." Barstow rolled his eyes. "He's a real water stud. You know—lifeguard, runs a surf school concession, related to half the families in Haleiwa. And guess what? He's the guy who runs the course for jet-ski accreditation, too."

"Your favorite type, eh? You think he's a member of the Blue Shorts?"

"Let's just say he offered to keep the beach clear of surfers during the holding period."

"Anything else?"

Barstow's lip curled in a half-smile. "Yeah, he wants to be in the line-up."

"Shit. Was he on your list?"

"No, but I think I'll give him a shot at it if he'll partner up with Nahoa Pi'ilani."

"Did you tell him that?"

Barstow shook his head. "Not yet. Let him knock himself out first." And Barstow grinned. It reminded O'Reilly of a tiger shark.

Chapter Thirteen

Storm got to Food Town at four forty-five. She dashed in the wheezing pneumatic door to see Ben at a checkout station, loading grocery bags into the basket of a very old man with flowing white hair and mahogany skin, a baggy T-shirt and shorts that hung past his knees. Too-large rubber slippers slapped against his wide, cracked feet.

"Is your daughter waiting in the parking lot, Mr. 'Oama? Ben asked.

The ancient nodded, and shuffled past Storm. Ben followed with the cart. "I'll be right back," he said to Storm.

He returned in less than a minute. "Thanks for coming by. Did my mom tell you where I was?" His expression was wary. Storm figured she wouldn't let on that Stephanie had confided her fears about the tow-in contest.

"No, Goober did. You heard anything from Nahoa?"

Ben shook his head. "But I haven't seen Sunny today."

Storm looked at her watch. "You think she'll be home?"

"I don't know. She works at Kimo's Pizzeria, so she might be starting a shift." He unpinned his name tag from his aloha shirt, which was covered with the Food Town logo. "We can walk over and check."

A petite young woman with curling dark hair that reached to her waist waved as they entered the front door of the small restaurant. "Hi, Ben." She beamed at him.

Lacquered wood-topped tables were crowded into the single room and people were already lined up at the counter for pitchers of beer. The combined aromas of basil, tomato sauce, and beer on tap made Storm's stomach growl. She was hungry, but didn't want to pause in her search for Nahoa.

"Naomi, is Sunny around?" Ben asked.

Naomi's smile diminished by a couple of watts, but she kept up her enthusiasm. "She's off tonight, but she'll be in at ten tomorrow morning." Her eyes wandered to Storm.

"I'm Storm Kayama." Storm put out her hand. "I'm a friend of Ben's and his mother's."

Naomi's smile amped back up a few notches. "You want a seat?" Her eyes flicked to a group of men on the other side of the room and she lowered her voice. "I can have a Kimo's Parmesan Special ready in about ten minutes."

"No thanks, but I'll come back later," Ben said.

Outside, Storm grinned at him. "You better go back tomorrow."

Ben shuffled his feet. "Yeah, she's really nice."

Storm got out her car keys. "You mind going with me to Sunny's?"

"Sure, she lives in Pupukea. We can check out Nahoa's at the same time."

"They don't live together?"

"Not technically, but she's there a lot. Sunny shares a house with two other women. It's kind of run down, but it's a cool place. Nahoa's cottage is just down the beach."

Storm led Ben to her car, which she'd left in the Food Town parking lot. As she made her way through the traffic in Haleiwa town, she realized how little she knew about Nahoa's lifestyle.

"What does Nahoa do when he's not surfing?" she asked.

"He's a shaper at the Tubin' Tanker. He and Mo'o Lanipuni are well known for their surfboard designs."

"That's a good job, isn't it?"

"Sure, Nahoa does okay. He's been getting some endorsements, too. Clothing and stuff."

Storm realized that Ben was a bit in awe of her cousin, who was kind of a local celebrity. Not only did Nahoa have a reputation for being a ballsy, red-hot surfer, the six years in age that separated the two seemed to be more than chronological. Ben was till a teenager, living with his mother, while Nahoa was a confident young man.

Sunny's house was a big rambling frame affair that looked as if it had undergone renovations by at least two different builders. Not even the paint matched. It sat on stilts on a large lawn shaded by two sprawling mango trees and a fringe of banana plants. Typical of old plantation homes, the place lacked a garage and driveway, and three older-model cars were parked in the grass, which was mowed and otherwise uncluttered. It reminded Storm of a college fraternity, except with the single-wall redwood construction and traditional hip roof common to Hawai'i. It had a certain scruffy charm.

Ben went right in the screened front door and shouted a greeting. No one was in the living room, which was situated inside the entry. Delicious cooking aromas were coming from the back of the house, and Ben headed in that direction, calling out a few more hellos. Storm followed and noted the comfortable, but unmatched furnishings, batik drapes, and high-end stereo equipment.

"Jenna, Charlie," Ben said. "Howzit?"

A pretty, rotund woman whose pareu barely covered a figure that conservatively could be called Rubenesque looked up from where she sat. The toddler she fed gurgled and banged his fists on his high chair tray. Storm wasn't sure if he wanted more of the pasty stuff she was feeding him or whether he was greeting Ben.

Both Charlie and Jenna grinned when they saw him and Jenna got to her feet and gave Ben a big hug. She went over to the stove to stir a pot, while Charlie hammered harder on his tray, and everyone but Storm ignored him. Flecks of food flew with each whack.

"What smells so good?" Ben asked. Storm thought he might be trying to ignore the big brown nipple that flashed where the flowing Tahitian garment gaped.

"Beef stew and rice," Jenna said. "What you up to?"

"This is my friend Storm. Sunny around?"

Jenna rolled her eyes at Storm. "She'll be back *bumbye*. It's getting dark out." Charlie sat open-mouthed, like a baby bird, and Jenna shoveled another spoonful into the chasm. "She's been *habut* ever since Nahoa broke their date. Can't hardly talk to her."

"He's not back yet?"

Jenna shook her head. Charlie shook his, too—with his mouth open. The front door banged.

"Maybe that's Sunny." Storm thought she heard a note of relief in Ben's voice.

She followed Ben toward the front of the house. It was nearly dark outside, but no one had turned on lights in the living room, and they could see a tall silhouette against the waning daylight that filtered through the screen. The figure leaned over and turned on a table lamp, then flung her wet blonde hair over one shoulder.

"Sunny?" Ben said.

Sunny's face lit up momentarily, then went blank. "Ben."

"This is Nahoa's cousin. Storm's—"

"Hi," Sunny said dully. "Are you first cousins?" She seemed to ask the question out of social convention, not interest.

Sunny looked familiar to Storm, but she couldn't place her. "Second. His mother was married to my mother's cousin."

Sunny gave her a second, harder look and shivered, then proceeded to wrap a beach towel tightly around her waist and do as deft a deck change as Storm had ever seen. Her bikini bottoms dropped to the floor, and in a swift move, she slid board shorts up legs that looked like they were half Storm's height. After that, she removed the towel and wrapped it around her broad shoulders.

It was when the light caught the myriad of earrings in her left ear that Storm remembered where she'd seen Sunny before. She was the woman at the surf contest who'd defended Goober's grumpy nature.

"I talked to you at last weekend's meet. My friends and I were there to watch Ben, Nahoa, and Goober surf."

"Oh," Sunny said. She whirled to peer through the screen door at the sound of a car passing.

"Did you see that package Nahoa got last Saturday?"

"Ugly thing, with shark's teeth?"

"Yes, do you know what happened to it?"

"No, but it pissed him off." Sunny gave up on the sound of the car and walked into the living room, where she dropped into a chair. She waved a hand in the direction of the sofa. "He called a couple people about it."

Ben hovered, standing, but Storm sat on the edge of the couch. "Do you know who?"

"No, but what's your interest in him?" Her voice was low, almost resigned, but she emphasized the "your" a tiny bit.

"I grew up with him. He's family, plus his mom and mine were friends."

Sunny sat unmoving, watching Storm as if evaluating her, while her eyes glistened in the lamplight.

"I haven't seen her for years," Storm said, "but she lost her husband when Nahoa was very young. I'm worried that the shark tooth thing was a threat."

Sunny's chin came up. "I'm worried, too, but I don't run his life. If a guy wants to move on, good riddance."

Sunny had apparently heard the rumors about other women. Storm felt sorry for her. She'd experienced cheating boyfriends, too. "Will you tell me if you see him? And that package, if you find it, would you let me know?"

Sonny looked at Storm out of the corner of her eye. Yes, her eyes were definitely wet. "Sorry, I need some time alone." She got up and walked out of the room, but turned to look over her shoulder. "I'll let you know, okay?"

Storm and Ben let themselves out the front door. Ben hadn't looked either woman in the eye for the last several minutes. Typical guy, Storm figured, paralyzed by a woman's emotions.

Ben slumped in the passenger seat of Storm's car. "I'd better get home."

"Want me to call your mom and tell her you're with me?"

"No." Ben's voice was much more abrupt than it needed to be, and Storm once again wondered about the dynamics between him and his parents. There were secrets in that family, and Uncle Miles' warnings about family secrets and how no one came out on top in a bitter divorce chafed like sand in a bathing suit.

Chapter Fourteen

Ben had only monosyllabic responses to any of Storm's attempts at conversation on the way back to Haleiwa. He did direct her down the street where Nahoa lived, and they crawled past his dark, closed cottage. Two newspapers in their waterproof plastic bags sat on the front step where the paperboy had tossed them. It was obvious no one was home.

Storm dropped him off at the townhouse where he and Stephanie lived and declined a polite, but perfunctory invitation to come in. On the way from Haleiwa to Laniakea, she stopped at the Food Town and bought a few grocery items, but her mind was occupied with whether she'd been as moody as Ben, Goober, and Sunny when she was their age. She'd probably been worse.

At sixteen, she had endured the Big Island police department's scrutiny for allegedly cultivating *pakalolo*, which she was definitely doing; they just hadn't located her patch in the sugar cane fields—yet. Aunt Maile and Uncle Keone didn't doubt her activities for a minute, so they shipped her to Oʻahu, Miles Hamasaki's household, and a much stricter high school. At seventeen, she was depressed enough to flirt with the idea of ending the struggle like her mother, with a bottle of pills. If it hadn't been for the Hamasakis, Aunt Maile and Uncle Keone, she'd have checked out.

With those thoughts, the beach cottage felt empty and lonely. She poured Yoshida's Teriyaki Sauce over a chicken breast and settled it on the grill, then went back inside to call Hamlin.

"Don't you ever check your phone?" he asked her.

Sure enough, there were four messages on her mobile phone. "I didn't hear it ring. But I was running around quite a bit."

"Were you back in the mountains?"

"Yes, Nahoa's girlfriend, Sunny, shares a house with some other surfers in Pupukea. The signal is probably weak back there." She went on to tell him about how Nahoa hadn't shown up for a date Monday, so she and Ben had gone to talk with Sunny. She also filled him in on her cousin's reputation with women, the upcoming tow-in surf contest, and Stephanie's fears.

"When are you coming back to town?"

"Could I talk you into coming out for the tournament?"

"When does it start?"

"From what Stephanie told me, the holding period started today and the surf is coming up. If the swell is big enough, they'll start the qualifying round Thursday or Friday afternoon."

"I've got two depositions on Friday, but I could leave town around five. Come back and we'll drive out together."

"I want to hang around and see if I can find Nahoa. I'm worried about him."

"You need to talk to the police."

"I did. I talked to Brian Chang." She told him about Matsumoto's injuries and how she wanted to ask some of the locals if he'd received a package like Nahoa's.

"Storm, I worry about you out there alone, asking questions."

"Chances are, Nahoa pissed someone off over a woman. He's probably lying low for a while. I'm mostly just going to surf. If I'm lucky, I'll see him. At least I'll see some of his friends."

"Be careful, okay?"

"I will and I'll talk to you tomorrow."

The next thing on Storm's list was to touch base with Leila and see if she'd been able to pick up Fang. She felt much better after talking to Hamlin, and she unwrapped a musubi she'd picked up at the supermarket. When Leila answered the phone, Storm's greeting was muffled by rice, Spam, and *nori*.

"She's already curled up with Pua," Leila assured her. They made their usual jokes about why Pua, Leila's grizzled English bulldog, let the fat cat into her bed.

"Pua can't see well enough to chase her out," Leila said.

"Nah, Fang's like a warm blanket. I should know."

"And she puts up with Pua's snoring."

When Storm hung up, the house felt considerably less lonely. Hamlin would be with her in two days, and the grilling chicken smelled heavenly. After dinner, she'd curl up with a good book and go to bed early so she could make dawn patrol.

Storm slept well until the crash of the surf and the watery morning light, filtering through the narrow blinds, woke her around six-thirty. Wind ruffled the gauzy white curtains and brought the smell of salt and sea into the bedroom.

She brewed a pot of coffee, just to warm up in the cool, damp morning air, and downed a large mug while she waxed her board and pulled a heavier-than-usual rash guard over her head. She still shivered, and contemplated that she'd probably never be able to surf where the water temperature dipped below seventy. Some hardship.

The morning was calm and the water glassy and smooth. There were already a couple of people out at the Laniakea breaks, but no one she recognized, so she tucked her board under her arm and strolled down the beach toward the break surfers called Himalayas. She set her surfboard in the sand and stood to observe for a few minutes.

A tiny rider cut away from a curling wave that looked twice his height. Good move, Storm thought. But that wave was a monster. She picked up her board; the waves were too big for her here, but the morning was beautiful and she'd find a smaller break down the beach a bit. Even if she ended up just going for a stroll, the sky above her was the hue of a fine Tahitian pearl, and it met the horizon in a hazy blue line, where the sun glowed the color of pale hibiscus. In those moments, Storm knew why many of the North Shore population eschewed the bigger salaries and faster pace of Honolulu.

Storm sighed with contentment and picked up her board. She'd heard Ben and some of his friends mention the Puaena Point break, and though she thought the waves might be too big for her, she would enjoy the walk and she might see someone she knew.

Sure enough, when she climbed over an outcrop of lava rock and down the other side to a flat sandy area, she saw Goober and Gabe, ready to head out into the water. Goober saw her and waved. He seemed in a better mood than when she'd seen him the day before.

"Storm, you going out?"

"You think I can handle it?" She squinted at the waves, where they broke about two hundred yards off shore.

"Sure, you can let the big ones go by," Gabe said. "Get off on the shoulder, or duck-dive under them."

Storm strained to see the surfers already on the waves. They looked smaller than the ones she'd seen at Himalayas, but she needed to get a perspective of a person's height against a wave's in order to judge whether the break was beyond her ability. And even that was no guarantee, because wave height varied within a set.

Storm did not want to get clobbered by a hefty wave that was closing out. She'd been tumbled in the washing machine before, lungs convulsing with oxygen deprivation. She'd also seen surfers lunge to the surface for air, only to have their surfboard, attached to them by the rubber leash, boomerang back to the water and slice the gasping person with a sharp skeg. And then there were the boards that got snapped in two as easily as ice cream sticks.

A couple of women were on the waves, and Storm judged the wave to be about their height. She suppressed a little shiver. "I guess I'll go," she said.

"You can do it. It'll be good for you," Goober said.

Storm shook her head, but he didn't see it. Good for her? Sounded like the kind of things guys say to each other before they tried some stunt that would either kill them or give them bragging rights, with nothing in between.

Gabe seemed to pick up on her apprehension. "There's a channel to our right, and the current will carry you out. The waves don't break as hard in there. Follow us, but stay on the inside."

In some circumstances, Storm would have been offended by Gabe's suggestion. It was sort of like saying, stay out of our way once we get out there. But this time, Storm's jitters told her it was a good idea. She had no need to go where the break was biggest, and if it weren't for the two women she could see out there, she wouldn't have considered following Gabe. Even Goober had shaken her confidence lately.

She plunged in after the guys, and gulped when the chilly water surged around her. There was a stronger current than she had ever felt, and she vowed to be extra attentive. Though the trio waited out a set of four or five big waves before they paddled through the break, going out wasn't as bad as Storm had feared. When they got to the wave lineup, she looked back at the shore and aligned two objects, a chunk of lava that rose from the sand and a lifeguard stand, so that she'd have a point of reference. A couple of rock formations on her left would serve to make sure she wasn't being carried out to sea by a rip tide, often undetectable in surging waters.

As Goober had instructed her last weekend, Storm paddled onto the shoulder of the first wave of the set and let it go by. He and Gabe left her there and headed fifty yards to the right, where a small group of men sat on their boards, facing the open ocean and waiting a turn on a wave. The two women Storm had seen were only about twenty yards out from where she sat, and Storm recognized Sunny, in tiny bikini bottoms and a long-sleeved turquoise rash guard, as one of them. Sunny hadn't seen Storm yet, because she glanced continuously toward the knot of men nearby.

She's searching for Nahoa, Storm thought, and squinted against the rising sun to try to identify the surfers. Though she couldn't make out any of them except Gabe and Goober, she was certain Nahoa wasn't among them. She shivered, then lay on her board to paddle out of the way of Sunny's friend, who was stroking hard toward her. Storm swooped over the curl as the young woman rose to her feet. Storm saw the flash of white teeth in her delighted smile.

Storm didn't see Sunny waiting for the next ride, and guessed the two women must have taken off together. Though it was hard to be sure with the water rising and falling around her, Storm assumed she was alone and in position for the next wave. Storm sat up, ready to kick her board around, and saw a flash of turquoise above a rising wall of water. She lay back down and moved to the side to watch Sunny's takeoff.

The woman was good. Those long, rock-hard legs were in an easy right-angle crouch, urging the short board at an angle across the face of the wave. Storm couldn't help but feel delight and admiration at the woman's strength and finesse. It was a big wave, whose vortex and thundering speed sucked air and water droplets back at Storm with a force that made her duck her head and squint. She exhaled with relief that she hadn't taken it, yet Sunny rode it as if she could handle twice its size.

Storm's relief was short-lived, though, because a black-clad rider that was hard to see shot out from the side, screaming at Sunny that she was in his way.

"Hey," Storm yelled.

That was before she realized that the surfer in black was Gabe. He had taken off on the wave a couple of seconds after Sunny, who had the right of way. It was a blatant snake.

Friends often rode the same waves, and safely negotiated their turns in opposite directions so that no one would be startled, or worse, injured. But in the split second after Storm saw Gabe, she knew he was deliberately bearing down on Sunny. It was a game of chicken, and anyone in Sunny's position with half a brain would bail out, rather than face a high speed collision in turbulent, roiling water.

But Sunny hadn't seen him yet, and the howl of wind and crash of the wave kept her from hearing his approach. Storm couldn't tell if he was shouting at her, but she wasn't going to wait around to see.

"Sunny," she shrieked, "watch out!"

Some high note of panic in Storm's voice carried over the rumble of tons of water, because Sunny glanced behind her. Just as Gabe reached her, she launched herself from her board.

Gabe looked back at Storm in surprise, which caused him to lose his balance and windmill his arms in an attempt to stay upright. Screaming a string of foul names, he tumbled backward and was swallowed by the breaking water.

Storm snorted in disgust. That act was just what Nahoa had warned her about, and she'd bet that he'd warned Sunny, too. However, from watching Sunny's smooth expertise, Storm would have bet there wasn't much the young woman hadn't already seen on the waves.

Sunny surfaced a couple hundred yards from where Storm sat. A smaller wave, probably the last of the set Sunny had taken, rose behind Storm. Storm looked around for other surfers, lined up her board, dropped onto her stomach, and dug into the water with deep, strong strokes as the wave sucked her into its crest.

Though smaller than Sunny's, the wave had excellent form and curled above Storm's head. Storm crouched, bending her legs as pistons, using her quadriceps to bear her weight and urge the board along its face. She was glad she'd had some experience over the last week on powerful North Shore waves, because she'd never had surf curve above her before. It was a left-hand break, which was perfect for her stance, and she let the board slow so that the water arched above her.

Jesus, she was actually in a tube. She couldn't believe it, and a moment of claustrophobic panic came over her. No, don't think about it. You can hold this position, you're strong, she told herself. And she did. She spurted out the side of the curl, stood upright with an excited whoop, jabbed two fists into the air, and tumbled exuberantly into the water.

When she popped to the surface, her excitement was squelched by the scene before her. Gabe and Sunny were thirty yards from her, and Sunny was ripping mad.

"I'll have you thrown off the ASP, you gutless fu—." A surge of water garbled some words after that, but Storm got the message.

So did Gabe. "Stupid bitch." He gave a cruel laugh. "No one gives a shit what you think. Not even Nahoa hung around for you."

"You jerk, you can't even catch a wave unless it's got a woman on it." Sunny's voice quavered, though Storm couldn't tell if it was with tears or rage. Maybe both.

Gabe narrowed the distance between himself and Sunny, which bothered Storm even more than Gabe's cruel words. Sunny was a strong woman, but if he got physical, she'd have real problems. Storm began to swim toward the two.

Gabe was within ten feet of Sunny, and Storm was still twenty feet away, with a good view of both of them. Sunny sat on her surfboard, arms crossed over her chest, and glared at Gabe. "Keep away from me, asshole. Always."

Storm wouldn't ever want Sunny mad at her, but she wondered why Gabe stopped without saying a word. He appeared to crouch into the water. Storm could see Sunny shift her weight, almost poise herself.

"Gutless bastard," she hissed at him.

And from under Gabe shot a sharply pointed, fiberglass missile. It was his surfboard, which he'd held underwater so that it would fly out of the water with the force of its own buoyancy. He'd aimed it right for Sunny's face.

"No!" Storm yelled.

Sunny had known what was coming, though, and she turtled. Gabe's board clattered on top of her upside down one, which made Storm wince. Sunny was safe underwater, but the clatter verified the violence of the act; both boards were going to need Mo'o's ministrations after this.

Sunny popped to the surface, her eyes wide with fury and loathing. "You really are a pathetic wimp."

By this time, Storm was beside her, and she grabbed Gabe's board to keep it from doing any more damage in the surging water. Sunny's eyes flicked to Storm's and Storm saw relief soften the blonde's face before she turned back to her attacker.

"You'll pay for this, you gutless suckerfish."

Both women stared at Gabe, who glared with unabashed hatred at the two of them. He now treaded deep, blue water, a quarter-mile from shore. No way would they return his board, which he'd just used as a weapon. Storm nudged Sunny's arm, and without saying a word, Sunny crawled atop her board and both women headed for shore, towing the extra board.

After a few minutes of paddling, Sunny steadied her breathing and looked over at Storm. "Thanks. He could have killed me."

"Yeah, that was scary. You're right—he's a coward." Storm shook her head. "But you've got balls for telling him out there."

"He needs to be told."

"You told Gabe, but you didn't want to tell Goober when he was being a jerk."

"Goober's different."

"Oh." Storm was about to ask why, but her thoughts returned to the maliciousness of Gabe's act. If his well-aimed board had hit Sunny as he'd intended, she would have been knocked cold, and probably drowned. Storm remembered Nahoa's warning about keeping an eye on Gabe. Could Ken Matsumoto or—God forbid—Nahoa have had an altercation with him?

She and Sunny had been making their way toward shore and were now close enough to see a group of eight or ten gathered where jagged black lava rocks formed a small cove. It was an odd place for people to assemble, and some of them were scrabbling for footholds as they grappled with something in the water.

The women paddled toward the group, but Storm had a bad feeling about this particular assembly. She glanced at Sunny from the corner of her eye and saw Sunny did, too. The woman's normally golden skin was ashen. Both women slowed their approach, glanced briefly at each other, and then away. Neither wanted to confront the dread in the other's expression.

Chapter Fifteen

Storm turned to look in the direction they'd come, but Gabe was nowhere to be seen. He'd headed away from this landing point. Meanwhile, waves carried the women closer to shore.

A jet ski roared up, with the driver waving frantically. "Stop. You don't want to come in here. You'll have to swim around these rocks to the next beach."

Sunny didn't even acknowledge that she'd seen him. Though she and Storm were still too far away to make out details, her eyes hadn't left the group on the beach. The man, who wore lifeguard shorts, tried to block the women's view with the machine and his body, but he had cut the engine and the heaving water buffeted him in its surges. One wave pushed him a few feet alee of Storm and Sunny. They caught sight of six men, struggling to haul a sagging body in colorful board shorts from the sea foam.

The breath caught in Storm's throat. Oh, God, she'd seen those shorts before. Sunny recognized them, too, for she made a noise between a moan and a whimper and slid from her board.

Storm reached out to her. "Hold on. You've got to hold on."

The lifeguard had maneuvered his way to them and reached out to Sunny. "Let's get her on the jet ski."

"She's afraid it's…it's someone she knows." Storm's voice caught, and she swallowed the bitter knot in her throat.

The man nodded wordlessly. Storm gripped Sunny's hand. She had to keep the young woman away from the shoreline activity. What was left of a human being after three days in the ocean would give the people that loved him nightmares. Storm choked back a sob.

By now, the lifeguard was unfastening the sled that had been lashed to the side of the machine. "C'mon, both of you, I'll take you to shore."

The wind and current had been pushing all three of them around the point toward land. By now, they were within a hundred yards of a long sandy beach.

"We'll be okay," Storm said to the lifeguard, though she meant that they'd reach the beach without help. Okay was a relative condition.

"Sunny, we're nearly there," she said.

Sunny squeezed her hand in reply. Storm could see the young woman's jaw muscles flex with the effort to gain control.

She looked up at the lifeguard. "Thanks."

With slow, heavy strokes, the women paddled toward the wide beach. The lifeguard followed them for a short distance, the powerful engine of the jet ski a rumbling escort. As soon as the women were within ten feet of being able to touch bottom, he turned, waved to them, and motored slowly away.

Storm and Sunny drifted as inconspicuously as they could. A small group had clustered at the end where the recovery took place, and Storm led Sunny as far away as they could safely come ashore. She didn't want to see anyone, and she figured Sunny would feel the same way. Disbelief, grief, and anger surged through her. She wanted to crawl away where no one could see her rail and weep for the handsome young man who had been so full of life, enthusiasm, and potential just a few days ago.

They were halfway into the trees that lined the beach when a long-legged brunette sprinted up to them. She gasped from the dash and emotion, then burst into tears. "Oh, God," she cried, and threw her arms around Sunny, who sagged against her. Storm recognized Sunny's friend from the surf contest.

"It's Nahoa," Sunny stated in a quivering voice. It wasn't a question.

The young woman nodded, and Sunny collapsed in the sand, which set the girl into a new burst of wails. Storm knelt beside Sunny, who dragged herself into a sitting position, with her head buried on folded arms.

"Dede," she said in a muffled voice, "please, I…I need quiet."

Dede gulped, then slowed to ragged breaths, interspersed with sobs. Storm felt her own eyes streaming. Dede's overt grief was unsettling, and Storm yearned to be alone to cope with Nahoa's death, but she knew that each of them was dealing with an awful blow in their own way.

Years ago, she'd come home from sixth grade and found her mother, composed and cold, on her bed. An empty pill bottle sat on the bedside table next to a spilled glass of whiskey. Storm had tried to wake her mother from her afternoon nap. Some of the confusion, anger, and disbelief she'd felt on that afternoon returned to her now.

But this time, Storm thought about the *lei o manō* that Nahoa had received, and the implied threat chilled her. It was one thing for depression to crush one's will to live, an entirely different matter to have your life extinguished by another person.

Dede's quavering voice brought Storm back to the present. "Sunny, I moved your van. It's right across the street." She turned to Storm. "Come on, we'll give you a ride."

"Okay." Sunny still mumbled into her bent knees and crossed arms. "Give me a couple minutes."

"Sure," Dede said, and put her arm around her friend.

The three women sat quietly, and Storm didn't know how much time elapsed. Shock and heartache numbed her thoughts, including the sense of passing time.

Dede was the first to draw a long breath. "People are starting to notice us. A couple of surfers are heading this way. You want to talk to them?"

Sunny looked up from her arms. Her face was pasty and her eyes swollen. "Let's get out of here."

"Jesus, there's Ben—and he looks like he's been gut-shot. And shit, there's a news van." Dede grabbed Sunny's arm and Storm's hand. "Let's go."

Dede's mission to get Sunny away from the media and curious onlookers had curtailed her grief. She hustled them efficiently through the trees and across the narrow highway. A white, rusting old Honda van with a neon pink bumper sticker that read Girls Just Want to Have Funds sat in a beach lot, surrounded by trucks and rusting sedans with surf racks.

A group of six or seven guys in board shorts scrambled from a pickup without giving the girls a glance. Their troubled faces were directed toward the activity across the street. The coconut wireless had begun to hum.

Dede retrieved the keys from a spot in the bumper, then managed to unlock the doors and bundle them inside before anyone recognized Sunny. Once she was in the driver's seat, she leaned over the driver's seat and offered her hand to Storm. "You're Nahoa's cousin, aren't you? I'm Dede Ward, and I'm so sorry for you—for your family."

"Thanks." It was all Storm could say.

Dede drove efficiently through traffic and a set of oncoming emergency vehicles. Storm gave her a few words of directions to the Laniakea cottage, but otherwise, no one spoke.

Dede pulled into the dirt drive that led to the small house. "You gonna to be okay?"

"Yes, thanks for the ride."

"You sure you want to be alone right now?"

"Yeah, I think so."

Dede nodded sadly and put the car in reverse. "Come over if you want."

"I'll call later." Storm raised her hand in a weak wave, and stumbled into the house. Truthfully, she didn't want to talk to anyone. For a while, she stood at the big picture window in the living room and stared out to sea. The sun was high in the sky, white spume laced the sand, and the turquoise shelf of the reef deepened to sapphire. The world looked like such a calm, predictable place.

Nahoa's death was different from her mother's, which had changed Storm's life. But here again, she stood at the abyss of loss and inevitability that humans faced. Death was not a situation anyone could fix, change, or solve. The phone rang from time to time, but she let it be part of another space, another time.

Storm had no idea how long she'd been standing at the window when she realized someone was banging on the door. Fuzzily, she wondered if they'd been there long.

"Storm Kayama?" Two police detectives stood on the door-step. "Detective Chang got in touch with us. We'd like to ask you about the package Nahoa Pi'ilani received."

"Come on in," Storm said.

The detectives, in plain clothes, introduced themselves as Steve Yamamoto and Jean Ursley, then entered and stood politely inside the door. "Could you tell us how and when he received it?"

Storm led them into the living room, where she sank onto the sofa. "He got it last Saturday." She described the delivery boy in detail, down to the zinc oxide on his nose.

"And you perceived it as a threat?"

"Yes. Nahoa did, too."

"Did he tell you it was a threat?"

"No, but it's known as a challenge to battle among the old Hawaiians. He didn't have to tell me."

"And you felt Nahoa knew the significance of the package?" Officer Yamamoto asked.

"Yes." Storm remembered how Nahoa had paled, then shrugged off his concern. But even the little boy knew something was wrong. Goober or Ben, one of them, had made a joke about Nahoa's 'aumakua protecting him. In a flash, she wondered about this. Had the two young men realized the significance of the war club? Or maybe they, like the little boy, had picked up on Nahoa's and her discomfort. Leila and Robbie certainly had.

"Yes, I'm sure," Storm repeated.

"Had you ever seen the boy before?"

"No. He told Nahoa some guy paid him to deliver it."

"You think it's possible the boy is staying nearby?"

"I don't know. Could be—lots of these homes are rented to visitors. He also could be from town—or staying at a hotel." Storm gave the officers the best description she could of the boy, and they left her with their cards in case she saw the kid on the beach again, or if she remembered any details that might be important.

They were halfway to their car when she ran after them. "What kind of injuries did he have?"

Yamamoto shuffled his feet and looked away.

"It's hard to tell." Ursley spoke in a soft voice. "In fact, we have to get positive identification through dental records. He's on his way to Honolulu now, but the ME won't have any answers for a day or two."

Storm wanted to ask if there was a chance it wasn't Nahoa, but she knew better. The police had been discreet. Kind, even. They were probably hoping the ME would have enough to work on. Jesus.

Disconnected suspicions, remorse, and misery ricocheted inside Storm's skull like hornets in a jar. She still stood in the sun, where she'd watched the police make their way back to Kamehameha Highway. Her head pounded and her salt-crusted skin prickled in the heat.

When she heard her cell phone ringing, she walked slowly inside. By the time she'd found it in the bedroom under the comforter she'd discarded sometime during the night, whoever called had hung up.

Storm didn't even check the number. Instead, she dialed Hamlin's direct line to the office and his cell phone. She got his voice mail on both phones and left a message for him to call her back. Then she dropped the phone back onto the unmade bed. She wanted to just climb in again, start the day over and pray it headed in a different direction. But she knew better. And she could do more about the day's sad events if she didn't crawl into a cocoon. First, she needed a shower, then she had some people to see.

Chapter Sixteen

"You think I should get the eight foot or the nine-six?"

O'Reilly had pulled two surfboards from the racks at the Tubin' Tanker and had them lined up for Barstow's opinion. "I've had my eye on these two."

Barstow squinted at the boards, then over at O'Reilly. "Depends. You weigh about 200? You want to do some turns, but still cruise, right?" He walked down the rack of vertical boards.

O'Reilly moseyed along with him, reveling in his feeling of well-being, which was due to the fact that he'd passed up the Strip and Go Nakeds last night. He could hardly believe the two words that had escaped his lips when those three hot babes offered him tastes. No Thanks. Jesus. The chicks were practically naked, too. He really was getting older. But wiser.

He knew his nerves would ultimately be what was naked if he imbibed in those radioactive concoctions, and this meet was too damned important. True, the cocktails would have helped him get to sleep, but he'd be awake again at three, wrestling with some of the steps he needed to take to make this meet a success. Even telling himself that some of them were necessary to triumph (ask any politician), he fretted.

It was good to unwind like this with Barstow, though that guy had nerves of titanium steel. Had to in order to surf like he used to, and they also served him well in business. The two of 'em were a good team.

"Here's a nine foot. You look at this one?"

"I hate purple."

Barstow rolled his eyes, then glanced toward the door. O'Reilly followed his gaze. All right, now. That was a beautiful woman, if you like them a little on the strong side. Tall and curvy, substantial. He'd like to let that dark, wavy hair out of that conservative French braid. It was trying to spring its bonds already, and yeah, he'd bet that dame was like her hair looked—a real handful.

She went right up to Mo'o, who'd been ignoring customers while he traipsed in and out of a back room, wearing a painter's mask and a resinous cloud that blossomed around him like an overwhelming cologne. She stuck out her hand and introduced herself, which was when Barstow nearly dropped the purple surfboard.

"Hey." Shit, he didn't want to have to buy that one.

"Sorry," Barstow muttered, looking over his shoulder.

"You know her?"

Barstow's poisonous glare cut him short. It sounded as if someone had said Nahoa's name, but O'Reilly hadn't quite caught the words. Maybe Barstow had, though, because he planted the surfboard against the wall and jerked his head toward the door. O'Reilly followed him out to the street. The early afternoon sun glared from the passing cars. Both men put on sunglasses.

"Who's that?"

"Stephanie's lawyer. I recognized her name."

"You're shitting me." O'Reilly grinned. "Introduce me."

"Grow up, O'Reilly."

"C'mon, I could be your spy."

"Like we need another spy."

"Jesus, what's with you? A major sponsor bag out on you?"

Barstow's reflective sunglasses shot a laser of light so intense that O'Reilly shifted. Barstow let his insect eyes rove up and down the street as if he were expecting a gunslinger to step out of one of the stores. "Let's go get something to eat," he growled. "Someplace we won't run into the Harridan. Or my kid, for that matter."

They found a nice, dark place. Like a cave from the blistering sun, ripe with the aroma of good beer on tap and something frying. Barstow didn't want to sit at the bar, so they took a table in a corner. O'Reilly ordered a bacon cheeseburger with a side of onion rings without even looking at a menu. Barstow seemed as tense as a violin string, and he ran his eyes up and down both sides of the page, then finally decided on a teriyaki chicken sandwich. And lemonade. O'Reilly figured he'd better get lemonade, too.

Barstow didn't say anything until the drinks came, just kind of let his eyes run around the room as if his mind was so busy he didn't want to distract it with words. When a teenaged waiter set the lemonades before them, he took a couple big swallows, and sat back in his chair.

"I'm worried the death of this second surfer is going to hurt us."

O'Reilly nodded. "I thought of that, too. But surfing's dangerous—it's part of the appeal. Like race car driving, you gotta have risk to have glory."

"Maybe." The cords in Barstow's neck seemed to slacken. "It'll depend on the spin the media puts on it. You talked to Gordon lately?"

"I've left a coupla messages, but I know he's busy. He's in touch with KZXM on a daily basis. They're planning a 'History of Hawaiian Surfing' docudrama for Thursday evening." O'Reilly waved to the waiter for a lemonade refill. "I'll talk to him before that. Don't worry."

"I asked Goober to be his liaison to local surfers," Barstow said.

"Goober? Please." O'Reilly's lips curled in a sneer. "Who's gonna talk to that loser?"

"You wanted me to handle the local surfers, didn't you?" Barstow's voice was calm, but cold. There was a line of white around his lips, which barely moved as he spoke.

O'Reilly took a deep swallow of his lemonade, nodded wordlessly, and felt the trail of icy liquid pass through his chest. Easy, now.

The nearness of the event and the tensions of making it happen were making them both short-tempered. Antsy. And of course, Barstow still liked to think of himself as a surfer. With local connections, like in the old days, though he hadn't been around for decades. He didn't even have the Hawaiian wife anymore.

O'Reilly looked Barstow in the eye. "What's he doing for us?"

"It's no big deal. He's keeping tabs on things. He can blend in."

"Okay, but let's not ask Gordon to interview him. He's barely articulate. At least Nahoa Pi'ilani could talk."

"C'mon, he's a good surfer. He's out there on the big waves."

"He doesn't have respect."

"He does. You know how arbitrary one contest is."

O'Reilly could see Barstow's left eyelid twitch. A bad sign. Now, if he could get Barstow off this topic. "You're right about that," he said.

Usually, a rant on the preconceived ratings of the judges did the trick. Barstow was convinced that judges got caught up in the popularity and charisma of certain surfers and ignored others' skills. "I meant he's a bit young, that's all. The judges will start to notice him soon."

It worked. Barstow set down his lemonade with a crack. "Judging is a crock. There are these gods of the moment, like—"

The waiter appeared with their plates and set them down. O'Reilly lunged for his burger. He chewed, grateful to exercise the jaw muscles that had been hard knots all morning. He hoped the good food would improve Barstow's ill humor. The guy was high-strung, but that's what also made him good for the job. O'Reilly reminded himself that he needed to stroke his partner a bit more. This would all soon culminate in a wonderful contest that would benefit everyone involved. Well, almost everyone.

Chapter Seventeen

"Are you Moʻo?" Storm held out her hand. "I'm Storm Kayama."

Moʻo shook her hand and pushed a painter's mask to the top of his head. His eyes were red-rimmed and the chemical tang of fiberglass resin hung about him. "Nahoa told me about you. You're his cousin, the lawyer."

"He's your assistant, right?" Storm wasn't sure if Moʻo had heard about the body that had come ashore.

"Yeah." Moʻo splayed his calloused hands on his display case and leaned heavily against them. "I don't know what I'm going to do without him."

"I'm so sorry." She'd been afraid she would have to break the news to him, but this time the speed of the coconut wireless worked in her favor.

"Yeh, me too. For your loss. You're family." Moʻo sighed. "Lotsa people going miss that boy."

"I wondered, did Nahoa tell you about a package he got?"

Moʻo frowned at her. "A package? You mean he ordered something? He gets stuff sent here, but I haven't seen anything lately."

"No, someone on the beach gave it to him."

"I didn't know."

"Do you know if someone was angry with him? I heard he was kind of a ladies' man."

"Nahoa's *kolohe*, that's for sure. Like most surfers—or young men, for that matter. But I never heard about anyone with a grudge." Mo'o turned on his espresso machine. "Sit, let me make you a cup of coffee."

Storm slid onto a stool. It was a relief to get off her feet. She'd been running on nerves and desperate energy since her morning surf session had ended on such a sad, disturbing note.

Mo'o poured beans into a grinder. "What kind of package you talking about?"

Storm told him about the delivery of the *lei o manō*. Mo'o's eyes narrowed at the mention of the Hawaiian weapon, and he opened his mouth as if to comment, then closed it when the door of the shop opened.

"Hey, Mo'o. I come to say I'm sorry."

Storm turned around to see an older, dark skinned man making his way through the store. His eyes flicked to Storm, but his attention was on Mo'o. He held out his hand to the surfboard shaper.

"S'good to see you, Buster." Mo'o stopped grinding the beans and stepped around the counter.

"I'm sorry, man, for getting all *huhu* the other day." The man's shoulder's slumped. "I just heard Nahoa wen' *make*."

"They found him this morning." Mo'o's voice trembled. "Thanks for coming. Life's too short fo' stay angry, brah." He clasped the man's hand, then threw his arms around him in a big hug.

The smaller guy held onto Mo'o, and patted his back. "It's terrible."

"Yeah. That boy. He make some dumbass mistakes, like any kid, but he was one good boy." Mo'o took a step back and gestured to Storm.

"Buster, you need talk story with this *wahine*. She's Nahoa's cousin. Storm, this here's Buster DeSilva. Tell him what you told me, okay?" Mo'o stepped back behind the counter and loaded the espresso maker with fresh grounds.

Buster looked between Moʻo and Storm, then back to Storm. His dark eyes were sharp and curious. Storm told him about the package Nahoa had received.

Buster sat down hard on the counter stool and grasped at the ceramic mug that Moʻo had placed in front of him as if it would give him strength. He took a sip of his coffee, and studied the surface of it for several long moments. Finally, he spoke. "You part Hawaiian, right?"

Storm nodded.

"I heard some rumors." He took another swallow of coffee. "You heard of *lua*?"

"A battle to the death?"

"An ancient fighting technique, with *aʻalolo*. The winner used *luaʻai* on the loser of the match."

Storm knew about the breaking of the victim's bones, but Buster had added a new dimension to Aunt Maile's lore. "What's *aʻalolo*?"

"Nerve pressure." Buster pressed on the inside of his arm, then touched his neck.

"How do you know this?"

Moʻo had been paying rapt attention. "Buster here runs a dojo. He teaches jujitsu."

Storm looked back and forth between the men. Buster hunched over his coffee, while Moʻo labored over the espresso machine.

"More coffee?" Moʻo could have been a waiter at Maxim's.

"No, thanks." Storm turned to Buster. "What were the rumors you heard?"

"You know Ken Matsumoto?" Buster asked.

Storm took a sharp breath. "I was going to ask you the same thing."

Buster took a sip of his coffee without looking at her. "Someone left a cord with a toggle hanging on the front door of his apartment."

"You think it was a *kaʻane*?"

Buster's eyes glittered. "I had a feeling you'd understand. Ken and his roommates thought the neighbor, who has a litter of Rottweiler puppies, left one of his training leashes lying around."

"You think it was a real strangling cord? Did you see it?"

"No." Buster sounded disappointed. "One of my instructors, a Chinese-Hawaiian guy, told me about it."

"Why would anyone want to hurt Matsumoto? I heard everyone liked him."

"Liked him, yeah," Buster said.

"Well? What else?"

"People are pissed about what's happening to surfing. No one owns the ocean, you know."

"Okay," Storm said, waiting.

"Hawaiians were surfing centuries ago, according to the chants. You can still see prehistoric petroglyphs of surfers in the lava rock."

"True."

"So, instead of a lifestyle that celebrated communion with the earth and ocean, we got holding periods, with certain groups getting paid to guard a break, keep local Hawaiians away." Buster's voice became derisive. "They even use jet skis to get out to the waves."

Storm figured it would be a bad idea to bring up how many Hawaiians either competed or made a living from the North Shore culture. It wasn't a simple problem. "You think activists are trying to discourage the contests?"

Mo'o made a snorting noise and ducked to get something out of his under-the-counter refrigerator.

"That's just part of it." Buster shoved his mug away.

"I've seen some signs, at schools and beach parks," Storm said. "People are getting together to protest the new tow-in contest, aren't they?"

"Think about it. Who was the guardian, the god of weather, sports, communion with the ocean?"

Storm didn't answer.

Buster slapped his hand onto the countertop. "It's Lono."

"Okay," Storm said slowly.

"He's trying to restore the balance we Hawaiians have lost. These are sacrifices, like in the old days."

"I don't know about that." Storm turned away from Buster and stared at the surface of her own cooling coffee while she ignored the glances of the men. She'd heard old-timers go on about legends before, and some of their tales were as far-fetched as Buster's. She'd actually seen phenomena with her own eyes that she wouldn't believe if someone had merely related the tale to her, and she knew many well-grounded locals who had claimed to see ghosts, live 'aumakua, and spirits of the Hawaiian gods. Aunt Maile was one of them.

But Storm had a hard time accepting the old stories when they tried to explain away violence. And though she couldn't identify what bothered her, there were some threads to this one that she needed to think through.

Storm looked up at Buster. "The guy that saw the *ka'ane*. He still around?"

"He teaches at my dojo."

"Could I talk to him?"

"Sure, we have a class at seven tomorrow morning." He swiveled on his stool to face her. "Come a little early. Once we get started, we don't want any distractions. It's an advanced class."

Storm stood up and tried to offer Mo'o money for the coffee. He pushed her dollars back at her, but she picked up a tube of sunscreen and bar of Sticky Bumps surf wax and insisted on making a purchase.

Outside, the bright sun made her squint and her stomach, which burned from too much strong coffee, growled loudly. It was the first time all day she'd thought of food, and it was two o'clock in the afternoon.

There wasn't much to eat at the cottage, and the restaurant that Stephanie managed was just down the street. She might as well check on her client, make sure the ex was behaving, and see if Stephanie had any information for her.

The hostess led Storm to a small table in the corner of the dining room.

"Is Stephanie around?"

The woman set a glass of ice water in front of Storm. "I'll check. She might still be here."

A few minutes later, Stephanie peered from behind the kitchen door. When she saw Storm, she walked over quickly and sat down. Her swollen and red-rimmed eyes startled Storm, and her first thought was that Barstow had caused her distress. So Stephanie's first words were somewhat of a relief, though they concerned an issue that sat heavily on Storm's heart.

"Did you hear about Nahoa?"

Storm nodded. Her own eyes burned. "News travels fast."

"He had so much to live for." Stephanie buried her face in her hands. "I'm starting to hate surfing. If anything happened to Ben, I couldn't survive it."

The hostess passed by, leading a young couple to a nearby table. The lunch crowd was thinning, but a number of parties lingered to finish ice cream desserts and coffee in air-conditioned comfort.

"Nahoa apparently had some enemies," Storm said.

Stephanie's eyes shot wide open. "What do you mean?"

"Did you know him well?"

"I...not really. Ben looked up to him, of course. He was a talented young man."

"Hello." The young woman that had just been seated stood beside their table, cracking a wad of chewing gum. "It's good to see you again. How's—"

"Ben?" Stephanie asked. "He's very well, thanks."

A confused look, surpassed quickly by a sly one, passed over the girl's face. "Oh. That's good." She hesitated a moment, then walked over to her own table.

"These young women," Stephanie whispered to Storm, "they follow the surfers around. You know, like groupies."

"I suppose," Storm said, and glanced toward the girl in question. The young woman looked more like a Brigham Young student than a surf groupie. She looked in Stephanie's direction with a little smile, as if she had a secret.

Stephanie waved her hand as if to shoo away a mosquito, then covered her eyes. Her face crumpled with tears.

Storm reached out to cover her hand. "You should go home."

Stephanie sniffed. "I might leave early. This is so upsetting, and I think I'm fighting a cold." She sighed and looked up at Storm. "I'm supposed to have put together the names of some of Marty's work associates for you."

"It would help. I'd like to get the papers served while Marty's still in town."

"I've left some messages with people who should call me back. Will Saturday be okay?"

"That'll work," Storm said. "I'll call you."

Stephanie got up slowly and exited the restaurant with dragging feet. Storm's lunch arrived soon after, and she found herself eating as if she were starving. She ate every crumb of her grilled *mahimahi* sandwich, and it wasn't until she faced down the last of the spiced curly fries on her plate that she pondered whether Sunny might be up to talking, or commiserating, with her.

When she got up to leave, she felt the young woman's eyes on her. Storm paid, walked through the door, then paused among the umbrella-topped tables. The girl looked like she wanted to ask a question. Nor did she look like a surf groupie.

Storm went back into the restaurant and approached the table. "My name's Storm. Are you a friend of Ben's?"

The young woman smiled, curiosity lighting her eyes. "I'm Susan. I could have sworn he had a Hawaiian name." She grinned. "And I highly doubt that he was her son."

Storm opened her mouth, then closed it again. "You mind if I sit down for a minute?" She dragged a chair over from an adjacent table. "Where did you see him?"

"I'm a desk clerk at the Kahuku Point Hotel and Resort."

"Was his name Nahoa?"

"That's it. Nahoa Pi'ilani. He was the one who always checked in."

"Holy shit," Storm breathed out. "They checked in together?"

"Sure, they'd come in mid-afternoon and no one would see them until the next day. They even got room service." Her grin widened. "We thought maybe they'd have a wedding on the grounds."

Chapter Eighteen

Storm leaned toward the young woman, who looked somewhat satisfied about spilling the beans. Susan apparently didn't know yet what had happened to Nahoa. "When did you last see them?"

"It's been a while. I'd say three or four months ago."

Storm slowly stood up, her mind whirling. "Thanks."

Storm made her way to the parking lot in a daze, but the jolt of her car's hot upholstery on the back of her legs brought her back to the present. Okay, so what if they'd had an affair three or four months ago? If you counted the fact that Stephanie had been long separated from Marty Barstow, neither was cheating on another person. And age differences had been ignored by lovers long before Stephanie and Nahoa. But she bet there was a handful of people who would find the duo offensive, and Ben, if he knew, would probably top the list.

Was Stephanie the woman who'd started phoning Nahoa again? If Susan had been correct about the last time the two of them had checked into the hotel, the timing was right. Then again, with his reputation, it could be someone else.

Storm stopped at a traffic light and squinted into the sunlight. If Susan's timetable was accurate, then at least it sounded as if Nahoa had been faithful to Sunny. With all the unhappiness suffered by the people who loved him, she felt good about this fact.

Several vehicles sat in front of Sunny's house, and Storm was glad to see Sunny's van among them. When Storm tapped on the door to the house, it was Dede who opened it.

"How's she doing?" Storm asked.

Dede shrugged. "One moment, she's okay. The next, she's a basket case." Dede's eyes filled with tears. "What a goddammed, fucking waste."

"Yeah." It was all Storm could manage.

"You okay?" Dede's voice was kind.

Storm shrugged. "I can't stop thinking about it. I wonder if I could have done something."

"What?" Dede reached out and touched Storm's arm. "You couldn't have done anything—who could?"

"I knew the *lei o manō* was a threat."

"Now you're sounding like Sunny. You two need to talk some sense into each other."

Dede led Storm into the kitchen, where Sunny sat, slumped, at the kitchen table, her hands wrapped around a mug of something that steamed. Her face was only about six inches from the surface of what looked like tea, and Goober sat across from her, with his hands gently encircling her forearms.

Sunny looked up. "Hey."

"Hey back. Hi, Goober."

Goober stood up and put an arm around Storm's shoulders. "I'm so sorry. He was family to you, and you were close." He offered his chair to her.

"Thanks." Storm sat. Goober's comment about her being close to Nahoa made her miserable. They hadn't been, and now she felt the loss of years. When his father died, Rochelle moved Nahoa and his sister, Storm's best friend, to Kaua'i. It was the island farthest from the Big Island, and Storm lost track of them. Nahoa had been the one to get in touch by sending a client her way.

"You talked to your family yet?" Goober asked.

Storm's stomach plummeted. "No. I'll make some calls later today." She'd call Aunt Maile. At least the burden of phoning

Rochelle Pi'ilani would fall on someone else. She couldn't stand the idea of bringing that family more grief.

"Have you seen Ben?" Sunny asked Goober.

"Not much. He's been hanging with his dad lately." Goober shuffled his bare feet. "I'd better get going. I've got a class at five."

Dede had been leaning against a countertop with Jenna, who put a fresh tea bag in Sunny's mug and poured hot water from the tea kettle.

"Thanks for coming by," Jenna said. She walked Goober out of the kitchen and to the front door, then came back a few minutes later.

"It *was* nice of him to come by," she said, and raised one eyebrow at Dede, as if looking for support.

"Right." Dede faced Sunny and poured a bottle of beer into a glass. "It's because of you. You know he wouldn't have helped Nahoa if he'd seen him floating by, face down."

"Shut up, you two." Sunny's tone lacked conviction, though.

Storm looked between Sunny, Jenna, and Dede. "He doesn't seem like your type," she said to Sunny. Jenna and Dede laughed out loud, and even Sunny smiled.

"That's not it," Sunny said.

"Hah," Dede snorted. "You're blind, woman."

"Not. It's because we—okay, I—tried to help him out. I let him crash here. He doesn't really have anyplace to stay." She looked reproachfully at her friends.

The other two women snickered. "The last time, we had to have the couch—"

"Fumigated," Sunny finished, smiling again.

Dede threw back her head and guffawed. "It got crabs."

"*Ule ukus*," Jenna shouted, and could barely squeal her next words. "We all got 'em. Everyone who sat there—Nahoa, Ben, even our neighbor."

"Not on our heads, either." This revelation set Dede into gales of laugher, and she gasped between words. "Mrs. Stern is eighty-two. Poor thing didn't know what they were."

At this point, Sunny joined in the laughter. "Jenna had to tell her."

This sent all three women into spasms. It was infectious, maybe comic relief from the sadness of the day, but it felt wonderful. Storm threw back her head, and Sunny's eyes streamed.

"Look, the guy's homeless. I feel sorry for him," she said.

Jenna, howling, slid down the front of the cabinet to sit, splay-legged, on the floor. She could barely get her breath. Dede pounded on the countertop and spilled her beer on Jenna's head, which set them all off again.

"He didn't look too bad today," Jenna conceded, while she licked beer from the back of her hand. "Okay, I'll admit. Sometimes he's not a bad guy. When he takes a shower, that is."

"He was actually wearing clothes this time." Dede handed a cold one down to Jenna. "Here, it tastes better in a bottle."

Sunny grinned and wiped away tears. "You guys are wonderful. No, you're awful. I can't decide."

They all laughed again.

Chapter Nineteen

O'Reilly wore an expensive pair of leather flip-flops, which Barstow told him made him look like a surfer-wannabe. Like a middle-class yuppie-slash-dot-commer from California.

Fuck Barstow. So what if he was a middle-class surfer-wannabe. He had a job to do. Fucking Barstow was his employee, for Christsake. And this sand was burning the shit out of the tops of his feet. Christ, it was high time to get this show on the road.

Gabe Watson stood right next to the lifeguard stand, a big, high wood edifice. A serious structure on a beach legendary for some of the best surf in the world. Three PWCs sat on the sand next to it, big honking jet skis that could rescue or tow a surfer, racing the monster waves.

Waimea Bay. A big swell was predicted and this is where it would happen. Tomorrow, if they could get the out-of-town surfers certified for operating the personal watercraft. O'Reilly eyed the machines and stifled a smirk of delight. Fucking Kawasakis, Yamahas, and one of their big sponsors, WhiteOut. Engines like the biggest motorcycles on the road. Impressive.

He needed to get Gordon out here to take some shots before the meet started. They'd look about the size of a water bug once they were in the ocean, sliding up a wall of water the size of the state capitol.

Watson watched them approach, his tattooed arms folded across his chest. He wore the infamous blue lifeguard shorts, which settled low on a set of abs that probably made babes cream themselves. O'Reilly wondered briefly if he'd be able to develop a set of those, then shoved the fantasy aside. Money was a better magnet.

Fucking Watson. He wished he didn't have to depend on him at this juncture of the game. The sonofabitch had an agenda, but at least he was where he said he'd be. And everyone had an agenda, didn't they?

Barstow beat O'Reilly to the first words. "What can you do for us?"

O'Reilly felt a twinge of irritation at Barstow's confrontational manner. Watson didn't have to do anything for them, except that he wanted a place in the Intrepid's lineup. But O'Reilly knew he and Barstow didn't have much wiggle room. There wouldn't *be* an Intrepid unless they could get the fourteen foreign contestants licensed. They were big names, and they needed to get certified today, or early tomorrow morning at the absolute latest.

Watson raised one eyebrow. "The law went into effect a couple months ago. All tow surfers operating a personal watercraft in the waters of Hawai'i need to have a state license." He sounded like he was reading the manual.

O'Reilly spoke up. "We've got seven pairs. How long will that take?"

"You want to start the first round tomorrow, right?" Watson asked with a smug smile.

Sadistic bastard, O'Reilly thought.

"Tomorrow, late afternoon," Barstow growled, and caught O'Reilly's eye.

O'Reilly knew a stink eye when he saw one. Barstow wanted him to shut the fuck up.

But O'Reilly couldn't contain himself. "How long does it take to get a license?"

"About six hours." Watson smiled again. "Per person."

This time, Barstow didn't bother to glare at O'Reilly. He moved so that Watson's eyes followed him. They turned in their own circle, away from where O'Reilly had his burning feet buried in the sand.

"How many people are certified to do this licensing?" Barstow's voice was low. O'Reilly could barely hear him, but he didn't budge.

"Five of us. Two on Oʻahu, two from Maui, and one from the Big Island." Watson's voice was equally low. It was a dance, a minuet of offer and counter-offer.

"There's a place in the lineup."

"Who would I be partnered with?"

"My son."

Watson's eyes narrowed. "Could be worse."

"Or Kimo Hitashi."

O'Reilly's eyebrows shot up. Barstow was gutsy, he had to hand him that. Goober had told them about the fist fight after Hitashi edged out Watson to win the Sunset Triple Pro last week. Hitashi had had eight stitches above his eye and he'd vowed to kill Watson if he ever got within ten feet of him. Tow-in partners had to trust each other with their lives.

"How are we going to get sixty-four hours of training into," Watson shrugged, "the next ten hours of available time?"

O'Reilly could only watch, his blood pressure rising and falling with Watson's thrusts and Barstow's parries.

"What do the other instructors want?"

A smile flickered at one corner of Watson's mouth. "Ten grand. Each."

O'Reilly couldn't watch any longer. He was starting to feel dizzy. It was a hyperventilation problem, from anxiety. He'd had it before. Jesus, this whole show could come down around his ears. He'd be bankrupt, disgraced. He walked away, sank into the sand out of earshot, and forced himself to take even, shallow breaths.

It seemed like hours before Barstow wandered toward him. O'Reilly watched his casual, meandering steps across the deep, soft sand and stifled the urge to lock his hands around the man's neck and scream at him for getting off on the wrong foot. Goading the stupid bastard from the start, when he knew what was at stake. What the fuck was he thinking of?

O'Reilly clenched his fists and shuddered with the effort of another calming breath. "So what happened?" he said between clenched teeth.

"Twenty-five hundred."

"Huh?"

"We pay each instructor twenty-five hundred."

"Including Watson?"

"Yeah, and he gets into the lineup. With Ben."

O'Reilly exhaled. He'd been thinking fifty grand. Twelve thousand five sounded like a gift. Hell, they could make that up with a minor sponsor.

"Way to go."

"You didn't trust me."

"Yeah, I did. Really. I just got nervous." O'Reilly clapped him on the back. "You saw me walk away, leave you alone with him. I knew you could do it, buddy."

"Right." Barstow stood up. "I've got to hand it to you for one idea. Giving Goober the guest room in exchange for information was worth the trouble."

"It's no trouble for you." O'Reilly pushed himself up from the sand and brushed his hands against his shorts. "I'm the one who has to live with him. He's got breath that smells like a Saint Bernard's. Plus, he whistles in the morning. Gets up all cheerful and makes espresso in his boxers."

Barstow laughed. "Maybe he'll have a good influence on you."

They started walking for the car, which they'd parked on the shoulder of the road that overlooked the bay.

"What's your ex going to say about Ben being in this contest?" O'Reilly couldn't resist getting a dig in.

"She's going to shit."

"That doesn't bother you?"

Barstow's mirrored sunglasses reflected light from a passing car. "Nope. She'll shit quietly."

O'Reilly unlocked the car. He didn't want to know anything more.

Chapter Twenty

By the time Storm left Sunny's house, she had eaten leftovers with the three lively women and Charlie, who had been at a neighbor's house with another toddler. She was grateful for the meal, as she probably would have eaten cold, leftover chicken and musubi, but even more for the sympathetic and rowdy company. Jenna and Dede had done a superb job of cheering her and Sunny, and cried along with them when their moods slumped. It was what friends did.

When she got to the beach cottage, it was dark and lonely and the telephone was shrilling.

"Where have you been?" Hamlin asked. "Brian called and told us about Nahoa."

"That's why I left you two messages. Is it on the news?"

"Yes, but the police won't release his name until they contact his relatives."

"Does his mother know?"

"I don't know. How are you?"

"Up and down. I ate dinner with Sunny and her roommates."

"If I didn't have a deposition in the morning, I'd head out there right now."

"I'll be glad when you get here."

"Call Aunt Maile and Uncle Keone tonight. They sent a birthday present to the office for you. I'll bring it out and we'll celebrate."

She could hear the smile in his voice. "I can't wait."

She used her cell phone to call her aunt and uncle on the Big Island, only to find that her phone held five voice messages she'd missed during the day. Uncle Keone picked up the phone.

His voice was gentle. "Wish we could be with you. It's your birthday weekend and the poor Pi'ilani boy—that family sure has had bad luck."

"Yeah, they have." Storm's voice was glum. "Any chance of you coming to O'ahu?"

"Wish we could. Maile's got a sick patient and I've got a roundup. We've got some late-born calves to castrate."

Storm had grown up around Parker Ranch, where Keone was a foreman. For a quick moment, she wished she could participate in the roundup and the inevitable cookout. Though Rocky Mountain oysters weren't her favorite food, there would be a great party.

"Uncle Keone, you ever heard of the Hawaiian practice of *lua*?"

"Sure, but it's pretty hush-hush. People around here talk of a guy named Henry Okazaki, who was the father of American jujitsu. They say he learned *lua* from a *kumu* in Puna, but no one knows for sure because it's *kapu* to teach *lua* to anyone who doesn't have Hawaiian blood. It's said he even taught *lua'ai*, or the bone-breaking techniques, by hiding them within his own martial art."

"Does anyone admit to practicing it?"

"No way. Funny, though, you hear whispers of it in certain dojos, around the time of Makahiki. Lono did *lua*—he was a wrestler, and he instituted the Makahiki games to honor the wife he beat to death."

"Nice guy."

"Yeah, well, most of the Hawaiian gods—and warriors— were fierce. Hell, some of those bastards used to eat the guys they killed."

"When was that happening?"

"It stopped around the time the white men showed up. But they kept collecting the teeth."

That got Storm's attention. "Teeth?"

"Sure. Used to put them around the rims of calabashes. Bishop Museum had a lot of those old bowls, but they took them out of public displays because they're human remains."

The hair on Storm's arms stood on end. "What teeth did they use?"

"In the old calabashes? Molars, usually. I can understand the museum putting those things in storage, you know. If you took your grandchildren to an exhibit and saw some bowl that belonged to Kamehameha I, and you knew your great-great grand-dad fought for Kiwalao, you prob'ly wouldn't want to explain it to the kids. Know what I mean? Uh, Storm? Are you there?"

"I'm here. You just got me thinking about something."

Uncle Keone's voice lost its jocular tone. "Storm, you better steer clear of the Pi'ilani family and their problems. Call the police."

"That's exactly what I'm doing."

"You want me to have Aunt Maile call you when she gets home?"

"I'll call her tomorrow, when Hamlin gets here."

"I mean it about calling the police."

"I'll do it right now." Her voice brightened. "Hey, my birthday present got here. Hamlin's bringing it to me."

"We figured someone would be in your office to sign for it." Storm could hear the smile in his voice. Uncle Keone loved surprises in the form of gifts. "We'll give you a call on Sunday, to celebrate."

Storm hung up the phone. Teeth. She had a very bad feeling about this. It was quarter to ten, but she dialed Brian Chang's cell phone. When he picked up, she could hear Leila's voice in the background, chasing Robbie off to bed.

"Brian, when your officers were here, they mentioned getting hold of Nahoa's dental records."

"Yes, unfortunately we'll need them."

"Has the ME had a chance to look at his teeth yet?"

There was a pause on the line. "Why do I feel like I shouldn't answer that question?"

"You just did." Storm took a deep breath and related what Uncle Keone had told her about *lua*, Hawaiian warriors, and the collection of teeth. "Your detectives asked me to call if I thought of anything, and I figured this qualified."

"You're right, Storm. Thanks." He took a deep breath. "The ME isn't finished, but it wasn't hard to see that Nahoa had lost some teeth."

"How many teeth are gone?" Storm asked.

"Six." Brian's voice was grudging.

"How many teeth was Ken Matsumoto missing?"

"Two."

"Molars?"

"Yes."

"Is Matsumoto's death still classified as accidental?"

"Yes, but we haven't stopped asking questions. And don't tell anyone about the missing teeth. We aren't releasing that information." Brian's tone had gone into official mode, and Storm knew better than to press him. She was lucky he'd told her as much as he did.

Chapter Twenty-one

The rumble of huge surf fills one's subconscious with an atavistic wariness before the conscious mind can identify the noise. It's like hearing distant thunder; a frisson of vigilance passes through a person.

Storm awoke to the pounding of waves and no sense of where she was. The bedside clock wasn't the one she was used to, though it was familiar, and it read 6:15, which was when she normally got up for work. It was the crash of surf and the smell of the ocean that reminded her she was at the beach cottage. Her head felt as if it was stuffed with steel wool, and she had a nagging feeling that she was forgetting something important.

Staggering into the bathroom, she groped for her toothbrush, and nearly yelped at her reflection over the sink. Dark-circled puffy eyes and hair that would send the bride of Frankenstein over the edge. Damn, now she remembered. She was supposed to go to that dojo this morning to talk to the fellow who thought he'd seen the *ka'ane*. Some of Buster DeSilva's theories had bordered on nutty—even Aunt Maile would agree. Storm hoped the trip to town was worth her time.

The warm yellow glow of the overhead light made last night's ominous thoughts seem much less threatening. But Nahoa's death was real. And the whole missing teeth issue tied in too well with the lore of *lua* and its weaponry.

It was now 6:30 and she didn't have time to lose. Even in the bathroom, she could hear waves pound the shore. It was going to be huge, and on big days it would often wash over the only road that led from the beach cottage into Haleiwa, causing traffic to inch along. Not only would the driving be slow, but people would be swarming in from the east, west, and south shores of Oʻahu to see it. A traffic jam on what was essentially a two-lane country highway could mean a half-hour drive or more, and Buster DeSilva had asked her to be early.

Storm pulled her hair back with two combs and a big rubber band, threw on a cotton sweater, jeans, and rubber slippers, and dashed through the mist, a combination of a soft winter rainfall and salt spray from the high surf. Traffic wasn't as bad as she'd feared, and at five till seven she pulled into the dojo parking lot, a rutted patch of gravel next to a simple frame building that looked like termites had been snacking on it since World War II.

When she opened the double door, she was immediately in a small vestibule, which let into a large room. The vestibule held a couple of benches and its floor was littered with footwear. Storm kicked off her own slippers and stepped into the large one-room interior of the building, which was covered with tatami mats.

Mirrors lined the far wall and a cluster of people dressed in traditional white gi knelt in two even lines in front of Buster DeSilva, who stood next to a young man. They both wore black. Buster caught her eye and bowed in her direction. Without saying a word, he nodded to the fellow next to him, who bowed also.

Storm returned their bows. Buster proceeded to lead the class in a series of breathing exercises while the young man jogged over to her and stuck out his hand.

"Thank you for coming. I'm Warren Yee."

Storm shook his hand. "Thanks for seeing me. I hoped I'd get here sooner."

Warren's grin revealed a dimple in one cheek, and his black eyes playfully reflected the overhead lights. "I'll bet the roads are busy. I'm going up to Waimea as soon as I'm finished here. I heard they're going to hold the first round of the Intrepid this afternoon."

"It's a pretty big deal, isn't it?"

"Yeah." His voice resonated with enthusiasm.

"Are you in it?"

"I wish. I have some friends in it." His face grew more somber. "But you're not here to talk about the tow-in contest, are you?"

"First I want to hear about the dog leash that Ken Matsumoto found. Where was it?"

"Hanging on the knob to the front door of our house. But it wasn't a dog leash."

"You're sure?"

"My grandparents used to have a trunk full of Hawaiian relics. I remember the *ka'ane*. My *popo* told me what it was."

Storm believed him. Some of Aunt Maile's and Uncle Keone's friends kept relics from the old times. That's how she'd recognized the *lei o manō*.

"Ken was one of your roommates? How many people live with you?"

Warren cracked his knuckles and shifted his feet. "There are just two of us, now. We need someone to share expenses." Warren looked hopefully at Storm.

"I live in Honolulu, but I'll keep my ears open for you. Did Ken know what the cord was?"

"No, I think I was the only one. And I didn't say anything, though now I wish I had. It just seemed too strange at the time."

"Right, you wouldn't necessarily think of it as a threat."

"Well, I didn't like it." Warren looked down at his bare feet, then up at Storm. "Actually, I thought it might be directed at me." He made a motion toward the class. "You know, because I'm into martial arts."

"Why? Does Buster teach *lua*?"

"No, of course not." Warren looked over his shoulder at the class, at Buster, whose voice was louder than it had been a few moments ago. The students were doing stretching exercises.

Storm thought he answered a bit quickly. She regarded him out of the corner of her eye, but Warren was still looking toward Buster, who had begun to break the class into sparring pairs.

"One last question," she said. "What was Ken like? Did he have a lot of friends?"

"That's two questions." But Warren smiled as he said it.

"Right. I meant, was he a nice guy?"

"Yeah. Yeah, he was. Generous, too."

Warren's response again seemed somewhat automatic, which made Storm think she should ask the same question of a few more people, and find out if others' impressions were the same.

She stuck out her hand. "Thanks for talking to me."

Warren grasped it and turned to face her, his back to Buster and the class. "The spirits of Nahoa Pi'ilani and Ken Matsumoto will be watching over the competitors today," he said quietly. "Come to my house if you have more questions."

Storm exited the dojo. Warren's friendliness had cooled a bit when she asked if Buster taught *lua*. Perhaps that was because the class was starting, and as Buster's assistant, he felt a responsibility to his job. It could also mean that Warren didn't want to answer her question, especially if he'd worried the *ka'ane* had been left for him. Uncle Keone had said that it was *kapu* for a non-Hawaiian to teach *lua*, and Storm wasn't sure whether Buster had Hawaiian blood. It didn't make any difference to her, but some Hawaiians took it very seriously.

Then again, Warren had offered to talk to Storm at home. She should take him up on that offer and talk to him away from the influence of the dojo. Away from any other ears.

Her stomach was now growling audibly and the aroma of a coffee-toting pedestrian's take-away cup was so enticing she felt like stalking the guy. The mist had increased to a drizzle, and clouds wafted in from the ocean. She knew if she licked the back of her hand, she would taste salt. Storm shivered in the damp, cool air.

Rosie's Diner, a popular spot known among locals for a great breakfast, was a half-block away, and Storm was as close to it as she was to her car. The door banged loudly behind her and the couple at the hostess' podium turned to see who had entered. They nodded a greeting and turned back to the hostess, who gathered a couple of menus and gestured for them to follow. Storm stepped up to wait her turn and noticed a man on the far side of the dining room look up at her. Their eyes met, and he quickly returned his attention to the woman he faced. The two appeared to be deep in conversation.

Storm hoped that her face didn't telegraph her surprise. She forced herself to calmly pick up a menu from a stack on the hostess stand and run her eyes over it. The woman hadn't turned around, but Storm recognized her from the back of her head. Even if she hadn't, she knew the Kate Spade handbag on the back of her chair belonged to Stephanie Barstow.

And the man with her was the wiry fellow she'd seen at the surf contest last week. So that was Marty Barstow, Stephanie's ex. His mirrored shades sat on the table next to his coffee mug, and his eyes bored into Stephanie's face. His right hand gestured fervently, as if he had to convince her of something.

Why was she meeting with him? Storm thought she'd always acted a bit afraid of him. Storm let her eyes slide over to the pair, then back to her menu. Marty was doing most of the talking, while Stephanie wasn't moving much. In fact, she sat with rounded shoulders, almost subdued.

"One?" The hostess broke into her thoughts.

"Yes, please."

The hostess took Storm around the corner to a side room. "Coffee?"

"You bet," Storm said. "I'll be right back." She draped her napkin across her seat and walked across the room to greet Stephanie.

When Storm appeared at her side, Stephanie lurched as if she'd been caught pocketing lipsticks at Macy's.

"Hi, Stephanie."

"Hi, Storm." Stephanie's tired eyes flicked from Storm to Marty, then back to Storm. "This is Marty Barstow."

Barstow got up and reached across the table to shake her hand. "Nice to meet you."

"Uh, it's my day off." Stephanie sounded as if she might be arrested for eating in a competitor's restaurant.

"This is a great place to have breakfast." Storm smiled at the two of them. She could see now that instead of providing the support she'd aimed for, she was making her client more uncomfortable. "Just thought I'd say hello. I've got to get back to my table before they give it to someone else."

"Nice to meet you, Storm." Barstow was repeating himself, but this had been anything but a scintillating conversation.

"See you later." Stephanie seemed to shrink.

Storm went back to her seat and poured herself a mug of the restaurant's good brewed coffee. She wondered what Barstow was telling Stephanie that unsettled her. Maybe he knew about the affair with Nahoa. But so what? In Hawaii and California, divorce was no-fault, so an affair shouldn't affect a financial settlement. Sometimes an affair could be used against a partner in a custody battle, but Ben was nineteen; he could choose where to live.

Storm took a deep swallow of coffee. She'd always had the feeling Stephanie kept aspects of the relationship to herself. For all she knew, Stephanie might be tired of trying to make it on her own and was begging Barstow to give the marriage another chance. Probably not, but Storm admitted that she knew little about the woman and her past relationship.

She still needed information about Barstow's business associates and partners. It would be a great excuse to have another friendly, woman-to-woman talk with Stephanie. Maybe Stephanie would tell Storm what this morning's meeting with Barstow was about, maybe not. But Ben's mother had asked Storm to protect her interests, and that's what Storm wanted to do. At least until her client told her to stop.

Right now she needed more caffeine and a stack of Rosie's maple pecan pancakes. She was halfway through them, enjoying every syrup-soaked bite, with a fresh cup of coffee and the day's *Honolulu Advertiser* opened to the police beat. It took her a moment to notice that someone stood by the table.

"I didn't want to interrupt you," Barstow said.

Storm was irritated. Not only with her own obliviousness, but with the fact that Barstow had stood by her for a few seconds without making his presence known. It made her feel like he enjoyed being sneaky.

"I'd like to talk to you when you have time," he said and handed her a business card. It was printed with his name, his company name, and his California address. "I wrote my local contact information on the back."

Chapter Twenty-two

Storm sat in her car for a few moments and read the back of Barstow's card. Stephanie was her client, and she wouldn't talk to him without telling Stephanie first. It might benefit Stephanie, though, if she could get a feeling for what he'd be willing to share with her. How he felt about Stephanie's participation in setting up his successful commercial real estate business, for example.

Storm used her mobile phone to call Stephanie, but no one answered and Storm ended up leaving messages. She decided not to initiate a meeting with Barstow. If he wanted to talk to her badly enough, he could make an appointment like everyone else. But then, she hadn't checked in to the office lately, and two of the missed calls on her cell phone had been from Grace.

Grace picked up on the first ring. "We're so sorry to hear about your cousin. It was on the news. How's that nice boy who was in the office last week?"

"Ben Barstow? Okay, as far as I know."

"Storm, you've had some important calls. Just a minute." Storm could hear Grace ruffling through papers.

"I've got a stack of message slips." More rustling. "Here we are. Rodney Liu from the Hawaii Building and Construction Trades Council. That's a big labor union. You better call that guy."

"Must be one of Uncle Miles' old clients." Storm dug for a pen in the glove box and jotted the number on the back of an old gas receipt, the shiny kind the self-service machines spit at you.

"That's what I thought. Okay, and here's another number." Grace read it off. "It was hard to understand this woman. I think she said her name was Pia, Puna, something like that."

Storm jotted down this number, too, and was filled with an emotion she couldn't identify. Anxiety, anticipation, a touch of fear. She labored to pay attention to Grace's next messages, which were from the Public Defender's office.

"Thanks, Grace."

"You're getting some good clients. Better get hold of Rodney Liu right away."

"I will. You have any idea when Hamlin is planning to drive out here?"

"He told me to tell you when you called that he'd be on the road by six. He wants you to make dinner reservations somewhere nice." There was a smile in Grace's voice. "Get yourself a slinky dress. It'll cheer you up."

"Right." Storm hung up the phone and sighed. Grace read her like the notes she'd spiked on her desk. The only clothes Storm had with her were the shift she'd worn when she'd visited Mrs. Shirome, now wrinkled and sweaty, two pairs of board shorts, her jeans, and two bikinis.

She looked around. The parking lot for Rosie's Diner wasn't full and no one seemed to be paying any attention to her. She called Rodney Liu's number and the two numbers for the PD's office and set up appointments for the following week.

She eyed the other number Grace had given her, then went into the call log on her mobile. Sure enough, there it was—twice. Grace didn't give out Storm's cell phone number to clients. It had to be Pua, Nahoa's sister, and with her name came a flood of memories.

Storm laid the phone on the passenger seat, and gazed out the VW's window into the dense branches of the overhead monkey pod tree. It had been many years and many tears. But she was a big girl now, she could do this.

Rochelle Pi'ilani, Pua's and Nahoa's mother, had been one of Storm's mother's best friends. When Storm's mother had been riding the roller coaster of her sweeping mood swings, Rochelle had been with her. Especially in the high times, the spending sprees to Honolulu, the opera fundraisers, the black tie events Storm's dad shunned.

Storm had her own reasons for avoiding Rochelle, who was always perfectly coiffed, and intensely critical of those who weren't. A stick, Rochelle would shake her head and cluck at Storm's chunky twelve-year-old physique. Storm never did call her Auntie, the affectionate name for a close family friend.

Pua had taken after her dad. Sensitive and unpretentious, she and Storm were inseparable. Storm remembered how, only a few weeks after her mother's suicide, Uncle Bert and Pua had invited her to go canoe surfing. A year before, she would have killed for this adventure, but now, with the whole neighborhood trying to console her, Storm would rather have slipped off to her secret spot in the sugar cane fields to puff stolen cigarettes, maybe even a little *pakalolo*, and try to sort out how she felt about life—and death.

That day, the waves turned out to be bigger than anyone expected. Any Hawaiian can tell you how unpredictable the ocean is. Bert, an experienced paddler, knew it as well as any one.

Storm suspected that at this point, her childhood memories were blurred and distorted. She remembered how the boat plowed through the crest of an overhead wave. It foundered to a halt so abruptly in the oncoming riff of curling water that she shot forward from her seat and banged her knees against the bow.

A salty deluge stifled her yelp of pain, and then the bow rocketed down the backside of another wave, only to crash into the face of a bigger one. Pua made a mewling noise, then Uncle Bert cried out.

"Try bail!" His voice was ragged and frantic.

She grabbed for the plastic bucket as it floated by, and scooped, again and again, until her shoulders burned.

Then Uncle Bert screamed again. "Jump!"

One moment, she heard Bert's frenetic command, and the next she was in the water, watching the red hull of the upturned boat, parallel to the curl of the frothing breaker ten feet above her.

Then she was in the green room, the ocean's lesson for ill-fated humans far out of their element. Tumbled like rootless kelp, the water pushed her down until her vision darkened. Without any feel for up or down, her eyes stayed open. It was this image that returned to her in nightmares, the darkening green. Powerless as a mote in space, she rolled through it. On and on, whirling weightless and without direction.

She would never know why the ocean spit her out a second before her convulsing lungs sucked in sea water. She didn't even remember how the roiling waters dragged her across a reef, tearing the skin off most of her back and both elbows and knees.

When the rescue canoe picked her up and took her to shore, she blubbered to a bereft Pua about a wild pig that paced the shore, but she shut up when Rochelle, hysterical, shrieked that the accident was Storm's fault.

Aunt Maile and Uncle Keone kept her home from school for the rest of the week. It wasn't until she went back that she discovered that Bert had drowned, and Rochelle had packed up her entire household, taken her children, and moved to Kaua'i.

Four years later, when Storm moved to O'ahu, she wrote Pua, but never heard from her. Her own family assured her that she bore no responsibility for Bert Pi'ilani's death, and she hoped they were right. But the cracked patella she'd sustained from the accident still throbbed from time to time, and reminded her of a deeper ache.

So why was Pua calling her now? Did she know Nahoa had sent a client to her? She must know they'd been in touch. Why else would she phone?

Sadly, when Storm thought about what she might say to Pua, the heavy object she'd seen dragged from the surf yesterday came vividly to mind. She also felt a strong surge of regret about the package that had been delivered to Nahoa. She'd done nothing. She'd known, deep down, that the threat was more serious than a mere warning to stay away from a woman. But she'd rationalized, and ignored the prickling sense of peril that hovered around the *lei o manō*.

Chapter Twenty-three

Reluctantly, Storm dialed the number. When Pua's message, in a voice that still sounded familiar, answered, she hung up. Pua would see the missed call and recognize Storm's number.

It was already early afternoon and Storm wanted to see Dede, Jenna, and Sunny. Sad as Sunny was about Nahoa's death, she and Dede might be up for going to the first round of the surf contest. They had friends participating, and it was scheduled to start mid-afternoon, when the tide went out.

Storm walked up the stairs to the front door, but jumped back when the door banged open and Ben barged out. She just avoided getting a black eye, because Ben had his head down and didn't look up at her.

"Hey there," Storm said, half in greeting, and half to warn him not to run into her.

He grunted something and jogged past her to a black Porsche Boxter that she'd passed on the way in. Storm hadn't recognized it, so she hadn't looked twice. Now she stared at the brand-new car in surprise. He got in without looking back, and pulled away from the house.

Storm stepped inside, where Dede greeted her. "Hey, we were just going to call you."

"What's with Ben?" Storm asked.

"Wait'll you hear," Dede whispered.

"Uh oh," was all Storm had time to say, because Sunny stomped into the living room.

"I can't believe he did this to Ben—or me." Her eyes were red again and her voice hoarse. "Bad enough that they got together," she wailed, "but he went back." Her voice rose through the tirade.

Storm knew right away to whom Sunny referred. "Wait, I talked to the clerk who saw them," Storm said. "That's not exactly what happened."

"What?" Dede and Sunny said together, though Sunny still looked angry.

"It happened four months ago. Before you and Nahoa got together." Storm directed the last comment to Sunny, who sagged into a chair.

"He didn't cheat on you," Storm added.

"Are you sure?" Sunny asked suspiciously. "Still, it was stupid. Ben's mother. I mean, we're friends with Ben."

"It was silly, but not traitorous," Dede said. She gave her friend a hug.

Sunny gulped a few times and wiped at her eyes. "Right before he died, a woman called him several times. It worried me."

Jenna walked into the room with Charlie on her hip. "He was a guy. Whaddya expect? Anyone want to try my brownies?"

"Men," Sunny fumed, but her mood wasn't nearly as black.

She regarded Jenna, who leaned against the door frame. Charlie had chocolate all around his mouth.

"Yeah, that's exactly what I need." She jumped to her feet and followed Jenna into the kitchen. Now that the immediate trouble had passed, Storm smelled the warm brownies. How could she have missed it before?

Some time later, Dede, Storm, and Sunny piled into Sunny's van and headed for Mahina Hou, a clothing store both Dede and Sunny liked. Jenna announced that she would forgo the trip because Charlie "hated shopping." Storm couldn't miss the expressions of relief that passed over Sunny's and Dede's faces. Charlie had chocolate smeared from his chin to his forehead, and was whining for more.

In a bit over an hour, Storm had found a dress by a local designer, and Dede had two tiny new bikinis. It was an activity meant to distract, and it worked for Storm and Dede. Sunny, however, meandered around the store, lost in thought except for the times she enthused about Storm's dress or Dede's thongs.

Dede tucked her bathing suits under one arm and marched to the counter, where a rack of lovely and unique earrings were on display. "I'll take these," she handed over the bikinis, "and these moonstone earrings." She pulled a tiny pair of dangling stones from the rack.

"Those are beautiful," Storm said.

Dede winked at Storm and turned to Sunny. "They're for you. You deserve a pick-me-up."

Tears filled Sunny's eyes. "Thank you. Moonstones are good luck," she said, and removed one set of her earrings so she could wear the new ones.

"They're perfect on you," Storm said, and they were.

Dede and Storm paid for their purchases, while Sunny's face relaxed in a gentle smile. It was an outing all three of them needed, where they could forget their sadness for a while.

Once on the street, Sunny looked at her watch. "I want to see how Ben does in the first round. He's paired with Gabe Watson, you know," Sunny said. "And he's not in a good frame of mind, as you probably noticed."

Storm looked at her. "Are you sure it won't upset you?"

"What if you see Ben's mother there?" Dede asked.

"It's okay." She looked at Storm. "I can handle it."

They weren't the only people driving to Waimea Bay for the first round of the Intrepid. Traffic moved about ten miles per hour along Kamehameha Highway, and came to a complete halt at Lani's and a couple of the more popular breaks, where drivers were either looking for parking, a nearly impossible quest, or braking for pedestrians and enthusiastic surfers, who were everywhere.

As they got closer to the winding climb to the Waimea Bay overlook, Dede muttered that they'd move faster if they were on foot. And it was true. Cars were backed up along the road as drivers waited to turn into the Waimea Beach parking lot. Hoping for a space in the small lot was an act of optimism about as realistic as waiting for a lift on the hovering helicopters. Between the roar of the surf and the cacophony of people, vehicles, and helicopters, even speaking was a trial.

"I've got an idea," Sunny shouted over the din. She pulled into the empty lane for oncoming traffic before either Storm or Dede could protest.

From the back seat, Storm saw Dede's eyes grow round, and Dede's right arm flew out to instinctively brace herself against the dashboard.

"It's the only way," Sunny said, with a sly grin.

Neither Storm nor Dede responded. An oncoming pickup stopped dead in their path, startled by the van's appearance in its lane. Sunny swung left, onto the shoulder of the road, and passed four inches from the side of the clean and shiny truck.

The driver's mouth hung open and Sunny waved at him. Dede, who had emerged from her startled state, flashed a wide smile and waved, too. "You want me to show some skin?"

"No need," Sunny grinned. "He's too scared to react. Probably spent the last two days detailing that truck."

Storm laughed out loud. She used to joke about how some local guys took better care of their cars than their girlfriends. A rusting and dented van in close proximity to their pet would lobotomize a guy like that—especially if a babe was at the wheel. She turned around to watch him. The man was still sitting there, though the car behind him tooted. His gaping face swiveled to follow their progress.

Sunny ignored the stares of oncoming drivers and stayed on the shoulder for at least fifty yards, until she got to the drive that entered Waimea Falls Park. "I've got a friend who works here," she said.

"You think he'll be here today?"

"It's Friday, right? He'll be here."

And he was. He asked about Sunny's welfare and consoled her on Nahoa's death, then led her to a grassy lawn where a half-dozen park maintenance vehicles were parked. "You can leave it here for as long as you want."

Sunny gave him a peck on the cheek and the three women locked the van and made their way down the driveway, retraced their path on the highway, and walked across the street into the beach park.

Though Sunny looked somewhat nervous about being at the meet, it was obvious to Storm that she and Dede had negotiated crowds at surf contests before. They waved and greeted assorted acquaintances. Some of them sadly commiserated on Nahoa's death. Sunny gave and received hugs and still led the way to a clearing near the clustered TV cameras.

There, Sunny and Dede folded their arms and looked around at the gathering. People stood in front of them, but they seemed to be officials: judges, sponsors, and organizers. A few surfers milled nervously and several powerful jet skis sat on the sand nearby.

"Here, I brought you a pair." Sunny handed Storm a compact set of Nikon binoculars.

"Hey, thanks." Storm followed her friends' leads and put the glasses to her eyes. "You know who's out there?"

"Coupla Australians," someone near them said. "They're hot."

Dede whispered in her ear, "Look, Ben's over there. That must be his dad."

Storm followed her glance. She recognized Barstow from the restaurant that morning. "It is. I've seen him before."

"That's right," Sunny said. "I kind of forgot you're his mom's lawyer."

"Yeah."

"What's she like?" Dede asked.

Storm thought a moment. "She's nice, but kind of sad. You'd like her under other circumstances."

Storm scanned the crowd, wondering if Stephanie would come see Ben surf. Maybe she was too nervous to watch. The surf report was twelve to fifteen and rising. Not as huge as some tow-ins, but it was going up. Plenty big for disaster, though.

There was a feel of electricity in the air, which amplified as if transmitted from spectator to spectator. Some of it came from the teams of surfers who milled on the beach next to their powerful watercraft, and some of it came from the elevated voices of media spokespeople. But most came from the escalating crests of waves, which thundered against the lava rock points at each side of the bay. Storm shook her head with wonder. If you came here in the summer, you could let children play in the placid waters of the bay and watch local kids do flips off the big rock that squatted near shore. Now, you wouldn't even go wading.

Storm licked the salt that saturated the air from her lips. Television cameras worked nearby, while another reporter, whose hair didn't move in the brisk wind, made his way toward Ben and his father. She'd seen the same guy at the surf meet last week. He'd been interviewing Nahoa.

Marty Barstow took a step back, out of the picture, while Gabe Watson appeared to stand next to Ben. Both of the young men wore red singlets emblazoned with the emblems of sponsors. WhiteOut Watercraft went up one arm, and the logo of a sports car manufacturer covered their chests.

More interesting to Storm was the fact that Ben would meet the reporter's gaze for brief moments, but he hadn't looked at Gabe during any part of the interview. Instead, he either squinted out to the bay or looked down at the sand. When the reporter addressed Ben directly, he looked up and answered the question, but if the reporter asked a general question, Gabe usually jumped in. While Ben looked away.

Uncharacteristically, Storm was more interested in watching the dynamics of the interview than she was the surfers. So when the crowd cheered a successful ride, she swung her attention back to what was happening in the water.

"That's the first guy, right?" she asked Dede.

"Yup, and that was an absolutely beautiful top to bottom drop. If his partner does as well, they'll definitely move up." She pointed over her shoulder at a big scoreboard propped in the sand not far behind them.

Storm had her eyes to the Nikons when a woman's shrill voice distracted her from the next surfer's takeoff. Sunny and Dede stood like statues, their binoculars trained on the tiny figure in the water, but Storm lowered hers. Though the wind and crowd noise distorted her voice, the woman seemed familiar to Storm, and she recognized the man the woman had confronted as the fellow she'd seen with Marty Barstow the week before.

He was tall, with the look of an athlete going to seed, and he held a hand up, as if to quiet the woman. She wore a pareu tied low around her narrow hips and a tiny bikini top. Long, dark hair whipped around her face, and people were beginning to notice her, partly because of their spat, but mostly because she was gorgeous.

Though the man continued to make pacifying motions, the woman leaned into him, her slender arms rigid with fury. The sound of her slap carried on the wind. Sunny and Dede lowered their binocs and glanced over, as did many of the people around them.

The man grabbed her wrist and began to lead her out of the crowd. He didn't appear to be as threatening as he was embarrassed, so most of the audience turned its attention back to the contest in the water.

Storm was fairly sure the man was one of the contest promoters, and was intrigued by the familiarity of the woman. She allowed herself one more peek at the apparent lovers' tiff when the woman wheeled and twisted out of the man's grasp, only to catch Storm's eye and come to a dead halt.

Chapter Twenty-four

Despite the changes eighteen years had brought, Storm recognized Pua Pi'ilani. Thinner and more graceful, her face shared the same high cheekbones and fine planes of her brother's. She'd also grown at least a foot, had her teeth fixed, let her jet black hair grow in gentle waves past her shoulders, and lost all her baby fat, which had been considerable.

Storm closed her open mouth and raised a hand in greeting. Pua, without glancing back at the man, squared her shoulders and walked toward her. With outstretched arms, she threaded her way through observers toward her old friend. Her eyes were wide, and a drying trail of tears streaked her cheeks.

Storm enfolded Pua in a hug, which the woman returned. She felt as frail as a bird in Storm's embrace.

"Storm, I've got to talk to you."

"It's been so long. I tried to call you back."

"I know. And no one could ever hear a phone ring out here."

"Who's that guy you were talking to?"

"Steve O'Reilly. He's the organizer-producer of the Intrepid and a complete asshole." Her words held more misery than fight.

"What happened?"

The two women had the attention of Dede, Sunny, and everyone within ten feet. Pua was hard to miss, and her low voice, almost a whisper, attracted attention even over the noise around them.

"That's what I need to talk to you about. Partly, anyway. Storm, I'm sorry I—"

Suddenly, three men loomed behind Pua. One was a local policeman, and one was dressed in a sweatshirt emblazoned with the Intrepid logo and the blue shorts of local lifeguards. The third was Marty Barstow. Barstow stood back while the two security men each took one of Pua's arms.

Pua looked resigned, and shook her arms free of them. They let go, but stood right by her. "You need to leave, lady. Or we'll take you in," the Intrepid guy growled.

"Complaints have been filed," the cop said. Storm thought he sounded a bit sheepish. He should be. O'Reilly was probably six-two, two-fifty. Storm bet Pua didn't weigh half that.

Pua didn't seem to want to make more of a scene, though. "Later," she mouthed to Storm, and walked away, chin high, ahead of the cop and lifeguard.

Barstow hung around. "I asked you to call me," he said to Storm.

Storm felt her face flush with anger. "Most people call me at the office."

His voice remained reasonable and confident. "I may need your help."

"Against hundred-pound brunettes?" Storm snapped.

Barstow shrugged. "She's my partner's problem. He had to get a restraining order."

"Call me sometime this evening," she snapped. "I'm tied up until then." By that time, she would have tracked Stephanie down.

Sunny and Dede had stood by her during this exchange, and when Barstow strolled away, they looked at her with raised eyebrows.

"Are you representing both of them?"

"No way. I don't know what he wants." She frowned. "But I should find out. You heard anything from the surf community about him and his partner?"

Dede shrugged. "I heard the partner's been trolling."

"Anyone you know hooked up with him?"

"He made a pass at me," Sunny said.

"No shit." Dede grinned at her. "I feel left out."

"He just hasn't seen you yet."

"How long has he been in the islands?" Storm asked.

Both women shrugged. "A month or two, and he gets around."

"The next surfers are going out," Sunny said. She and Dede raised their glasses to view the next pair buzz out into the bay on the back of a jet ski. One of them was Goober, whose bleached dreadlocks were unmistakable.

"He got in the lineup," Dede said with some wonder in her voice.

"Yeah." Sunny's forehead was creased with a deep frown. "He's paired with Kimo Hitashi."

"He hasn't even won a major tournament," a nearby surfer complained.

The tiny figures were visible in the rise and fall of the water by their bright yellow singlets. Storm observed Goober slip from the back of the PWC and paddle into a rising swell, while Kimo zipped well away from the break zone.

Binoculars were critical to watching the surfers' moves, but they also made it difficult to judge incoming swells because of their tendency to make the waves appear closer together than they were. She could tell by Goober's reaction, though, that he felt the rising water promised a good ride.

Sure enough, with the audience's collective gasp, Goober rose to his feet. To Storm, his takeoff looked solid and aggressive, but she heard Sunny utter a small groan.

"What?" she asked.

"He's late," she muttered without lowering the glasses.

Now Storm could see it. Goober seemed to be trying to compensate, but the wave was ahead of him and started to curl. It had to be an awfully scary feeling, Storm thought, and watched him crouch into a drop, his only hope to get far enough ahead of the lip.

She could feel Sunny, whose shoulder touched her own, relax a bit, but Dede turned to Sunny with a question.

"How are they judging this? The waves aren't big enough to give the biggest ride the most points."

"In surf like this, they give points for a combination of things. Nahoa told me they'd look at everything from aerials to classic tube riding. They're looking for the best snaps and cutbacks, too."

The wave, a mere twelve- or fifteen-footer, still showed what was probably more than a twenty foot face. Storm's method for judging literal wave height was to try to figure out how far above a man the wall of water towered. This wave was three or four times Goober's height. To Storm, that was a big honking wave.

Goober was in what appeared to be a safer zone, and he got enough speed for a nice cutback, which encouraged applause from the fans. Storm knew there was no way he could hear the crowd's approval, but he must have been stoked by his move, because he next tried to fade up the wave, and lost some of his momentum in the process.

Part of the challenge of surfing is that every wave is different. Like snowflakes wrought by Mother Nature's ingenuity, each has its own personality in thickness, curl, speed, and direction. A surfer needs to continuously evaluate these factors and adjust to them. Storm suddenly saw that with his last move, Goober had miscalculated where the wave would break first, and consequently, the angle of his ride.

Dede's yelp confirmed her fears. The wave's leading edge was directly over Goober, and he was about a foot too low on its face. There was no way, even if he rocketed into a drop, that he could beat the speed of the wave, and he knew it. So did the crowd, which let out a collective gasp.

The viewers moaned as tons of water folded on top of him, turned to one another in dismay, then craned to see when and where his head would appear in the rolling lather of the broken wave.

Everyone watched Goober's board tombstone in the frothy whitewash. Kimo Hitashi zoomed in on the duo's big jet ski, warily keeping an eye on the next incoming set, but the crowd could tell by the frantic whine of the engine and Kimo's overlapping circles that he hadn't found his partner.

Long minutes elapsed before a yellow blur, the color of the vest Goober wore, appeared like a speck on acres of foam. When Kimo got to him, the spectators exhaled their pent-up breath in relief. But people tittered with anxiety, because they could see Kimo lean over and struggle to haul Goober onto the watercraft.

When Goober was finally visible behind his colleague, a cheer went up from the beach. In the interest of time, the next set of surfers was hustled into the water, but all eyes were on Goober and Kimo as they wobbled to the medical tent. It didn't take long for word to spread through the crowd that Goober had suffered a blown eardrum and would require further medical examination. Kimo would get a chance to finish his part of the competition the next day.

"Poor Goober," Dede said. "He's out. No way he'll be allowed in the water for a few days."

"Lono's revenge," Sunny said in a voice only Dede and Storm could hear.

Dede nodded soberly. "Maybe."

Storm started. "What do you mean?"

"Let's get out of here," Dede said, looking around.

The three of them walked to the car, and Sunny talked. "Lono punishes those who break certain *kapu*. Spiritually, Hawaiians believe that humans need to coexist with nature, to be part of the *'aina*."

"Goober grew up in foster homes. He's sacrificed some of his *hanohano* the last couple of years." Dede winced as she said this. "He became a bit desperate."

Storm nodded. The fact fit with what she'd observed in him. "So he entered the surf contest for the prize money. Is that what brought on Lono's revenge?"

Sunny shrugged. "More like he did a complete reversal of the philosophy he had when he came here. He used to surf for the athletic challenge and for a kind of purity, a oneness with nature." Sunny pulled onto the highway. "Then he got desperate to compete. And yes, his motive was mostly the money."

"You know the feeling," Dede said, "that there's a much greater power than yourself, and for a few brief moments, you're part of it?"

Storm nodded. She knew, and the wisdom of these two young women impressed her, not for the first time. "Has Goober finished high school?"

"Not yet," Dede said. "He's on and off with it. Since he moved here from California a couple years ago, he hasn't had a permanent place to stay or a steady job. He's almost twenty, and though there are probably a couple other juniors and seniors at Waialua High School his age, he's touchy about it."

"Like a lot of us, he grew up surfing," Sunny continued, "though some of us are lucky, and have an education." She looked over at Dede, who rolled her eyes.

"Sunny's more forgiving than I am," Dede said. "I think he should make a job and school his top priorities."

Sunny continued, undaunted by Dede's comment. "He moved to Haleiwa thinking that he could get a job either teaching surfing or as a lifeguard."

"And the local boys shut him out," Storm muttered, almost to herself.

"You've got the picture," Sunny said.

Storm winced. "It's hard to get a job as a lifeguard even if you're born and raised here." She didn't need to mention if you were a blond Californian, it was even harder. As much as Hawai'i people wanted to deny it, some racism still existed, often against newcomers from the Mainland—and particularly if they sought prestigious, high-profile City and County jobs that didn't require advanced degrees.

"But he's teaching surfing," Storm said.

"Gabe gets him a few jobs. It's not enough to live on," Dede said.

"Nahoa believed in the sheer challenge of surfing, too," Sunny said, almost as if talking to herself.

"He told me." Storm had been wondering about this aspect of Nahoa's surfing, and she was glad the other woman had brought it up. "But he still competed."

"He and Buster DeSilva used to argue about that," Sunny said. "If you listen to Buster, he'll tell you we need to change the Western values that reinforce the concept of ownership and encourage taming the forces of nature. Nahoa felt it was possible to compete and still be true to the spirit of surfing. After all, Lono started Makahiki, which included surfing contests."

"And DeSilva didn't agree?" Storm asked.

She watched Sunny's shoulders rise and fall in an easy shrug. "Buster used to compete in surf contests, too, you know."

Storm sat up straighter. "I didn't know that."

"Sure, he was good. Great, even. This was before tow-ins, when guys paddled themselves out in big waves. He used to surf with the Aikau brothers."

"That was the sixties and seventies. No one could get out when it got much over twenty feet. What the Civil Service Defense Alert calls Condition Black," Dede said. "When it gets that big, you need a jet ski or boat, because of the speed of the wave."

"Buster thinks using watercraft defies the art and spirit of surfing. The huge waves are sacred to him, an act of nature to be revered, not conquered by noisy machines."

"Does DeSilva feel strongly enough to take action against the organizers or participants of the tow-in contests?" Storm asked.

Sunny watched her from the rearview mirror, and Dede looked over her shoulder. "No, no," Sunny said quickly. "He'd never do that. He and Nahoa were kindred spirits. If anything, they thought people brought bad luck onto themselves."

But there was now a spark of apprehension in both women's eyes, as if Storm had voiced a concern they hadn't wanted to consider.

"What do you think?" Storm asked.

"About Buster's beliefs?"

"Yes, and about what happened to Goober today."

"Buster's got some good points, practical ones. Beaches are supposed to be public property, but you know that isn't always what you find when you try to get to some beaches on this island."

"True." Storm thought of the retaining walls popular among estate owners in the Diamond Head area. Paradoxically, the walls caused erosion of the sandy beaches the estate owners were trying guard.

"I don't think Goober was a victim of Lono." Sunny looked at Storm in the rearview mirror. "I think he crumbled under his own self-doubt." She shrugged. "Although, maybe that's how Lono's curse works."

Storm didn't doubt that people could sabotage their own efforts due to guilt or ambivalence. Aunt Maile told her it happened all the time. She even believed some illnesses worked that way.

But this thought brought another question to Storm's mind. "Usually the tow-in contestants have a lot of experience in big surf, right?"

"Good point," Sunny said. "Goober has less familiarity with tow-ins than some of the guys watching from the beach today."

"There's some talk going around," Dede added. "There's a rumor he got into the contest by doing favors for that guy O'Reilly."

"But Goober fell on his own," Sunny stated.

"Still, how did he get into the contest?" Dede asked.

"I don't know," Sunny said, but she sounded worried.

Chapter Twenty-five

Just as the women pulled into Sunny's and Dede's yard, Storm's cell phone rang. It took her a few minutes to dig it out of her bag under the seat, and when she got to it, the caller had hung up. Storm looked at her missed calls. She had two, and the most recent was from Stephanie. The other was from Pua. Storm wanted to talk to both women.

"I'd better go," she said. "Thanks for a great afternoon. It was just what I needed."

"Me, too," Sunny said, and Dede echoed her. "We'll see you tomorrow for the second round."

"I wouldn't miss it."

Storm grabbed her packages, tossed them into the passenger seat of the VW, and called Stephanie.

Stephanie must have been sitting next to her phone. "I need to talk to you," she said, her voice low and hoarse.

It was five-thirty, which still gave Storm plenty of time to get ready before Hamlin arrived. "I can be at Starbucks in ten minutes."

Stephanie was sitting in a back booth when Storm got to the coffee shop. Storm stopped at the counter long enough to order an oat cake and a cup of the day's brew.

Though Stephanie looked relieved to see Storm, Storm thought she looked even more haggard than she had at breakfast that morning. Her hair stuck out in brittle tufts and her skin was blotchy and rough. Her hands were wrapped around a frothy hot drink that looked to Storm like a latte, in the biggest size. The cuticles of her formerly manicured nails were chewed raw.

Even her eyes were bloodshot, and Stephanie wiped at one of them before she spoke. "I didn't tell you some things."

"I figured out the one about Nahoa."

Stephanie drew a ragged breath. "That's one of them. I'm kind of relieved, you know."

"I don't judge you. But it's probably a bit hard on Ben."

Storm had always thought it unfair that men could date or take second wives younger than their daughters. Let a woman try that and she's excoriated. Stephanie and Nahoa had not only tried to be discreet, they'd convinced the hotel personnel that they had a real love affair going. Even Susan, the clerk who had relished passing on the gossip, believed in their affection.

"I'm very sorry for your loss," Storm said.

Stephanie's eyes streamed and she blotted them with a paper napkin. She opened her mouth to speak and closed it again. Storm watched her throat muscles convulse in a swallow.

"We broke up several months ago. I still cared, though."

"Sure, that's normal."

"He had a new girlfriend. I was trying to stay away and let him get on with his life." Stephanie looked at Storm and blew her nose into the napkin. "I…I guess I loved him. I didn't want to mess up what he cared about."

"You called him after you broke up?"

Stephanie nodded. "I just wanted to see how he was doing."

"Is that how Ben found out?"

Stephanie's eyes narrowed. "Marty told him."

"When? You have any idea?"

"I'm not sure. A few days ago, I think."

"And Ben told you about this?"

"He didn't have to." Stephanie's eyes filled again.

"But he knows how Marty treated you, doesn't he? He seemed sympathetic to the divorce."

"He told me he doesn't know what to believe anymore."

Stephanie was tearing the napkin into shreds, and tiny pieces fell into her latte and all over the table. As Miles Hamasaki had taught her when she first started working with him in the law office, Storm waited for Stephanie to fill the uncomfortable silence. It didn't take long.

"You saw Marty this morning," Stephanie said. "He's a strong, convincing man."

"Yes. Did you know he came to my table and gave me a business card? He wants to meet with me."

Stephanie's eyes popped wide. "Don't go."

"I can't hide for very long. He came up to me on the beach this afternoon, too."

Stephanie made a choking sound.

"What's he going to tell me?" Storm asked softly.

Stephanie covered her face with her hands, but Storm could hear her words. "I took money from him. He told me if I made a fuss about Ben being in the surf meet, he'd tell his lawyers and go to the police."

"Did you?"

"It was mine, too. I worked hard and he kept all the money. I got two hundred dollars a month for all the household expenses." Her voice broke with anger and emotion. "Two hundred lousy bucks. Groceries, clothes, school books for Ben. Marty kept a checkbook and paid the bills so I wouldn't know how much money we had or where the accounts were."

"How much did you take?"

"About eighty." Her voice was muffled. She still hadn't looked up from her hands.

"Eighty dollars?" Couldn't be, Storm thought.

"Eighty thousand."

"Oh." Storm sat back in her seat. A few seconds later, she asked, "How'd you do it?"

"I worked in the office, answering phones and stuff. Remember?"

Storm nodded.

"Marty had a safe, a big one with a combination that only he knew. He kept a lot of cash in there, because some of the people he worked with couldn't be paid on the books." Stephanie took a deep breath. "He was starting to drink more. He met people he wouldn't talk about, and callers hung up when I answered the phone. I couldn't get hold of his cell phone bill, and I got more and more concerned. I started watching him carefully, you know, when he opened the safe. It took me a while, but I figured out the combination."

"And you took eighty grand in cash?"

"Yeah, and we came here." She dropped her hands to the table top and her puffy-lidded eyes met Storm's. "You know everything now."

Storm believed her. The woman looked wrung out. Storm reached out and touched Stephanie's hand. "I might have done the same thing."

Which was true. Before Storm was forced to move to Oʻahu from the Big Island, she'd sold zip-lock bags of *pakalolo* from a patch she'd cultivated in the cane fields. Hawaiian pot was a hot item in those days, and Storm had been ready to make a down-payment on an old Harley when Aunt Maile and Uncle Keone had intervened. They'd probably saved her life, but it took years of being a pissed-off, bitter teenager to realize it.

"Can he prove it?" Storm asked.

"He says the contractor who paid him will back up his accusations and talk to the authorities."

"Do you think that's true?"

"I don't know what the money was for." Stephanie paused. "But I doubt if it was legal, all in cash like that."

"I doubt it, too."

"But that's not the problem." Stephanie's voice was sad again.

"Ben?" Storm said.

The miserable expression in Stephanie's eyes said yes.

"You can't control Marty," Storm said. "He can use this emotional blackmail against you forever. He may have already told Ben."

The look on Stephanie's face was excruciating, so Storm wanted to say something positive and encouraging. "You have to stand up to a bully at some point."

Stephanie twisted her hands together, and slowly nodded. "You'd better go talk to him. It's better if we know what he's up to," she said.

"I think so, too."

Chapter Twenty-six

Storm watched Stephanie drive out of the Haleiwa shopping center parking lot before she picked up her mobile phone.

"Pua, sorry I took a while to get back to you. I've been tied up."

"At the surf meet?"

"I needed to meet a client, too."

"Sure, I understand. Storm, I'm sorry I didn't get in touch. Like a long time ago, before…before Nahoa," her voice quaked, but she went on, "died."

Storm wasn't sure how to respond. The ball had been in Pua's court about fourteen years ago. "We have a lot of catching up to do."

"Yes. Do you have any time?"

"Right now?" Storm looked at the old, dial-type clock on the dashboard, which amazingly still kept accurate time. Though daylight was fading fast, it was only a few minutes after six. Hamlin had probably just left Honolulu, if he was on time. It would take at least an hour and a half in Friday afternoon rush-hour traffic to get to the Laniakea cottage.

"I've got a little more than an hour before a friend gets here. I've got dinner plans."

"Would you meet me? I'll come to you," Pua said.

"Where are you?"

"I'm at Damien's. I needed a drink."

Damien's was the restaurant Stephanie managed. That was the problem with a small town; it was nearly impossible to rendezvous unnoticed—as Stephanie had found out.

"Can you drive?" Storm asked.

"Sure, I just had one."

"Here's where I'm staying." Storm gave directions to the cottage. "Come on over, we'll talk there. I can jump in the shower, too."

"Thanks so much. I'll give you a head start." Storm could hear the person she once knew in Pua's grateful answer.

Storm took the time to dash into a market for a couple bottles of wine, sodas, some pistachios, and kaki mochi. She hovered over a sushi platter, but decided she didn't want Pua to stay that long, and she didn't want to spoil her own appetite for dinner with Hamlin. Not that she had to worry much. Lack of appetite was not one of her most pressing problems.

Since there was no car sitting next to the cottage, Storm knew Pua hadn't arrived, so local style, she left all but the screen door opened, taped a note on the aluminum frame for Pua to come in, set out a bowl of nuts and a couple of wine glasses, and hopped in the shower.

When she got out of the shower, she heard a faint thump and figured Pua had seen the note. The sound of a creaking floorboard carried through the bathroom door, which Storm had left slightly ajar. "Pua? Pour yourself some wine. I'll be out in a minute."

No answer. In fact, the silence was conspicuous. For the first time, Storm had the bad feeling she shouldn't have left the front door open. She hurried to pull on her underwear and the night shirt she'd left hanging on a hook that morning, then quietly pulled the bathroom door closed and locked it, then leaned her ear against it. She knew from the local papers that drugs, particularly ice, were a big problem and accounted for the majority of home break-ins. Some of those people could be pretty desperate, so the last thing she wanted was a confrontation.

She eyed the narrow, louvered window above the bathtub/shower, and knew she'd have to be nearly airborne with terror to scale those wet, shiny tiles and squeeze her size ten hips through that small space, only to be face to face with the ground six feet below.

The intruder knew where she was. She'd already invited him to pour a glass of wine, so stealth wasn't an option.

What was that noise? Jesus, it was the chiming sound Windows made as it booted up. The asshole was using her laptop. Why he didn't just steal it was a question she couldn't answer—she wasn't a thief, after all. Although she insured her laptop against theft (she had learned the hard way), she had data in client files that she hadn't yet backed up.

A commotion might be her best defense. She began pounding the door with her fists. "I'm calling the cops," she screamed. The door rattled in its frame with a gratifying racket.

She listened for a moment and thought she heard a rustle. She hammered again. "Beat it, you dickless scum-sucker." More banging. "I've got a phone in here, you squid-sucking fuckweasel."

No noise in response. Could the guy be trying to gauge whether she could get a radio signal in the bathroom? If only, she thought, and quietly turned the lock. But when she tried to open the door, it wouldn't budge.

The sonofabitch had somehow jammed the door. Now she was really pissed.

She rattled the door with renewed effort and added a kick or two. Maybe she could draw the attention of neighbors, who weren't too far away. "Get out of my house! Now!"

She paused for breath and lay her ear against the door again. Not a sound. No computer noises, nothing. What was he doing now? Going through her lingerie? It wouldn't hurt to hurl more abuse, just in case the gangrenous specimen was still within hearing range.

Storm drew in a lungful. "Get a life, you smoke-swilling, syphilitic swamp—"

"Storm?" The voice was timid.

"Pua?" Storm seized the doorknob with both hands and renewed effort. It flew open with a slam that blew the towel off her wet hair.

Pua stood there with her hand still extended in a knock. The other hand, which held her cell phone, dropped to her side and she peered at Storm's face, then around her into the small, steamy bathroom to see if she was alone. She looked back at Storm, her mouth open in surprise.

"Pua, there's someone in the house." Storm reached out to pull her old friend into the bathroom.

Pua looked around. "I didn't see anyone. I went in the living room and kitchen before I figured out you were in here."

Storm stared at her. "What about the bedroom?"

Pua looked to her left. The room was three feet down the hall, and the door stood open. "I don't think so."

Storm peered around the corner and took a step out of the bathroom. She could see her computer, alone and running, on the floor. She put her hands on her hips and glared at Pua.

Pua's perfect lips twitched.

Storm reached up and realized by the tangled halo of frizz that her towel had fallen off some time ago. Her hair felt as if it stood on end, a mishmash of homeless Rasta and mental hospital decrepitude.

Pua made a snorting noise, one that her mother would have disapproved of. Then she threw back her head and laughed out loud.

Storm grinned at her. At least she hadn't run away. But had the intruder?

"You scared me to death," Pua gasped.

"I can tell. You're absolutely terrified."

"Really." Pua leaned against the door frame and wiped at her eyes. "You sounded so serious. Are you auditioning for something? You got a part in a play?"

Storm grabbed her arm. "Didn't you unlock the door?"

"No, it was open."

"This door?" Storm pointed toward the bathroom. She felt like she was doing "Who's on First?" by herself.

"No, the front one." Pua pointed down the hallway, and broke out in a new set of giggles.

"Did you see my note?"

Pua's laughter hiccupped to a stop. "Sure, I saw your note. And I called your name about three times, but you were shouting so loud you—"

"I know, I know." Storm pushed by her and walked down the short hallway to the bedroom where she'd left her laptop and handbag.

Both women stood in the doorway and looked at the strewn clothes, upended purse, and computer disks scattered all over the floor.

"Oh boy. I scared him off, didn't I?" Pua whispered.

"I think so."

The laptop was on the floor, plugged into an outlet in the corner by the unmade bed. Her handbag had been emptied on the rumpled sheets, and the clothes Storm had discarded before her shower were on the floor, but not in the heap where she'd originally dropped them. They'd been scattered, as if someone had kicked through the pile. The contents of her briefcase were also dumped on the floor.

"Maybe you scared him with your shouting. You were pretty colorful." Pua's voice was hopeful.

"I don't think so. He trapped me in the bathroom. Did you see anyone?"

Pua shook her head and watched Storm open her wallet to see if her money was missing. "I can loan you some money."

Storm frowned. "It's all here."

The women glanced simultaneously at the laptop. The screen showed the desktop image, all the icons lined up on both sides of a pretty mountain scene.

"I gather you didn't start your computer," Pua said.

"Right."

Both women stared at the computer as if it might tell them who had been there.

"Maybe you can figure out if he opened your files. I think there's a way," Pua said softly.

"I'll have to ask someone about that." Storm walked into the room. It didn't feel like anyone was lurking. The closet door, which slid on a track, was already open, and there were few places to hide. Unless the prowler was under the bed, he'd left. Storm knelt down and peeked. Nothing but dust.

She turned and walked into the living room with Pua close behind. The sliding glass door that led onto the front lanai stood open about a foot.

"Looks like he left this way," Pua said. "But you should call the police and report it."

"He went down to the beach, where no one will notice a stranger. Smart." Storm watched a couple of chickens cross the sandy expanse in front of the cottage. Between them, the thick tropical grasses, and the brisk breeze, footprints would be nearly indistinguishable.

Pua held out her cell phone. "Call the cops right now."

Storm did, and handed the mobile back to Pua. "Thanks for letting me out of the bathroom. I'm glad you came when you did."

"Yeah." Pua sounded as if she wondered if it had been a good idea to come over at all.

"Maybe he'd already gone. He just left me in the bathroom to give himself time to get away."

"Probably."

Storm looked at the bowl of nuts and wine glasses, which looked undisturbed. "Want a glass of wine?"

"I could use one."

"Me, too." Storm poured two glasses, then looked down at her attire. She still wore only underpants and a T-shirt. "I'll be back in a minute. I don't want the cops to catch me like this."

Pua grinned. "They've probably seen worse."

Storm found the shopping bag with her new dress undisturbed in a corner of the bedroom. She slipped the dress on, a spaghetti-strapped number in a subtle midnight blue floral pattern. It had its own little shawl, which Storm threw around her shoulders for comfort, as well as warmth. She caught sight of herself in the mirror over the dresser and almost laughed out loud at her hair. The natural waves, as if excited by the break-in, stood out in an electrified Afro. She spent a few extra minutes twisting the mess into an almost civilized French braid.

Meanwhile, an old Gabby Pahinui tape was playing from the living room. Pua was still messing with the stereo boom box when Storm went out. "'Moonlight Lady' is one of my all-time favorite songs."

"Me, too," Pua said. "Hope you don't mind my looking for music."

"No way, it's what we needed."

Storm sat down on the sofa and picked up the untouched glass of wine. Pua sat at the other end of the couch and picked up a half-empty one. "I'm sorry I never wrote you."

"What happened?"

"Mom seemed so unbalanced after Dad died that I was afraid to." Pua twisted her wine glass. "Actually, I did. I bet I wrote you ten letters. I just never mailed them."

"Why not?"

"At first, I was afraid she'd find out. As time went on, I figured we lived separate lives. By the time you moved to O'ahu, I wanted to leave the past behind so badly, I didn't reach out to anyone."

"She blamed me for Uncle Bert's death?"

"Look, Storm. It's all in the past. Nahoa and I always knew she was irrational."

"She blamed me." Storm blinked a few times. She'd always suspected this, but hearing the words hurt more than she'd thought they would. She got up, went to the kitchen for the bottle of wine, and came back to refill both glasses. She set the wine bottle down on the coffee table. At this rate, she wanted it nearby.

"She was a nut case, remember? Take it from me, I know better than most people."

It was Storm's turn to look into her own wine glass. "Did she blame my mom's death on me?"

"No, of course not." Pua answered too quickly. "Look, my mom never accepted responsibility for anything. She always blamed other people. She couldn't even accept that she might just have bad luck."

"You're talking about her in past tense."

"She died ten years ago. Pancreatic cancer. Of course, she smoked and drank like a fifties film star." Pua tried to smile at Storm, but her eyes were filled with tears.

"I'm sorry," Storm said.

"Yeah, me too."

Storm looked at her old friend and found that she wasn't mad at Pua, not even for letting their friendship go. They'd been young and burdened with loss. She had mixed feelings for Rochelle Pi'ilani, who'd never seemed as mature as either of her children. Storm was old enough now to know that her memories of Rochelle were those of a sensitive, insecure twelve-year-old.

Tonight, some of her lingering questions had been answered, and she felt a kinship with Pua. They'd both had crazy mothers, but Storm's at least had been a kind, loving mother when she was able. With a lot of help from loved ones, she'd left most of the feelings of responsibility over her mother's death in the past. Every now and then, though, she still wondered if she could have been a better daughter, a less self-involved or more agreeable twelve-year-old. Would it have made a difference?

Don't even go there, she told herself, and went back to Pua's story. "Did you get your chance to fly the coop?"

Pua nodded. "Got a modeling contract when I was seventeen." She looked wryly at Storm. "Agencies were looking for 'exotic' girls."

Storm laughed and Pua joined in. "Exotic as muddy sugar cane fields."

"If only they knew," Pua added. "They thought I was eccentric for taking my shoes off when I went into someone's home."

"I bet." Storm had had the same experience when she went to college in Michigan. "Where were you?"

"New York, mostly. I had a great time, but it's a hard life for a kid. And believe me, I was still a kid. Got my GED between shoots."

"Were you in magazines?"

"Some, but I ended up doing more runway work. I got to travel to some great places."

"And you got paid well?"

"Yes, but I spent most of it. Part of the problem with being a kid." Pua shrugged. "Then Mom got sick and I came back to the islands to help out. Nahoa was fifteen and playing high school football. When Mom died, I took him to California. Job opportunities were better there, plus he was falling in with some bad influences on Kaua'i. I used an old business contact to hook me up with TV work."

"More modeling?"

"No, I'd taken some community college courses in communications and I got a job as a weather person for a Los Angeles TV station."

"Lucky you. Are you still doing it?"

"Yes, but I've moved to a San Diego station." Pua frowned. "I left LA because of Steve O'Reilly."

"The surf promoter?"

"That's what he is now." Storm detected a note of scorn in her voice. "He was a sports announcer at an affiliate station."

"How long did you go out with him?"

"About six months."

"What's he like?"

"He's an arrogant womanizer." The hand holding her wine glass trembled and Pua took a swallow.

"He cheated on you," Storm said.

"Yup." Pua set her glass down and folded her hands in her lap. "Got fired for it, too, the creep."

Storm watched Pua, whose knuckles showed white. Pua had been studying her wine glass since the topic of O'Reilly had come up. Pua had pushed for this meeting tonight, and Storm didn't think it was only for the purpose of reestablishing an old friendship, though she was glad it had happened.

"Someone found out he was cheating on you and fired him?"

Pua's lips twisted in an attempted smile. "I wish. No, the other woman happened to be the producer's wife."

"How did the producer find out?"

Pua poured herself what was left of the wine. "DeWitt—that's the producer—got some photographs."

"They just arrived on his desk?"

"Something like that." Pua looked back down at her hands.

Storm handed her the bowl of pistachios and Pua took a handful. "You sent them?" Storm asked.

Pua's smile was sardonic. "Nahoa did. Walked right in and handed them to DeWitt's secretary."

Storm had to admire Nahoa's nerve. "Nahoa wasn't into job security, was he? Did he get fired, too?"

To Storm's relief, Pua laughed out loud. "No to both questions, to DeWitt's credit. Nahoa had been doing some commercial work, but mostly he'd been surfing. He knew he wanted to come back to Hawai'i."

"How long ago did this happen?"

"He came back about a year ago," Pua said softly. "I just got here. I came because the police notified me of his death." Her voice started to quiver. "We were close, you know."

Storm reached over and took her hand. "Pua, what happened on the beach today?"

"That arrogant prick told me Nahoa was a loser. Always had been, always would be." Pua choked on the words and tears flowed down her face.

Storm felt her own eyes fill. Even if he and Nahoa and had been at odds, O'Reilly's comment showed unbelievable cruelty. The guy must be bearing a grudge the size of Mauna Kea.

"Would O'Reilly be vindictive enough to hurt him?" It would be so easy to stage a surfing accident.

Pua's eyes blazed. "I wouldn't put anything past him."

Chapter Twenty-seven

"What's with the woman?" Barstow asked. They sat at one end of the crowded bar at Pipeline Pub and Grub. People eyed the two men with curiosity, recognizing them from the well-publicized surf event that had inflated Haleiwa's population and changed its sleepy ambiance to a star-studded media fest. But their body language and simmering hostility kept admirers at a distance. There were other, more appealing targets: brown-skinned surfers, scantily-clad women, and local celebrities drifted among the bar's patrons.

O'Reilly knocked back half of his scotch, which he drank neat. "You know women. Break up with 'em and they bear a grudge the size of my dick."

Barstow didn't smile. His hands lay flat on the counter. "Who is she?"

He had only drunk about a quarter of his draft, a Gordon Biersch pale ale. O'Reilly considered asking him for some, just to quell the shaky feeling in his gut.

"Her name's Pua."

"And?"

"We used to work together."

"In California? She looks Hawaiian."

O'Reilly ground his teeth. Barstow was going to find out anyway and the situation would look stranger than it did now. He finished his scotch. "Her brother's Nahoa Pi'ilani."

The muscles in Barstow's jaw twitched. "When were you going to share that little tidbit with me?"

O'Reilly gestured for the waitress. "I just did." He pointed to Barstow's draft. "I'll have one of those."

"You knew Nahoa from California?"

O'Reilly shrugged. "I knew who he was, of course."

"You obviously knew his sister."

O'Reilly couldn't help himself from smiling. "Yeah, it was good while it lasted."

She'd looked more beautiful than ever. Too bad her brother had fucked things up. Alicia DeWitt, the producer's wife, was a whimsy, a two-or-three-night fling. He would have gone back to Pua and made it up to her.

"Just in case you'd forgotten, Nahoa's dead," Barstow snapped. "And the cops don't think it was an accident. They came by asking me who he hung out with, if he had any enemies. You got anything you want to tell me?"

O'Reilly stared at him. "They haven't talked to me yet." He leaned forward. He had a slow fuse, but Barstow was starting to push his buttons. His vision narrowed on his partner's face like a cold, blue laser. "I'm going to say this once and I don't want to hear another word about it. They can come talk to me anytime. I've got nothing to hide."

"Right," Barstow said in a low voice. "The cops said they'd shut down the meet if someone in it had anything to do with Pi'ilani's death. I'm here because you asked me, and I'm going to be very pissed if you fuck this up." His hands clenched into fists. "We'll never get a chance at surf like this again. You know how lucky we are with the timing of this swell?"

"You're forgetting who put this together, buddy," O'Reilly said between clenched teeth.

"No, I'm not. And you've done an awesome job with the media coverage. But I got the big names here and that certification—"

"Hey, I forgot to tell you. Two credit card companies came in today." O'Reilly stretched his cheeks in what he hoped was a big toothy smile. "One of them signed Ben."

"Good, that's good." Barstow's Adam's apple rose and fell. "A half mil, year's contract."

Barstow sat very still for a moment. "Thanks." He whooshed air through his nostrils and made a visible effort to rein in his temper. "We can't have any negative publicity at this point. None."

"I get it."

Barstow stared at the amber in his beer glass as if it were an oracle.

O'Reilly's hackles still stood on end, but he knew what Barstow said was true. His ale had appeared at some point—he hadn't noticed—and he now took a slow swallow. Time to change the subject to more practical matters.

"What are you going to do about Goober?"

"It's out of our hands. The judges gave him a four point six and the doctors told him to stay out of the water for a couple of weeks." Barstow seemed relieved to be on another topic.

"Kimo's still got his ride. He could bring up the average."

"To what, a six?"

"Doesn't he have another heat?" O'Reilly asked.

"Not at that average."

"What happens if Kimo is outstanding?"

"There's no provision for a partner change if one guy bombs his ride. That's the chance a rider takes. The only way that would happen is if another surfer gets hurt or disqualified and we've got an odd number."

"Well, Goober's hurt. So who's going to drive the jet ski?"

"One of the other guys." Barstow looked around the room. "I might ask Gabe to do it. He owes us."

O'Reilly nodded. "He's going to hate it, but what's he gonna do?"

Barstow grinned at him. "I figure he'll see it our way."

Chapter Twenty-eight

"Nahoa was never a loser," Storm said softly.

Pua now cried freely, and Storm put an arm around her shoulders. Storm's eyes also filled with tears, and she was filled with helplessness at her friend's grief.

A knock on the door stirred both women from their misery. "Must be the police," Storm said. She went to the door, unable to shake off the sadness that filled the room.

"Come in," she said, and the two police detectives who had visited before stepped into the room.

Their attention turned to Pua, who sat sniffling on the sofa. "Was anyone injured?"

"No. This is Nahoa Pi'ilani's sister, Pua."

The officers looked from Storm's sad expression to Pua's swollen eyes. "We're sorry about your brother."

"Thanks," Pua said dully.

"We think Pua scared the guy away," Storm explained. "She let me out of the bathroom."

"How was the door blocked?" Detective Yamamoto asked.

"I knocked something out of the doorknob," Pua snuffled.

"There's a nail on the carpet here," Detective Ursley called from the hallway. "Probably was jammed in that little hole. You'd locked the door from the inside?" she asked Storm.

Storm shuffled her feet. "I was scared."

"I would be, too," Ursley said. She gestured toward the bedroom. "Have you checked to see if anything is missing?"

"Not really. We made sure he was gone and called you."

"Why don't you take a look now, while we check out the house?"

"He started my computer."

"Really?" The cops looked at each other. "Usually they steal 'em."

"Can you get fingerprints or anything?"

"Maybe, but the powder will make a mess. Let's see if we can get prints from the doors first. Of course, to do us any good, they've got to be on file."

"The Department of Motor Vehicles takes them, don't they?" Storm asked.

"Only your thumb. We'll need a whole set, which means either your intruder has a record or was printed for some other reason, usually work-related."

Storm followed Ursley into the bedroom and showed her the dumped briefcase items, scattered floppy disks, and strewn clothing. The computer screen was in sleep mode.

Ursley put on a pair of orange goggles and lay on the floor to examine the laptop. "I don't see anything on the keyboard at all. It looks wiped clean, though I see fingerprints all over the screen. Those are probably yours."

After a few minutes of watching Ursley scrutinize the computer screen and housing, Storm sat on the floor and began to sort through the contents of her briefcase. She had four floppy disks stacked next to her. "A floppy is missing." She poked through the briefcase pockets. "I had five. The missing one was labeled 'January cases.' Damn, I'd typed in information on Mrs. Shirome."

Officer Yamamoto walked into the room. He carried a mobile phone on a newspaper. "I heard this ringing. It was outside, in a hibiscus hedge."

Storm gave a little gasp. "It's mine. I hadn't even noticed it was gone."

Yamamoto handed it to Ursley. "Let's check it for prints." He addressed Storm. "Was it turned on?"

She nodded.

Ursley examined it with her orange goggles, then handed it to Storm. "You might want to check the call log."

"It's already at the call log," Storm said. An ominous weight sat on her. This person had been looking for information, and he'd found a lot of it. Who she'd talked to, their phone numbers, what was on her computer, whose cases she was handling. For once, Storm was glad she didn't have many high-profile clients, plus she was behind in her recordkeeping. Her call to Rodney Liu, the labor union official, would be on the phone, but she hadn't had time to record the details of her conversation. She certainly hadn't recorded today's revelations about Nahoa's and Stephanie's affair, not that she ever would. Nor would she be inclined to write down anything with regard to the 80K Stephanie had taken.

Storm stared at the face of the phone and thought about what could have precipitated the break-in. She'd witnessed a couple of confrontations in the last two days. Gabe's surfboard assault on Sunny might have been deadly. Stephanie had used bad judgment in two ways that she knew about. The affair was probably fairly widely known, but Storm assumed that the stolen money was not. Except for Barstow, who knew about it? More important, who cared that she knew? Storm didn't know the answers to these questions. But what bothered her even more were the questions she didn't know to ask.

If anyone had been following her, she'd left a trail a kid could follow. From her open conversation with Moʻo and Buster yesterday and her meeting with Warren Yee, the jujitsu sensei, to her contact with Pua in front of hundreds of people on the beach this afternoon, she had been marching in plain view up and down Haleiwa's narrow and congested main street.

There was nothing she could tell the detectives that would lead them to her trespasser. Nothing in particular that she could pinpoint as the incentive for a burglary.

The two officers got back to work on the house. Ursley picked up the briefcase with a coat hanger hook, and shone her flashlight carefully over it. "I don't see any prints here, either. We prefer not to fume electronic equipment with superglue, but if you want, I could take the computer case and a floppy or two back to the station."

"You think you'll find anything?" Storm knew the answer to that question by looking at their faces. They were going through the motions, trying to make her feel better.

"Never mind. Work on finding who killed Nahoa, okay?"

"There's a whole team on that one," Ursley said.

"Any progress?"

Ursley and Yamamoto looked uncomfortable. "We can't talk about an ongoing investigation."

"I understand," said Storm.

Yamamoto walked out of the bedroom and came back a few minutes later. "Looks like he came and went through the sliding door on the *makai* side of the house," he said.

"That's what we thought." Pua had wandered into the bedroom.

Storm, meanwhile, stowed all items back into her briefcase and purse without noting anything else missing. She probably wouldn't notice until she needed it. She fought the urge to hide her purse and left it with the briefcase on top of the unmade bed. She might never know if the intruder had found what he was looking for.

She and Pua went out to the kitchen, where Yamamoto handed Storm a form. "Better fill this in for insurance purposes. And call us if you find anything else missing."

"Thanks for coming out."

"Lock your doors, okay?" Ursley said, and the two left.

Pua began to wash out the wine glasses. "When's your friend getting here? I don't want to leave you alone, but you need to get ready for dinner."

"I'm okay. I'm sure the burglar's long gone. The police car was pretty conspicuous."

"I guess so." Pua fumbled with the soapy sponge.

Storm touched her arm. "How are you doing?"

Pua's face was pale and drawn. "Not so well. I don't know what I'm going to do without Nahoa."

"It's got to be awful for you," Storm agreed. "I'm here if you need me."

"Even after all this time? I should have called you long before today."

Storm shrugged. "I'll be here."

Pua clasped her arms across her chest as if she were cold and turned to face Storm. "Storm, there is one thing. Will you help me find who sent him the package? Who hated him enough to leave him in the water," her voice dropped to a choked whisper, "for the sharks?"

Storm could see Pua struggle with her emotions. The image of the somber group on the beach, hauling the heavy mass to shore, returned to her. She also remembered Gabe's maliciousness and how easy it would be to cause a death, even if it resulted from a flash of temper or a perceived insult in the water.

"The police are asking the same questions."

"You and I both know that people here won't talk to them as easily as they will to a pretty face, one with ties to the community."

Storm wanted to disagree, but she knew better. Both women remembered a boy who'd been a leader at school, and who'd attended Ke Kula Maka'i, HPD's training academy. He'd come back to work on the Big Island, and though he was still a local boy, people got a little quieter when he was around. They'd report something outright dangerous, but they wouldn't discuss the size of someone's *pakalolo* patch or whether Auntie so-and-so's sixteen-year-old had too many beers before he drove home. She and Pua knew that it was often these gossipy tidbits that led to a truth, like pebbles along a trail.

Pua's sad eyes beseeched her. Nahoa's death hurt even Storm, who hadn't seen him for years. It must have shattered Pua's world.

Storm sighed. "I'll keep poking around."

Chapter Twenty-nine

Storm had brushed her teeth and was finishing with a touch of mascara when she heard banging on the screen door, which she'd locked after Pua's and the police detectives' departures.

"Storm?" Hamlin's voice sang out.

She ran to open the door. "I'm so glad you're here."

"I'm late." He dropped his briefcase on the floor and returned her embrace.

"It's okay, so am I. It's been a busy day."

"Are you all right?" He held her at arm's length and examined her face. "You look upset."

"Pua came by."

"Nahoa's sister?"

"Yes, and something else." Storm leaned into him. "Someone broke into the house and locked me in the bathroom. The police just left."

"Oh, no." Hamlin pulled her to him. "I wish I'd been here."

Storm put her arms around him. "It might have been better that you weren't. I was scared, but safe." She didn't want to think about what might have happened if the intruder had felt the need to disable her, or anyone else, in order to perform his search.

"Pua got here in time to scare him off and let me out of the bathroom," she explained.

"And the police checked the house?" He looked around as if the house needed to be searched again.

"Yes, it's fine. He went out the sliding glass door in the living room."

"Good grief, Storm." Hamlin hugged her with a burst of strength that took her breath away. Storm knew that they both remembered all too clearly the close call they'd had when Miles Hamasaki's killer confronted them. Storm couldn't help but recall that it was Hamlin who'd suffered the more serious injuries.

He loosened his embrace. "I'll have to thank Pua when I meet her."

"I hope that's soon."

"You made up for lost time?" Hamlin looked concerned. He knew the families' history.

"I'll tell you about it over dinner. Where do you feel like eating?"

"I'll run out and pick up something," he said, and held her at arm's length to carefully examine her face for signs of stress. "You can't feel like going out after the experience you just had."

"Are you kidding? I want to get out of here for a while." Storm caressed the back of his neck. "Then I want to come back together, check over the place—and relax." She smiled at him.

"You're sure?"

"I'm sure."

"Somebody told me Damien's has the best seafood. I made a reservation, but we can cancel it."

"No, I want to go. That's where Stephanie Barstow works, and the food's great."

A half hour later, Storm and Hamlin had a romantic corner booth with candles and a vase of dendrobium orchids on the tablecloth.

"What's Pua like?" Hamlin asked.

"She's beautiful. If she hadn't looked like Nahoa, I might not have recognized her. She's changed a lot."

"She wasn't pretty when you were kids?"

"I never thought of her that way, but I don't think so. For one thing, she was shorter and heavier."

"Like a lot of girls on the brink of puberty."

Storm had to grin. "Exactly. Like I was."

"But she's still a nice person?"

Storm gazed thoughtfully at the candle. "I think so."

"Did she come by just to talk? Because you guys hadn't seen each other for so long?"

The waitress delivered a bottle of wine to their table, and Storm, grateful for the interruption, waited for her to serve it. Storm didn't want to reveal that Pua asked her to question Nahoa's friends and surf colleagues, because she knew he would strongly oppose the idea.

Hamlin hadn't forgotten his question, though. He raised his wine glass to her, and then, like the smart trial lawyer he was, went at it from a different direction.

"She's here to set up services for Nahoa?"

"I suppose. We talked about a lot of things. Family stuff, you know. She works for a TV station in California now."

Hamlin elevated an eyebrow. "You haven't seen this woman since you were twelve, right?"

Storm examined the rich red liquid in her glass. "Right."

"And you still feel a connection with her?"

"I guess so. I mean, we have history. We each had a parent die when we were young."

"And she just lost Nahoa, who had reached out to you. Showed you a kindness."

"Yes." Storm drew out the word and met his gaze. "So?"

"Storm, you don't owe her anything. Please don't get involved in trying to track down who killed him. The police are working on it, and they'll figure out what happened."

Storm leaned her head on his shoulder. "Hamlin, thanks for wanting to take care of me."

"I worry, you know."

"I know, and I love you for it."

The waitress showed up to take their orders. Storm had been too preoccupied to spend much time on the menu, but the pear, candied walnut, and arugula salad caught her eye. Another waiter passed nearby, with two sumptuous plates in his hands. A heavenly aroma trailed in his wake.

"What's he carrying?" Storm asked.

The waitress glanced over her shoulder. "Looks like *opak-apaka* Chinese style, with ginger and sesame oil. The other dish is our special seafood curry, with *ono*, scampi, scallops, and calamari." She winked at Storm. "We serve it with lots of condiments, including homemade mango chutney."

Suddenly, Storm was ravenous. "I've got to have the curry. It sounds wonderful."

Hamlin, meanwhile, had been studying the menu. "I'll have the osso bucco, with rosemary polenta."

They handed their menus to the young woman, and Hamlin turned back to Storm. "What did she ask you to do?"

Storm sighed. "She wants me to figure out who sent him the package."

Hamlin shook his head. "Let the police do that."

"I will. I figure I'll call Brian and find out what the cops have discovered so far and get back to her. She just wants someone who knew Nahoa personally to pay attention."

"Do you think the break-in this afternoon had anything to do with Pua or Nahoa?"

"I don't know, but I'm glad I don't have anything written down about Nahoa. Whoever broke in wanted information in my files. I only keep information on clients there." She winced. "I should probably call some of those clients and warn them."

"Like Rodney Liu."

"And Mrs. Shirome." Storm sighed. What a way to start out with Uncle Miles' former clients. She hoped they didn't think she was a risky flake.

Hamlin read her mind. "It'll be okay. It's not like your laptop got stolen from a restaurant or someplace public."

"Right." She was unconvinced.

"You need a cheering-up." Hamlin reached into his pocket and pulled out a long, slender box, wrapped in bright yellow paper. It had a slightly flattened, off-kilter bow. "Your Aunt Maile and Uncle Keone wanted me to give it to you tonight, instead of waiting until Sunday."

"I guess they figured we'd be celebrating your arrival on the North Shore."

"Maybe. Aunt Maile definitely wanted you to have it early." He handed it to her. "Leila and Robbie are going to come up Sunday, and I'm going to give you my gift then. They're helping me with it."

Storm gave him a puzzled look, but he just grinned. "You'll have to wait and see."

Storm tore off the wrappings and revealed a black velvet jewelry box. "Good grief, I'm supposed to downplay my thirtieth birthday. Looks like they splurged."

She opened the box, gasped, and then beamed. Carefully, she unfastened a gold chain from its protective nest and held it up. Hanging from the chain was a plump little gold pig with emerald eyes. It looked over its shoulder, head cocked, and mouth slightly open in what might have been a smile.

"It's adorable." She cradled the pig in the palm of her hand to see it better.

"It's *kolohe*, like you." Hamlin peered at it. "Beautiful, too."

The waitress arrived to carry off their empty plates. "What a great charm. She looks like a Vietnamese potbelly pig. My friend has one as a pet—they're so smart. It's a birthday present?"

"Yes, and it's my *'aumakua*," Storm said.

"Perfect," the waitress said, and made off with their dishes.

"I'm glad Aunt Maile didn't ask me to bring you the real deal," Hamlin said when she left.

"That'll probably happen next year."

They were still chuckling over how far Aunt Maile's devotion to their shared *'aumakua* might extend when the waitress returned with three waiters. They carried a dessert plate, with something that smelled delicious and was lit with a single candle.

Their harmonious version of "Happy Birthday" masked Storm's groans—especially when most of the tables around them joined in. The waitress set a warm chocolate soufflé before Storm. She moaned again, with anticipation. This was one of her favorites.

"I'll get you for this," she whispered to Hamlin.

"Good, I can't wait," he grinned.

And about an hour later, she did. So when the phone jarred them from a dead sleep, it took several rings to find the shrill annoyance.

Storm, slightly more familiar with the bedroom, got to it first. "Hrmmph?" she croaked into the receiver.

"He's not here," a woman's voice wailed. "He didn't come home."

"Stephanie? Is that you?" Storm still couldn't open her gritty eyes. "What time is it?"

"Almost two. He never stays out this late."

"Stephanie, he's an adult. He's probably with friends." Storm rubbed her eyes and thought about how Ben had pushed by her earlier in the day. He'd just told Dede and Sunny about his mother's and Nahoa's affair, which in retrospect seemed spiteful, as if he needed company in his disillusionment. Storm guessed his staying out was another attempt to punish his mother.

There wasn't any easy way to do this. "Ben knows about the affair. Call the police and report that he's missing. Tell them about you and Nahoa. The whole story."

"They don't need to hear about Nahoa, do they?"

"They probably already know."

Storm kept talking over Stephanie's renewed whimpers. "I saw Ben earlier today, er, yesterday. He was upset, but he'll get over it."

"There's something else, Storm."

Storm was now completely awake, and an anxious knot lurched in the area of her stomach. What now?

Stephanie got control of her tears, but her voice quivered. "I heard some people talking about Nahoa and that other surfer who died."

"What? Where'd you hear this?"

"A couple of surfers who were hanging around the beach. They said Matsumoto and Nahoa had been killed by Hawaiian ghosts."

"Who said this? Was it Buster DeSilva? Do you know him?"

"It wasn't Buster. These were young guys, and they talked about a sacrifice to Lono. They said Nahoa and Ken both broke *kapu*. Their bones were shattered, their teeth pulled, and the bodies were hidden in the caves around Pupukea."

Storm sat up abruptly. The police had withheld the information about the surfers' missing teeth.

"Stephanie, you think you could find out who those guys were?"

"I'll ask the woman I was walking with, see if she knows. What's wrong?"

"Nothing, I'm curious," Storm said quickly. "Did they say how Ken and Nahoa supposedly broke *kapu*? There are thirty people in the contest. Why would Nahoa and Ken be singled out?"

"Nahoa used Mo'o, who supposedly comes from *ali'i*, to get in. Ken comes from real estate money, a lot of it."

"Both of them were experienced big-wave surfers. Plus, people pull strings to get in these things."

"But the rumor is, they didn't get in the contest with integrity."

"I didn't know Ken, but Nahoa had a great deal of integrity. He went out of his way to teach wave etiquette and good will. Contrary to some other guys I've seen," Storm couldn't help adding.

"That's true. It's probably just jealous gossip." Stephanie drew a deep breath and switched topics. "Ben might be at his father's."

"And I'll bet he's safe in bed. The police can check that for you."

"Storm, I don't want to call the police. If the police show up at Marty's, he'll tell them...well, he'll tell them about the money. He'll make it sound really bad."

"It's your word against his. You're going to have to work that out, you know."

"Not today, not while Ben is in this contest. Please, will you come over?" Stephanie pleaded.

"What do you want to do? You want to go knock on Marty's front door at this hour?"

"We'll just drive by. We can see if Ben's car is parked by the house. All I want is to know he's safe." Then she added, "And I want you there in case Marty sees me."

"Have you tried phoning?"

"Yes, but neither of them answer. I've only got a cell number for Marty, and it's been busy for an hour."

Storm could understand Stephanie's concern for Ben's whereabouts, but if she was certain he was at Marty's, why didn't she just wait until morning? Though she probably wouldn't get much sleep. Storm thought about how Leila fretted over Robbie's safety. She'd be a quivering mess if she didn't know where Robbie was.

How much did Storm's duty to her client obligate her? She remembered Mrs. Shirome's tales of how Uncle Miles had gone out of his way to help her with a case that required behind-the-scenes activity.

Storm suppressed a ponderous moan and swung her feet over the side of the bed. "I'll be there in about fifteen minutes," she said.

Hamlin reached out and toyed with a lock of her hair. "What's happening?" he mumbled.

"It's Stephanie Barstow. She's worried about Ben, who hasn't come home." Storm stood up on legs that ached almost as much as her head. Her mouth felt like it had been tarred and feathered. Too much wine, too little sleep.

Storm pulled on a pair of jeans and a sweatshirt and shivered in the damp, chilly night air. Wind rattled the palms alee of the cottage, but even above the susurration of the branches rumbled a jagged, incessant thunder. Open ocean swells, powering in from massive storms in the Aleutians, were quaking the shore and blasting their salty spume along the coastline.

She reached up and touched her new necklace, which lay heavy and cool against her bare chest. Aunt Maile and Uncle Keone had sent it not only because they knew she'd love the mischievous little critter, they'd given it to her for protection. It made her feel better about going out into the black, thundering night.

Chapter Thirty

Stephanie was out the door of her modest duplex before Storm came to a stop in the gravel drive. In the light of the open door, Storm could see the figure of another woman, who waved from behind the screen.

"Who's with you?" Storm asked when Stephanie got in the car.

"The condo's a three bedroom and Ben and I share it with a flight attendant. She travels half the time, and spends a lot of her time in Honolulu with her fiancé. It's a great deal for us, because she pays a third of the expenses."

Storm waved back at the woman, who slowly closed the door on the night. She could see that Stephanie's eyes were swollen and red.

"I'm glad you've got someone with you," Storm said.

Virtually no one was on the road, and salt spray drifted over the pavement, thick as fog. Storm rolled up the car windows against the blustering wind, and kept the windshield wipers moving against the salt that hazed the glass and saturated the air.

The night was opaque as a velvet cloak, partly because the spray obscured any moonlight that might have shimmered on the water. Streetlights were reduced to an anemic blur. Where the road ran close to the beach, around Ehukai and Pipeline, the ocean's presence was a palpable but invisible force that sent shock waves through the earth. The car's headlights shone feebly through the mists, and Storm leaned forward, squinting to see past the clouding windshield. Stephanie quietly twisted a wad of tissue in her lap.

"You know where he lives?" Storm asked.

"Just past Sunset Beach." She sounded tense. "There's a little road. I'll show you."

"You've been there?"

Stephanie didn't say anything right away. "I drove by. I wanted to see what kind of place he'd rented."

"Is it nice?"

Stephanie nodded. "Probably rents for three or four thousand a week."

The women lapsed into silence again, as the car, in its cocoon of light, pushed through the darkness. The murky air limited the scope of the headlights, and just as Storm caught sight of the water flowing across the road, the little car plowed through it. Stephanie drew in a sharp breath as their momentum faltered.

Storm downshifted into second and kept the car's velocity at a steady, slow pace.

They must be close to Sunset Beach, and about thirty yards from the ocean. Wind battered the VW, and Storm gripped the wheel with both hands.

Whenever the surf got high enough, the road washed out. Though she couldn't distinguish the beach or water to her left, Storm knew some of the waves were big enough to surge over the sand and reach the road. She wished she could see them. She desperately didn't want to miss the timing of a gigantic set across this narrow stretch of road. But the night, outside the halo cast by the headlights, was an impenetrable wall, and the ocean, several yards farther out, a heaving, unpredictable mass.

"I see the Sunset Beach sign," Stephanie said. "We're close."

Storm didn't answer. She hunched over the steering wheel, trying to see into the blackness on her left, attempting to judge whether the splashing water under the car's wheels was rising or falling. It wasn't getting any deeper, she decided, which was an immense relief, because this was the only road. They had to come back the same way.

"We're just going to drive by, that's all. We can't hang around and take the risk that the waves will rise and the road will be blocked."

"Yeah, that sounds okay." Stephanie sat forward in her seat, as if she, too, were physically urging the Beetle along.

"I see his street," she said. "Turn left up there."

The road climbed onto a raised point of land that was the site of a lovely housing development. Enormous houses with spectacular views sat shoulder to shoulder in a high-rent neighborhood.

"There it is." Stephanie pointed to a home at the end of a cul-de-sac, lit by low modern globes that illuminated a short driveway. The house was a modern design in all-over cedar shake, with towering windows. Lights were barely visible in a front room facing the ocean.

"I don't see Ben's car," Stephanie whispered.

"It's probably inside," Storm said. Three wide, paneled garage doors were closed tightly.

"Yeah." Stephanie sounded dejected.

"We can't stay," Storm reminded her.

"I know." Stephanie's eyes raked the structure and she rolled down her window to peer toward the lighted area. "That's probably the living room. Can you see anyone?"

"No." Storm squirted fresh water on her windshield to clear it. "I guess no one will notice if I turn around in the driveway."

She swung the VW into the driveway and set off a motion-sensitive spotlight over the garage doors. By the time she'd put the car in reverse, Marty Barstow had opened the front door.

Stephanie rolled down her window. "We're looking for Ben. Is he here?"

Barstow squinted into the night. "Stephanie? Who's with you?"

Storm rolled down her window. "I am."

"What do you mean, you're looking for Ben?" he shouted.

"Isn't he here?" Stephanie had the door open before Storm could coast to a stop.

"No," Barstow shouted. "He lives with you, remember?"

Stephanie climbed out of the car. Her hands gripped the top of the car door. Storm put the car in neutral, set the hand brake, and leaned out the window. The wind whipped her hair around her face. "Stephanie was worried because he didn't come home. Have you seen him?"

"Not since this afternoon." Barstow's voice climbed with concern.

"When was that?"

"After the meet, around six. We wanted to take him out for dinner, but he said he wanted to get home."

Stephanie's hands tightened on the doorframe and her face began to crumple. "Come on, Marty. Don't play games with me."

"I'm not!" There was enough alarm in his voice to convince Storm he told the truth.

"What are you doing still up? Has he called you?" Stephanie asked. Tears streaked her face and her long hair rose in the stiff breeze.

"I was on the phone to Australia." Barstow looked at his watch. "But I'm going to call the police."

"We'll report it together." Stephanie slammed the car door and walked toward the house.

Storm could smell the ocean on the buffeting wind. She would just have to hope the waves didn't get any higher. "Does he have a girlfriend? Did he leave the contest with anyone?" she asked.

"He might be with Gabe Watson," Barstow said.

"Let's phone him," Stephanie pleaded.

Barstow frowned at the two women. "You might as well come in for a minute."

"We can't stay," Storm said. "The surf's rising."

"It's supposed to be twenty-five feet or more by morning," Barstow said. He picked up a phone on a table in the foyer. Storm and Stephanie watched him wordlessly for a few moments. "No one answers. But that doesn't mean anything," he added quickly. "I sometimes turn off the ringer at night, too."

Stephanie made a despairing noise. Storm had to hand it to Barstow, who patted her hand, even if he looked uncomfortable doing it. He pushed three numbers on the handset and made a report to the police. He gave a description of Ben and his car, and the names of some of Ben's friends, then repeated a series of phone numbers where he or Stephanie could be reached.

"They're starting now." His shoulders drooped with relief. "I was worried they'd want to wait until morning."

"They're looking for him?"

"Yes, they'll be in touch with us. You'd better get going. They'll probably call your home."

"Thank you," Storm said. Stephanie was ten feet in front of her, and making a dash for the car.

"Storm, are you free to meet me tomorrow? I won't take much time," Barstow said in a low voice, out of Stephanie's earshot.

"I'll be at the contest," Storm said.

"I'll be too preoccupied once it starts." Barstow rubbed his chin, which was dark with a day's worth of beard. He looked tired and drawn. "Look, I'll be at my partner's house tomorrow morning. Could you come there?"

He dug in his jeans pocket for a scrap of paper and jotted some words. "Here's the address. It's closer to you than this place. You know where Chun's Reef is?"

"Sure," Storm said. She'd had some good rides at that break a few days ago, before Nahoa's body had rolled ashore.

"Any chance you could be there by eight?"

"Does this have anything to do with Stephanie?"

Barstow shook his head. "No, a local guy has been harassing me about the holding period we've had."

"What's his name?" Storm said, though she had the feeling she already knew. Buster DeSilva's name was popping up frequently.

Barstow didn't surprise her. "DeSilva. Old-time surfer with issues."

Storm didn't doubt that DeSilva had issues. From her discussion with him, she knew that he was a passionate believer in the old ways. He'd be strongly opposed to contest organizers who "reserved" a beach using local muscle.

Her gut told her he was harmless, but she knew it would be unwise to overlook conflict, with what had happened to Ken and Nahoa. She also wanted to get a feel for Marty Barstow, to see if he brought up anything about Stephanie and the divorce. It might help her represent the woman's interests.

"Okay, I'll talk to you," Storm said.

She trotted out to the car, where Stephanie waited. Eight o'clock was going to arrive way too soon. All she wanted at that moment was to safely negotiate the road ahead and climb back into bed with Hamlin.

Chapter Thirty-one

It was nearly four when Storm fell into bed beside Hamlin, who was fast asleep until she nuzzled up next to him.

"Your feet are cold," he said, and draped one leg over hers.

"Yeah," Storm said, and didn't know anything further until light peeked through the closed blinds and she smelled the aroma of strong coffee. She rubbed her eyes and turned over. Hamlin was already up and the bedside clock read seven-fifteen. What she really wanted to do was drag him back to bed, but she'd told Marty Barstow she'd meet him at eight. Damn. At least she had time for a cup of coffee.

"Why don't I go with you?" Hamlin said, when they both settled with their full mugs on the lanai overlooking the ocean. "We can be co-counsels."

"Hamlin, what would you say if I decided to come along on one of your depositions, or to visit one of your clients?"

He frowned at her. "We're not at the office."

"So what? This guy has a legal question. If it turns out to be in conflict with my representation of Stephanie, I'll be the first one to suggest that he talk to you." She slurped from her coffee mug. "I doubt it, though. He mentioned another, unrelated concern."

Hamlin glowered in the direction of the ocean. She could tell he knew she was right, but he didn't like it. Not with Nahoa's death hanging over their heads.

"I won't be alone. His partner will be there," Storm assured him. She went into the cottage to get dressed. On the way out the door, she called Stephanie to see if Ben had shown up, but the roommate answered the phone.

"I gave her a couple of Valium when she got in last night," the woman said hoarsely. She sounded exhausted. "We haven't heard from Ben."

"I'm going to meet with Marty Barstow, and I'll ask if he's heard from him. Hopefully, he's over there."

"I'll tell her," the roommate said. "She'll give you a call later."

Finding O'Reilly's beautiful beach rental was no problem, though parking was an issue. A Porsche Boxter sat next to a Corvette in the short driveway, and Storm's hopes leaped for a moment, until she realized the car was navy blue, not the black one Ben had been driving. Storm made a U-turn and found a parking place off the shoulder of the highway. Hers wasn't the only car on the stretch.

The house sat just far enough back from the beach to be out of the high-surf zone, but Storm could smell and taste the tang of the ocean from the back of the house. She pushed the doorbell.

"Come in," a man's voice hollered.

Storm pushed open the door, which was already slightly ajar, and walked past what looked like an office. That door, too, was partly opened and she could see the glow of a computer screen. It made a "you've got mail" sound as she passed. Men's voices came from the front of the house, which smelled of good coffee.

When Storm got to the kitchen area, she stopped in admiration. The entire front of the house was one big room, and the wall facing the ocean was almost entirely glass. A fireplace sat in the corner of one side of the area, with comfortable leather furniture clustered around it. The other side of the space was a modern, stainless steel kitchen, cluttered with coffee mugs, dishes, and cooking utensils.

Barstow sat on a bar stool at a granite-topped island, and the man Storm knew as O'Reilly stood on the other side of the island. He operated what looked like a commercial espresso maker. The aroma coming from it was divine, and much more appealing to her than O'Reilly himself, who wore nothing but a loosely fastened, drooping lavalava.

He leaned over the counter, offered his hand, and held on to hers for a moment too long. "The exotic and alluring Ms. Kayama. I've heard about you."

"Nice to meet you." Storm didn't mention that she'd heard about him, too. Instead, she kept her eyes on the guileless, blue-eyed smile, and hoped that his sarong didn't catch on a drawer pull. Storm had the feeling he'd already checked her bra size, and was so skillful at it that she hadn't noticed.

"I make a great latte, if you'd like one," he said.

"Take it," Barstow growled. Dark circles underscored his bloodshot eyes. "You probably had less sleep than I did. You hear anything from Ben?"

"No," Storm said. "Have you?"

Barstow just shook his head.

"I told you," O'Reilly said, "he's pissed at both of you." He gestured with the cup he handed Storm. "Not you, the ex." He glanced back at Barstow. "He's probably with that blonde."

"Does he have a girlfriend?" Storm asked.

O'Reilly shrugged and his lavalava slipped an inch. "I meant that gorgeous dame Pi'ilani was hooked up with. Aren't she and Ben good friends?" He raised an eyebrow and smirked.

"You're just jealous." Barstow glared at him over his own coffee cup. His cell phone rang, and he picked it up, barked a few orders into it, and disconnected.

"True, but I'm a patient man." O'Reilly shrugged again and Storm directed her gaze to the glorious view out the window.

Barstow, in her line of sight, rolled his eyes. His phone rang again, and he said a few short sentences before hanging up. "Questions about the set-up for today's rounds," he said in explanation.

"It starts at noon?" Storm asked, and he nodded. A sliding screen door opened behind her and she turned at the noise. "Goober," she said, surprised. "Howzit?"

Goober was coming in from the side of the house, and he barely glanced her way. He looked like he'd awakened and put on the same board shorts he'd been wearing all week. Or maybe he'd just slept in them.

"Sunny wouldn't go out with you if you were the last man on earth," he snarled at O'Reilly.

"Ooh, someone's in a bad mood this morning," O'Reilly said.

"How's the ear?" Barstow asked.

"Fine. I can surf."

Barstow's voice was kind. "It's out of our hands. Those are the breaks."

"You need someone to drive the jet ski for Kimo," Goober said.

"Sorry, kiddo. Doctor's orders." O'Reilly turned on the steamer attached to the espresso maker.

Barstow waited for the racket to stop, then spoke kindly. "It happens to the best of surfers, and you need to heal before you head back into the water. You could get an infection."

O'Reilly handed Goober a mug of coffee, but the young man ignored him. Storm noticed that O'Reilly's hand trembled. He quickly set the mug on the counter, and turned to the sink.

Goober stared, pale and somber, at Barstow. "Please," he said softly.

"It's out of my hands this time," Barstow said. "You'll have other opportunities."

Goober held Barstow's gaze for a half-second longer, then turned on his bare heel and headed for the front door.

He was halfway down the hall when Barstow spoke again. "Did you see Ben yesterday?" He used the same soft tone he had when Goober stood right in front of him.

Goober glanced over his shoulder. "He met a tourist. Maybe he's with her."

The circles under Barstow's eyes seemed to become less pronounced with this news. Storm was relieved, too.

She turned to him. "What did you want to ask me?"

Barstow had mentally shifted gears and wore a thoughtful expression. "What do you know about this guy DeSilva?"

"Not much."

"You ever met him?"

"Once."

Barstow nodded, as if he'd already known the answer. "What's your feel for him? You know, from the coconut wireless."

"As far as I know, he has a good reputation in the community."

"Teaches martial arts, doesn't he? You know if he has an arrest record?"

"I haven't had reason to look."

"Is that difficult?"

"Might be. Has he threatened you?"

"Yes." Barstow looked thoughtful. "Yes, you could say that. I also heard that he'd threatened Nahoa Pi'ilani."

That got Storm's attention, which was exactly what Barstow had intended. And while O'Reilly had his back to them and kept busy by scooping coffee into the espresso machine, his head was cocked as if he didn't want to miss a word.

"How so?" Storm asked.

"Something about being a sacrifice to Lono. You ever heard of that?"

"I don't put much store in those things." Storm looked directly at Barstow. Though circled with fatigue, his eyes glittered, as if he'd been waiting to see how she'd react to this inflammatory tidbit.

Storm wasn't in the mood to play games. "What's your concern in this?"

Barstow looked down and took a sip of his coffee. "He sent a letter to our parent company and threatened, as a Native American, to sue for loss of public access to the shoreline."

"When?"

"A few weeks ago, when we established the waiting period."

"Have you received any verbal threats or experienced vandalism against your property?"

"No, but he called me names. They were of a threatening nature."

"Are you physically afraid of this man?"

O'Reilly seemed to stifle a snort, but Barstow didn't react. "Not yet, but I don't want the situation to escalate. Especially in a crowd, like we expect at today's contest."

"You've got security, right?" She remembered the bouncer-type who'd hovered over Pua yesterday.

He nodded.

"Have them keep DeSilva at a distance. But don't let your security guys start a confrontation. Let him keep face." She looked him in the eye.

Barstow met her gaze. "I understand."

"Good." Storm looked at O'Reilly, who was now watching the two of them. She wanted to make sure he knew she addressed him, too. "That's very important."

Storm looked back at Barstow. "And if you want to take this further, I'll refer you to an attorney who's very good at countering threats."

Barstow grinned widely, which was not the reaction Storm had expected. "Your uncle taught you well."

"Did you know him?"

"Wish I had. He had a good reputation."

Storm allowed her eyebrows to rise, and she waited to see if he'd explain why he'd brought up Miles Hamasaki. But he took a slow swallow from his coffee mug. O'Reilly started the noisy coffee bean grinder.

Storm was hit with the impression that she'd been on trial. She wasn't sure what their opinion of her was, but she was peeved at the assessment. In fact, she doubted either of these guys was disturbed by DeSilva's actions, if there had even been any. The meeting was starting to irritate her. She had better things to do.

Storm stood up. "I've got to go and you've got a tournament to run. Hope I was able to help you."

"Send me a bill," Barstow said.

"Not this time," she answered. Or ever, she thought to herself. She had no desire to do further business with these two. "I'll let you get to your meet."

"Thank you." Barstow stood and shook her hand. O'Reilly came around the island to thank her, too. This time when he shook her hand, he didn't hold on.

Chapter Thirty-two

When Storm got back to the cottage, she found a note from Hamlin, telling her he'd run to town for groceries. She wandered into the bedroom and tidied up while she thought about the meeting with Barstow and O'Reilly. She had the feeling they thought they could manipulate her, perhaps on the basis of their self-appointed celebrity status. In some ways, they'd struck her as juvenile. Game players, both of them, but of a different sort. One thing she'd hand Barstow was that he'd handled Goober gently, despite the young man's hostility. He'd seen past the boy's bravado to his need and disappointment.

Both O'Reilly and Barstow were showing signs of stress. They were in the middle of an enormous operation, complete with prima donna surfer personalities and media scrutiny. Throw in a bit of local antagonism, and it was probably hard for them to sort out the critical issues from the stuff they could let wash over them. On reflection, though the complaint about Buster DeSilva had seemed trivial, it was probably worth following up. She wouldn't do anything major, but asking Brian if he had an arrest record wouldn't take much effort.

Her own impression of DeSilva was that he was an eccentric, and possibly even an extremist who believed Hawaiians had been hoodwinked by Western concepts. But he hadn't struck her as someone who would use violence. He'd seemed genuinely concerned about the *ka'ane* and Nahoa's package. On the other hand, he taught jujitsu, and possibly even incorporated *lua* into his martial arts instruction. She had no idea how his dojo operated, and perhaps this was something she should look into. In her experience, martial arts philosophies ran the gamut of inner control and "oneness with the universe," to cinderblock-smashing, bokken-flailing aggression. If he were in the latter group, he might be more of a threat than she'd thought.

Storm walked into the kitchen, where she'd seen a phone book. Buster and Evangeline DeSilva lived on Kawailoa Drive, which was on the way from Laniakea to Haleiwa. She also looked up Warren Yee's address. After all, he'd invited her over to talk about something he hadn't seemed willing to go into at the dojo. His address was in Haleiwa, not far from the dojo where he and DeSilva taught.

Storm found Kawailoa Drive without any problem, but once she'd made a left onto it, the road headed back toward the mountains for miles and became more potholed as she went. By the time she got to the DeSilvas' plain frame home, which was on a large plot of land and surrounded by mature mango, lychee, and avocado trees, she was glad the old VW had a stiff suspension.

The first person to answer her knock on the screen door was a baby in a one-piece blue romper. He'd crawled faster than most people could walk, and then stood up at the aluminum door. Storm figured he'd be running upright in about a month, when the parents, or grandparents, would really have their hands full. He beat on the rattling frame with both fists. The more noise he made, the wider his smile grew, and the louder his verbal greetings became. It was close to "hi," but he couldn't quite form the word yet. But he didn't care.

A slender, longhaired girl in low-rise jeans and a cropped top ambled about two seconds behind the little guy.

"Sorry to bother you," Storm said. "Your little brother is going to be fast, isn't he?"

The girl, who appeared to be about fifteen, laughed. "Sparky's my son. And yes, he'll be fast. Like his father."

Teen pregnancies were nothing unusual in the islands, but this girl looked like she should be learning to neck, instead of dealing with parenthood.

Storm kept her smile in place. "What's his dad do?"

A flicker of sadness passed through the teen's dark eyes. "He's a surfer."

Storm's stomach twisted. She surmised the two were no longer together. "Well, your son is adorable. Is Buster DeSilva around?"

The girl picked up the baby, who squawked at having his noise curtailed. "My dad's at the dojo. You know where that is?"

"Yes, thanks. Does he have classes this morning?"

"No, he goes in on Saturdays to tidy up."

"Thanks, I'll drive over." Storm said. "Take care," she added, and meant it.

When Storm reached Kamehameha Highway, she called Hamlin's mobile phone.

"Where are you?" he asked.

She told him where she'd been and how she planned to head into Haleiwa. "Have you had breakfast?"

"No, and I'm starving." He sounded a bit grumpy.

"I'll meet you at Rosie's Diner in an hour."

"An hour?"

"Okay, a half hour. Go ahead and order. I'll have huevos rancheros. With sour cream and extra guacamole."

"Working up an appetite?"

"Yeah, aren't you?" Storm hung up. She was sorry to keep him waiting, but she'd have to make it up to him later.

Storm pulled up in front of Warren Yee's house. A rusting pickup and a van, even more beat up than Sunny's, sat in the carport. The pickup looked familiar, and she thought she'd seen it in the dojo's parking lot.

Warren answered the door. "Hey, I thought you'd be getting ready to go to the surf contest."

"I am, but there's still time. You have a few minutes?"

"Come on in." He held the door open for her and led her into the kitchen. Another young man sat at the table, drinking a long-neck.

"This is my roommate, Justin. Justin, this is Storm."

Justin jumped up from where he'd been reading the paper and almost knocked over his beer. "Hey." He extended his hand and shook hers enthusiastically. "Want a beer? I went out for dawn patrol and worked up a thirst."

"No, thanks."

"How about some orange juice?" Warren didn't wait for an answer. He handed her a glass.

"Thanks. I wondered if you'd mind if I asked you a few more questions." She glanced at Justin.

"No problem. Justin knew Ken Matsumoto, too. We all worked out together." Warren gestured to the table. "Have a seat."

Storm sat down across from Justin. This was better than she'd hoped; she'd have two points of view. "The other day, you said Ken was a generous guy. Did you mean with his money?"

"You said Ken was generous?" Justin looked in surprise at Warren.

Warren shrugged. "He was if it got him somewhere."

"Like if it got him exclusive use of a break." Justin's voice was derisive. He met Storm's surprised glance. "Don't get me wrong—I'm as sorry as the next guy that Ken bought the farm, but I did think he was headed for a pounding."

"Did someone threaten him?" Storm asked.

"About a dozen someones," Justin said.

"I didn't want to talk about it at work," Warren explained. "We try to keep only positive energy in the dojo. No anger or resentment. It's counterproductive to developing our mental focus and our search for self-knowledge." He swirled his orange juice and sighed. "I'm trying to be less negative in my life."

Justin wasn't. He rolled his eyes, stretched his legs out, and leaned back in his chair. "Ken was an asshole. He paid these guys, the Blue Shorts, to keep certain breaks clear. Especially if the conditions were good."

"Did Buster know this?" Storm asked.

Warren looked down at his feet. "Yeah, I think so. He looked disappointed one day, and wouldn't talk about what was bothering him." He looked at Storm. "That's how he deals with problems, though. He considers all aspects before he'll talk about the solution."

"Buster wasn't the only one who was upset," Justin said. "Half the surfing population was pissed. Goober tried to get him blacklisted from contests." He looked at Warren. "You saved Ken from getting thrashed, remember?"

"Maybe. I don't know what that group would have done."

"Who?" Storm asked.

"Bunch of local guys. Even Gabe Watson had had enough, and he's part of the Blue Shorts."

"Yeah, Gabe keeps a careful eye on public opinion," Justin added.

"So Ken wasn't such a popular guy," Storm said. "What about Nahoa?"

"Oh, he was great," Justin said. "Everyone's devastated at what happened."

"Wait a sec." Warren looked at his roommate. "Nahoa wasn't any saint, you know."

Justin took a swallow from his beer. "Hey, that's water over the dam."

Warren paused, then seemed to reach a decision. "Not for everyone. Sometimes a bad decision is something you live with forever."

"Come on, she was sneaking him in her bedroom window," Justin said.

"But she was fifteen."

Storm felt her hands go cold. She had a very bad feeling about this. "What happened?"

Warren examined the surface of his orange juice. "Well, Nahoa messed around."

"I see." Storm nodded, not sure she wanted to hear the rest. "How long ago was this?"

"At least a year and a half," Justin said, as if it were over and done with.

Right, Storm thought. And the kid is not quite a year old. "Buster's daughter?" It wasn't really a question.

"Yeah, her name's Evie."

"Shit." Storm dropped into a chair at the table.

"Yeah," said Warren. "But Nahoa had a good heart."

"He really did," added Justin.

Storm gulped down her orange juice without asking about the state of DeSilva's heart.

Chapter Thirty-three

Storm drove directly to Rosie's Diner, where she was already ten minutes late for brunch with Hamlin. She couldn't have faced Buster DeSilva right then. Any questions she had for him would have revealed her newfound knowledge and her anguish and disappointment with Nahoa's judgment.

She couldn't help but stew over the story Warren had related. Evie had been afraid to tell Buster she'd missed her period—five of them, in fact. She'd just worn baggier clothing, which her father never questioned.

Though Warren and Justin deduced she was pregnant before Buster, they knew exactly when he caught on because one morning he appeared at work snarling and uncommunicative. At the dojo, he'd barked out the most rudimentary of commands to his classes and flattened unsuspecting students with lightning-fast moves. This had continued for about a month, when he'd apparently risen above his rage. He cheerfully informed Warren that he'd felt the baby move. After that, he gave frequent reports on the progress of the pregnancy. Class attendance rose, too, though Warren doubted it was because Buster had again become personable. Warren's opinion, which was substantiated by Justin, was that many martial arts devotees have a streak of masochism. Buster's reputation as a tough and skilled instructor had spread across the North Shore.

Storm went straight to where Hamlin sat. He had a pot of coffee on the table and the morning paper propped before him.

"Hi," he said, and rose to greet her. "The food should be here any minute. I was afraid yours would get cold." He gave her a second look. "What's wrong?"

She told him. Hamlin sat back in his chair and listened without interruption, his face impassive, though the set of his mouth was grimmer than usual.

"Damn," he said. "You've met this DeSilva?"

"Yes." Storm paused while the waitress set their heaping, fragrant plates before them. Her appetite wasn't what it had been an hour ago.

She tore off a corner of a tortilla and nibbled on it. "He's an activist, but no one's mentioned that he's ever done anything violent."

"Have you asked Brian Chang to run a check on him?"

"Not yet. I'll do it after we eat."

Storm ate about half her huevos rancheros and let Hamlin finish the rest. Since they'd come in two cars, they agreed to meet back at the cottage and drop one off before driving to the contest.

Storm called Brian before she got into the highway traffic, and asked him to check if DeSilva had an arrest record. Brian said he'd call her back, and Storm followed Hamlin back to the cottage. As she drove, she reflected on how everyone she'd met during the week connected to one another. Pua's request to find who delivered the *lei o manō* had led to DeSilva, which coincided with Barstow's problems with the man. Stephanie, Ben, Gabe, and even Goober were in the mix of people who'd had difficulties with Ken Matsumoto and/or Nahoa. Not necessarily both, though. She still had some digging to do.

Brian didn't take long to ring her back. "Buster DeSilva got arrested for a civil disturbance about ten years ago. He and some other activists were evicted from some beach land near Ka'a'awa and resisted arrest." He paused. "I know the arresting officer and he's not usually a hothead. DeSilva must have done something he considered dangerous."

"Thanks, Brian," Storm said.

"You got anything you need to tell me?" Brian prodded.

"I don't think so. One of the surf promoters said DeSilva had sent him some hostile letters. Wanted to know if I thought he should get a TRO."

"Any threat of physical confrontation?"

"He said no."

"He probably won't get one without it."

"That's what I told him. But thanks for your help."

"You're welcome. If I find out anything else, I might get to tell you in person. Leila, Robbie, and I'll be out tomorrow late afternoon."

"Great," Storm said. They disconnected, and she crawled along behind Hamlin in slow-moving traffic. People were beginning to crowd the North Shore in anticipation of the contest, which was scheduled to take place at a break called Outside Log Cabins. The inner break, Log Cabins, was already closed out, unsurfable. Storm turned on her car radio to follow what was happening.

The Intrepid was following a format different from most surf contests. Sports enthusiasts breathlessly announced that, thanks to a storm surge and an unusually large swell along North Shore beaches, the contest could take place at a different break each day. This not only showcased O'ahu's spectacular beaches and its variety of surf conditions, but was a concession to the O'ahu Surfing Alliance's complaints that the holding periods closed beaches to non-contestants.

Hamlin waited for her at the front door. He unlocked it, stepped into the house, then looked and listened for any signs of a repeat break-in.

"I don't think he'll be back," Storm said. "He either got the info he wanted, or found I didn't have it."

"Let's hope so." Hamlin went into the living room and turned on the television. "I saw some TV vans in that line of cars."

"It's a big event. The traffic's going to get worse. We should probably get going." She picked up the phone. "Let's see if Sunny and Dede have left yet. They may have parking suggestions."

Dede answered. "We were just leaving. Since we're on the way, why don't you come over here and we'll drive together? I've got a friend who lives about a half-mile from Log cabins."

Storm hung up and turned to Hamlin. "You're going to meet Sunny and Dede."

"The girls you told me about?" He looked very happy.

She rolled her eyes. "You're spoken for."

"I can look, can't I?" Hamlin bounced his eyebrows.

"Sure, I will be."

"I knew it," he said, feigning disgruntlement. "All those young surfers."

"Yeah," Storm said, and waggled her eyebrows back.

When they got to the girls' house, Sunny and Dede were outside, waiting by the van. Dede eyed Hamlin's 1965 200SE convertible. "Let's take your car."

"Okay," Hamlin said without hesitation. Storm knew that he'd have ridden in Sunny's van without protest, but the spotless old Mercedes had been willed to him by a grateful client. He not only loved to drive it, she could see he relished the idea of driving a carload of beautiful women.

Dede directed Hamlin, who got a lot of amused and envious stares in the stop and go traffic, to a narrow residential road that ran parallel to Kamehameha Highway. When they got to the house she pointed out, the front yard already looked like a parking lot. Dede's friend had been standing on the last patch of grass, and she watched them pull up with an expression that combined relief, impatience, and amusement.

"Thank God," the young woman shouted at them. "Hey, nice car. You probably want to put the top up."

Hamlin did, and they gathered their hats, binoculars, and water bottles before joining the throng of pedestrians marching along Kamehameha Highway. People trekked along the narrow shoulders of the highway like pilgrims on their way to Mecca, small packs of supplies slung over their backs. A nimbus of excitement moved along with them. The aura grew more charged as they got closer to the contest site and saw signs of the hoopla surrounding the event.

Television vans, studded with satellite dishes and antennae, already lined the highway. To get so close, they must have parked the day before, and some of the technicians who climbed in and out of the vehicles looked like they'd spent at least one night on site. Large Starbucks cups were apparently part of their gear. Razors weren't.

The logistics of getting to the site kept the crowd from getting as unruly as the highway. There were no parking lots, and the road was lined with cars as far as they could see. Like the vans, anyone with a nearby spot had to have staked it out the day before.

Sunny apparently was thinking along the same lines as Storm, because she turned to Dede. "Thank heavens your friend saved us a spot. Some of these people won't get in."

"Yeah, a bicycle is better than a car when it comes to attending one of these," Dede replied.

The four of them followed the majority of the spectators along a public beach access. It led through a stand of tall ironwood trees, which separated two large beachfront homes. Many of the arrivals paid no attention to the public walkway, and made their way across private yards and driveways.

Sunny led the way across a stretch of the beach to a makeshift hut, where a cluster of media personalities and TV camera operators came and went. A board that announced the teams, the color of their singlets, and their standings loomed behind it. Storm could see O'Reilly inside, waving his hands and gesticulating at one of the sports announcers.

On the way by, Storm could hear snatches of his diatribe. "…don't give a fuck about any floating leis in their memories…let the goddamn girls cover the heart-warming stuff…" His voice sneered at the word "girls," and Sunny and Dede exchanged glances.

Storm caught Hamlin's eye. "A few hours ago, he was in his lavalava, making lattes," she said out of the corner of her mouth. "He was downright jovial, then."

"High pressure job," Hamlin said.

"Yeah." Sunny jutted her chin toward O'Reilly's partner, who was planted not far away on the sand. Barstow stood, feet planted in a wide stance, arms folded tightly across his chest. He glowered at Goober, whose back was to Storm and her friends. The muscles in Barstow's jaw stood out in knots.

"Makes me tense just looking at him," Dede said. "Let's go farther down the beach and see if we can figure out who's in the water."

"Looks like the judges are sitting over there." Storm pointed to a large, square tent that had been pitched on the sand in a prime spot.

"That's a good place to hang," Sunny said. "If any of us get separated in this crowd, let's meet behind it."

"Good idea," said Storm. She squinted at the back of a wiry, dark-skinned man who had stopped to shake the hand of a surfer. Sure enough, when he turned to face the water, she could see it was Buster.

Storm took a deep breath. She'd had time to digest Warren's news about Nahoa, and she figured now was the time to tackle Buster. He looked happy and relaxed. "I'll be right back," she said to Hamlin, who had put his binoculars to his eyes.

Before Storm reached Buster, though, a lovely woman holding a microphone intercepted him. Storm stopped dead in her tracks. Pua wore TV makeup and a tasteful dress. A graceful puakenikeni lei encircled her neck, and a cameraman hovered over her shoulder. Her hair drifted in the offshore breezes. She looked happy and relaxed, a magnet for the camera and anyone she approached to interview.

Pua saw Storm at the same time, and gave her a brilliant smile. Buster followed her gaze, and looked over his shoulder. He grinned, waved gaily, then turned back to Pua, who asked

Buster about the conditions today's surfers would have to deal with, then held the microphone out for his answer.

Overhead, a couple of helicopters hung above the shoreline, one of them emblazoned with the call letters of a TV station. Between the surf, the helicopters, and the blats of the contest announcer's public address system, Storm could only hear snatches of their conversation. Buster said something about how the lateral current would pull the surfers and all their equipment toward Haleiwa, and then Storm lost the rest of his words in the noise.

She looked around at the media activity. This was turning into a well-publicized event. And there was Pua, in the middle of it, talking knowledgably about conditions, wave form, and prevailing currents. Some weather woman. Storm couldn't wait to hear how she'd pulled this off.

Meanwhile, other camera operators honed in on the inevitable scantily clad beauties and buff beach boys. There were always a few. Naturally, the cameras ignored the majority of the spectators, who, like Storm, had dressed for the cool onshore breezes by pulling sweatshirts and jeans over their bathing suits. The bathing suits were an optimistic touch. No way did she want to get in surf conditions like the ones today.

Storm realized these shots would be transmitted across North America, which the morning's paper announced was suffering its first major winter storm of the year. It might be warm compared to Wyoming and Saskatchewan, but no one was getting a tan that day. The swell was high and still rising. Arctic storms, part of the same weather system that swept across the continent, generated waves that grew as they accelerated, unimpeded, across the North Pacific. NOAA ocean buoys pinged their warning of these monsters, which barreled toward Hawai'i's reef system, a veritable welcome mat.

Impenetrable gray clouds draped the skies, and the surf, already approaching twenty feet, sent salty mist rolling across the shore and land. A tiny young woman, wearing a thong bikini that would fit in one of Storm's B-sized bra cups, scampered by. The breadth of her lower back was tattooed with a hawk's wings, and goosebumps pimpled her lithe and exposed body. Of course, the cameras that followed her like flies at a picnic wouldn't see those.

DeSilva finished his interview and walked over to greet Storm. Pua mouthed "later" at her, and turned to a famous Australian big wave surfer, who towered above her, wearing a very pleased expression.

"Hi." Storm intercepted DeSilva. "Do you know Pua?"

"I'd heard of her, but this is the first time I met her," DeSilva said. "She's my grandson's auntie."

"Um, I just heard about that."

"I wondered if you knew," DeSilva said. He gave her a wry half-smile.

"You must have been terribly upset with Nahoa."

"I was, at first." But he sounded cheerfully unperturbed. Storm watched his face carefully, but his eyes met hers without hesitation. "I thought about having him arrested," he admitted.

"For what it's worth, I thought Nahoa used terrible judgment." The anger in her voice surprised her, but DeSilva just shrugged.

"Most people did," he said. "But Evie was part of the act, and by the time I found out, it was too late to do anything about it. The little guy was on his way, and he needed a family to love. Why not us?" This time, his smile held a touch of sadness.

Storm wondered about DeSilva's wife, Evie's mother. Warren hadn't said anything about her, and Storm hadn't seen anyone else at the house.

As if he knew her thoughts, DeSilva spoke again. "My wife died in a traffic accident when Evie was five. My brother and sister live on Maui, so it was just the two of us most of the time."

"Still, it must be hard for you and Evie to have a baby around."

DeSilva squinted toward the edge of the beach, where two contestants gathered their gear to head into the waves. A shout had gone up from the crowd, and Storm noticed that Kimo

Hitashi, who had been with Goober yesterday, was now paired with the tall Australian Pua had just interviewed.

"You know, she was never good at school before," DeSilva continued. "Her grades have been better since Sparky was born. Like she's starting to see a reason for it."

"What about Nahoa? Did he accept any responsibility?"

Storm had been carefully watching DeSilva for his reply, so when his eyes slipped from her own gaze to something behind her head, she turned, though she sensed he was relieved at the distraction.

Goober was stomping toward them, and the scowl on his face would distract most people. He still wore the board shorts she'd seen that morning and had added a faded red sweatshirt to counteract the chilly day. His dreads were more matted than usual, and the wind, which swept from behind him, carried unwashed body odor. His arms were rigid and his hands clenched into fists. Though she and DeSilva stood shoulder to shoulder, Goober's stare bore into Storm. So intense were his emotions, and unwavering was his focus, that she doubted he even saw DeSilva.

He marched right up to her. "Better watch yourself," he said and grabbed her arm. He shoved something into her hand, then shot a quick glance over his shoulder. Without another word, he dashed away from the water, toward the tree line and beach homes.

Chapter Thirty-four

O'Reilly finished sorting out Gordon, his former colleague from KZXM TV. Honestly, why would the man think a national audience would be interested in a local memorial service for the two dead surfers? Hell, he'd straightened him out on that sappy idea, then sent him off to do some surfer interviews. That's where the juice was. In fact, the idea had come to him while they stood there. One of KZXM's competitors had zoomed in on a babe's tattoo—across her nearly bare ass—and it had given him an idea. One of the girls in the local pizza joint had told him that Sunny, Nahoa Pi'ilani's girlfriend, was a big name on the women's circuit. So he'd sent Gordon off to talk to her on camera. People would eat it up. Good grief, the woman was gorgeous, a champion surfer, AND her celebrity boyfriend had just died doing the sport he loved. What a story.

Gordon trotted off with his panting cameraman in tow. Next conversation, he'd have to tell him to lay off the hairspray. Looked like a Viking in a fucking helmet. It was bad enough he wasn't a natural blond.

Sunny, a girlfriend, and a man O'Reilly didn't recognize all stood shoulder to shoulder, binoculars growing out of their faces. The guy was too pale to be a surfer, plus he walked with a limp. Maybe he was a relative from the mainland. And whoa, there was Ben, about twenty feet away from them. Where was Barstow, anyway?

"Hey," O'Reilly shouted, when he finally caught sight of his partner, face to face with fucking Goober again. Poor kid was still trying, but he had to hand it to Barstow on this one. The guy treated the young man with more patience than he would have been able to dredge up. For crying out loud, the little prick had blown it himself, after they'd given him the chance of a lifetime. Handed it to him on a platter, just for doing them a few favors. Barstow might not even know about some of the favors O'Reilly had asked of the kid. Still, Barstow treated him with respect.

Barstow's expression was pretty grim when O'Reilly finally got his attention. He shrugged and turned his palms up in the universal, "What am I to do?" gesture, and made his way toward the media hut.

"Over there," O'Reilly shouted again and pointed to Ben, who was talking to Pua Pi'ilani. Christ, what the fuck was she doing here? O'Reilly felt his face flush and forced himself to take a deep breath. She was doing surfer interviews, too. And he knew the station she worked for had as much pull, or more, than KZXM. She was a lot easier to look at than Gordon, too. Fuck.

O'Reilly would have to deal with Pua later. He mouthed "Ben," and pointed again. No one could hear over the racket of the surf, helicopters, and PA system, which blatted and crackled. He needed to get a technician to look into that problem, too.

Barstow finally saw where O'Reilly pointed and veered off to intercept his son. O'Reilly could see a mixture of relief and frustration on his face. Barstow loved that kid, and he must have been worried as hell last night. That morning, in the short time they'd had together before the Kayama woman and Goober showed up, he'd related how Stephanie had shown up at his house.

O'Reilly had seen the fear in Barstow's eyes and deep lines of fatigue that bracketed his mouth. In fact, the thought had gone through his mind that Barstow might actually still care for Stephanie. Nothing he'd said, just a niggling suspicion.

Whatever, O'Reilly was himself relieved that Ben stood there on the beach, the big gun his dad had bought him for the contest propped beside him. One of Moʻo Lanipuni's special designs, a primo board. There was Gabe Watson, too, never far away from anyone with a microphone. Or a beautiful woman, O'Reilly thought with a surge of emotion he couldn't identify.

A roar from the crowd distracted O'Reilly. Jesus, Kimo Hitashi was having a spectacular ride. O'Reilly shouted at a nearby cameraman, a fellow with a tripod and a huge lens. "You getting that?"

The guy didn't answer, which was a good thing. He was too busy getting footage. O'Reilly held his breath and watched Kimo's maneuvers. He couldn't help being captivated. What a sport! They'd have it on ESPN this evening, by God. Even more sponsors would get on board. This was turning out just as he'd hoped and prayed. He only had a few loose ends and another day to keep up this momentum.

Then he'd pay attention to some personal issues he hadn't had time to deal with. Women, for one. And Goober. He was a good kid, but he was getting kind of wacky.

Chapter Thirty-five

"What the hell?" DeSilva said, watching Goober's disappearing back. "That kid getting so *pupule*. What'd he give you?"

"Keys." Storm stared at the item in her hand. "To my house."

"You just notice?"

"The Honolulu one. They were in my purse."

DeSilva frowned at her. "How'd he get 'em?"

"I'm not sure," Storm said. Unless he was the person who broke into the cottage. But why would he return them? And in this manner?

"I better find out," she said, looking around for Hamlin. Hamlin, who stood with Dede and Sunny about thirty yards away, lowered his binoculars. Their eyes met.

"I'm going after Goober," she shouted, and pointed toward the trees. A gust of wind, crowd noise, and static from the loudspeaker system whipped away her words. She looked in the direction Goober had gone, then at DeSilva.

"Will you tell him?" she asked DeSilva. "Tell that man I'll be right back."

Storm kicked off her rubber slippers so she could run more easily, and headed away from the swarm of people on the beach. Spectators were still arriving, and Storm made her way against the flow, weaving among the beach-chair, mat-schlepping individuals who staggered in after having to hike along the highway for at least a mile.

A low beach scarp, left by the combination of high surf and receding tide, slowed her down a bit. To save time, Storm tried to climb right up the face, and the two-foot soft sand cliff collapsed and carried her back with it. The incoming stragglers avoided this pitfall, and headed for a shallower slope. Since the mini-avalanche had already come to rest, she clambered up the rise on her second try and trotted across an apron of deep sand to a wide-leafed ground cover.

Most of the arrivals got to the beach via a sandy path that was a public access, but Goober had taken a less-traveled route. Storm saw movement some distance away, in the private space between two large beach homes. It was the combination of the faded red sweatshirt and blond hair that caught her eye. If he hadn't turned to watch his former partner's progress into the water, he would have been long gone, but he stood with a hand shading his eyes and a droop to his shoulders.

Though she wanted to confront him with how he'd had possession of her keys, she also felt a surge of pity for the young man, so she stopped and observed him for a moment. She'd grown up with kids like him. There had been a boy in the tenth grade whose parents were notorious drunks, and who came to school with bruises, cuts, and one time, a black eye. He'd been a surfer, too.

The kid Storm had known had won local events and eventually dropped out of school and moved somewhere—word was he'd gone to Australia with the World Surfing Tour. Storm hoped so.

She could understand Goober's disappointment. Not only was surfing the ultimate in cool for his peers, it took balls the size of coconuts to face waves like Goober did yesterday. Surfing like that demanded respect, no matter what your family life or income level might be.

But Storm doubted he gave himself any credit for having braved yesterday's challenge. He would want at least enough points to rise above his existing anonymity.

She would bet that Goober had been counting on the Intrepid to carry him out of the mire of mediocrity and hopelessness that had probably dogged him all his life. A chance like this didn't come often.

How often do people like Goober hear the word no, Storm thought. No job, no credit, no down payment, no car, no hope. She'd felt the same bleakness she saw in him, before Miles Hamasaki had given her a shove and powerful encouragement—along with trust, maybe the most potent boost she'd ever had.

Barstow had told Goober he was out of the Intrepid. His chance, however he had come by it, was *pau,* gone with one ill-timed fade on a treacherous wave. And though Storm thought Barstow had done his best to be gentle, he'd done it in front of her, which had to hurt Goober even more. O'Reilly had also witnessed the rejection, and had done nothing to defend the kid.

Consequently, Storm stood for a few seconds and observed Goober watching his own partner catch a gorgeous wave. Experience, strength, courage, and athleticism all play a part in a surfer's performance, but Lady Luck also has her role. Picking the right wave, and then having it turn out to be even better than anticipated, can catapult a surfer to greatness. Kimo Hitashi had one.

Kimo's first cutback brought a round of applause from the audience. Then the young man, his feet solidly in the foot straps, rocketed down a twenty-foot face. At that speed, ripples acted like ramps, and even from where she stood, Storm could see Kimo and his board bounce along the surface of the water, getting at least six feet of air. When he landed in a crouch, he took stock of his position and seized the opportunity to fade up the wave and disappear into the tube.

Storm and every other spectator froze, riveted on how, when, and if the speck-sized human would emerge. Time slowed. Storm held her breath, unable to tear her eyes from the thundering mass of water.

And Kimo appeared, a mote of yellow, careening on the oblique across the slope of a mountain that began to fold in on itself. But he was ahead of the closeout. And his teammate, the Australian, was already revving the powerful PWC through the boiling soup left in the wave's wake. A roar went up from the crowd, a bellow that carried over the helicopters and blaring PA systems to Storm and Goober. Storm, her mouth still agape, turned her gaze to Goober.

His posture was straighter, and he held a fist in the air. A reflex of triumph, a cheer for his partner, for the ride Goober had himself wanted so badly.

The breath caught in Storm's throat at Goober's uninhibited and selfless reaction. She shouted to him, but her voice was swallowed by the wind and surf. Though she wondered if he hadn't paused for a split second, he turned and dashed through the trees and hedges that separated the two beach houses.

Storm sprinted after him. Her feet sank in deep sand for another thirty yards before she got to a ground cover of lantana, ironwood needles, and a harder packed surface. By then, she was between the two dwellings and out of sight of the beach. On her left was a low fence, whose function was to impede drifting sand, and several dense hibiscus and oleander bushes. On her right was the wrap-around lanai to the nearest house, which showed all the signs of an unoccupied vacation home. Draperies covered all the big, sliding glass doors and picture windows. A couple of wood chaises sat forlornly on the lanai, their cushions stowed until the owner's next visit.

Storm stopped and looked around. She also used the moment to catch her breath and knock the hard little round seeds from the ironwood trees from beneath her toes. She had a nasty bruise on the bottom of one heel, which made stepping directly on it painful.

She brushed at a cut on the ball of her foot, where sand adhered to the beads of blood.

Gusts of wind still loosened strands of her hair, but she was more protected here by the rise of the beach and the house than she had been down by the water. A line of trees and sprawling philodendra blocked her view of the highway, which passed about two hundred secluded yards from her. Goober was nowhere in sight.

Wait, had a curtain twitched on the second floor? Storm had the uncomfortable feeling that she was being watched. She looked around, pivoting slowly in the sand.

The windows on the higher story were mostly large casements, completely draped. There were some wood louvered windows on the bottom floor, next to several large sliding glass doors, also curtained. All the doors and windows appeared to be closed, so she doubted that a breeze had stirred anything inside the house.

It must have been her imagination, or a spark of paranoia, but she still felt as if someone was nearby. She swallowed. Even the little hairs on the back of her neck began to stand on end.

Though she hadn't heard anything she could pinpoint, Storm wheeled to see if anyone stood behind her. Before she could complete the turn, she felt a sharp jab under her left shoulder blade.

A shock followed, so powerful that all her muscles contracted, then went into spasms. Her jaw clamped tightly and her teeth painfully bit into the side of her tongue. The sinews of her neck contracted, and her eyes, beyond the scope of conscious direction, rolled back in her head. On some level, she knew that she was getting an electric shock, and that she'd fallen onto the sand. But any conscious thoughts were overwhelmed with the knowledge that her limbs stiffened and twitched, completely beyond her control. Her heart pounded with terror and confusion.

Struggling against the effects of the shock, she found she could roll her eyes. Who was doing this to her? She was just beginning to regain control of her neck muscles when another shock convulsed her. A part howl, part squeal escaped her, then a white cloth covered her face.

Storm's muscles couldn't respond to her brain's signals, though she wanted to hold her breath. Her gasps were a reflex, beyond her conscious control. She knew that cloying chemical odor. Ether, a common solvent and powerful anesthetic.

Blackness rolled over and around her, enfolding her in a mantle of nauseating oblivion.

Chapter Thirty-six

Storm fought her way back to consciousness with an uneasy stomach and spinning head. The sickening sweet residue of ether still clung to her, and she swallowed hard to quell a fat knot of nausea.

She cracked open one eyelid, closed it against the spinning, and opened it again, more slowly. She lay on one side, in the dark, with her hands bound behind her. Pinpricks of light stabbed through what she sensed was a small, closed space. She shivered with cold, and the abrupt movement induced another onslaught of green whirlies.

Her churning stomach was worsened by the fact that whatever she lay on rocked gently. The sensation of instability was exacerbated by pounding, a sort of sub-sensory vibration that thrummed around her. This pulsation was punctuated with an imbalance of pressure similar to the feeling one gets when a car window is opened at high speed, and it worsened her queasiness.

Storm could taste salt, and the swaying motion corresponded to the irregular movement of waves, as in a protected area. As if to reinforce this impression, a wavelet splashed her face, which caused her to jerk her head up and away. This brought about a wave of nausea so strong that she retched with dry heaves, then sagged from the head-spinning the sickness had brought on.

Another surge of water rose around her. This time, Storm sensed its approach from the change in air pressure, and she lifted her head a few inches. Droplets splashed her face, but she held her breath this time, and the coolness washed away some of her disorientation.

Each boom was accompanied by the buffeting sensation. Storm labored to sense the reason for the pressure change. In seconds, she knew, and the knowledge caused her to catch her breath. The rhythmic pounding was caused by huge waves beating on rocks, and she was within them.

She was in a cave, and she lay on a sticky, scratchy surface that swayed with a grating, breaking noise. Storm turned her head and eyed its rough, tacky exterior. She'd seen these sticky bumps a thousand times. She was on a surfboard, a beat-up old thing, which rested on a ledge in the cave. The water covering the rocky platform was two or three inches deep, and caused the surfboard to rock erratically, as if one of its skegs had been broken off.

How long had she been there? She had no recollection of anything that happened after she'd collapsed on the sand next to the beach cottage. Her arms were tied behind her, which caused her shoulder muscles to cramp and burn. Even that wasn't as bad as the fact that her hands were senseless lumps, either from cold or from lack of blood flow.

Storm craned her neck to look around. Her captor had removed her jeans and sweatshirt. Her bikini was all she wore, and she was thoroughly chilled. A sense of rage and violation at being undressed nearly choked her. Fear at the possibility of having been otherwise abused passed through her, but she let fury overtake alarm. Anger would be a much more effective tool, and she yearned to find the guy who put her here.

Another pounding resonated through the cave, accompanied by the shift in air pressure. She forced herself to take a shaky breath, then another. Panic, like the pulsation of the huge waves, battered her senses. But she held it off, and made herself analyze her surroundings. She needed to attract someone's attention. Lava caves riddled parts of the coastline, and they were often excellent fishing sites. If anyone would be out when the surf was big.

"Help." She sounded like a sick puppy. "Help," she called out, louder. This time she managed a cry that sounded like a child's.

Water rose around her again. Like a tide, Storm thought. An incoming tide, each wavelet a little higher than the last. The effects of the ether were fading, and this realization gave her enough strength to struggle to her knees. It took several minutes, and she could only do it because her legs, fortunately, were free. Even so, the surfboard rocked and tilted with her efforts.

Crouched on her knees, she surveyed the cave. Sharp-toothed rocks loomed only an inch or two above her unprotected back. When the next wave surged through the space, Storm had to lean forward to avoid hitting the back of her head. Even so, the craggy lava scraped her shoulder.

Now that her head had cleared and her eyes had adjusted, she could make out the entire cave: a ceiling a few inches above her bowed head, a sloping wall near her right shoulder, and a diminishing oval air space that ended in the rocky barrier fifteen feet away. The few inches of water on the ledge had deepened to almost a foot.

The water was rising. Since she had no concept of how long she'd been unconscious, she didn't know how much higher it would get. She thought it had been low tide when she went after Goober, which meant that the water could rise a couple of feet in the small space. It would fill the cave.

Panic broke through the pretense of calm she'd wrapped around herself, and she screamed for help again, this time with a full, lusty roar. Though her voice was strong, it was muffled by water and dripping walls. Storm shouted again, shuddered with an effort at self-control, then moaned with despair. Screaming for help was fine, but she didn't have the luxury of succumbing to panic. She needed to do two things: get her arms loose and get out of the cave.

A scattering of small holes allowed narrow rays of sunlight to stab through a porous wall opposite the ledge on which she huddled, and the beams briefly bounced off the surface of a rippled and seemingly bottomless black pool. Though volcanoes hadn't erupted on Oʻahu for a couple million years, volcanic rock existed all over the island. The pencil-thin rays had penetrated porous *aʻa,* the type of jagged lava that would slash a body as easily as the teeth of a Moray.

Storm squinted with the effort to stay calm and scrutinize all the visible aspects of her enclosure. Think. Someone put her in here, so there had to be an entrance. She twisted her neck until it hurt to examine the ceiling, which was getting closer and closer to the top of her head. There was no place to drop a five-eight, hundred-forty-pound woman and a nine-foot surfboard through the ceiling. So the entrance had to be under water, at least once the tide came in.

Storm's throat closed with desperation, and tears burned her eyes as she looked at the tiny rays of light that seeped through the rock like the mockery of some ethereal fairy. Is this what happened to Nahoa? Her gaze flitted around the cave again, this time so frightened she didn't take in any information. Had he been in this very place?

Storm remembered the police detectives' comments about the damage to Nahoa's body. Sharks loved caves, didn't they? And they sensed blood from miles away. Was there one in the dark water beneath her, circling to defend its territory?

"Help!" she shrieked again. Her voice worked at full volume, a hoarse and desperate shriek that died in the closed acoustics of the cave. At the same time, she pulled herself back from the abyss of terror and told herself to think about the entrance to the cave. Even if it was under water, tides in Hawaiʻi weren't the twenty-foot changes that occur in other parts of the world. She could dive to it—if she could get free.

Storm shuddered. She'd just have to take her chances with sharks. Weren't reef sharks the ones who liked caves? They were smaller than tigers, hammerheads, or whites, and not as apt to attack humans. She was counting on it.

She jerked at her bonds. Her hands were numb clubs on the end of burning arms and she had to get them loose. As she yanked, the surfboard jerked, then teetered. It was rising with the water, of course, and becoming less stable on its rocky shelf. If she fell off with her hands tied, it would be nearly impossible to get back on the board—or the abrasive ledge. She tugged again, this time more gently. Yes, she was attached to the surfboard itself, by its rubbery leash.

Storm found comfort in this knowledge for the simple reason that a leash was something she knew. At one end, the rubber tubing would be attached to a hole in the tail of the board, usually by a narrow nylon cord. At the other end, which would normally go around her left ankle, should be a Velcro band. Not that she expected to be bound by Velcro; that was hopelessly wishful thinking.

She had to get the feeling back in her hands. She needed to move her wrists and arms to get the blood flowing, and maybe, just maybe, loosen the tubing. If it was as old and abused as the board she sat on, it may have hardened, even cracked, with age.

Nahoa would have tried this, too, she thought with a stab of desperation. And pushed the fear away. Anger was okay, but terror would only freeze her and keep her from considering her options.

A sucking sensation, a whalloping thump, compression of air, and more water rushed into the cave. This time, it nearly washed her from the board. Storm sucked in a jagged breath. On its heels, another wave rolled through the little cavern, and the old surfboard, for the first time, lifted completely from the uneven shelf and teetered beneath her knees.

Storm twisted her wrists, grimacing against the rough, tight truss. She rotated them one way, then the other, slowly at first, as she tried to ignore the friction of the rubber against her skin. Slowly and carefully, she rotated on the board so that she could rub her wrists against the knobby lava wall. She needed to find a small, sharp outcropping at the right level. Her abraded shoulder hit the wall and she winced. Damn, the entire wall felt like knife blades. Salty, stinging blades.

Her hands were so numb from cold and diminished blood supply that she could barely manipulate them. But she felt the salt in her fresh wounds, by God. And when her sawing efforts didn't hurt quite so much, she figured the lava was scraping more rubber than skin. So she used her pain. With each ripping millimeter, the elasticity of the leash diminished. Instead of retaining its tightness, the resilience of the rubber seemed to lessen. Either that or the blood she imagined now circled her wrists acted as a lubricant. Whatever was happening, she had to keep it up.

Meanwhile the incoming sea water floated her higher in the small chamber. Her chest now lay directly on her thighs, and the awkward pose not only increased the strain on her shoulders, but caused the bones in her knees to grind against the gritty, hard surfboard. Tears of effort filled her eyes.

A particularly loud crash, with subsequent gush of water, bumped her head against the ceiling. She yelped, then allowed herself a bellow of rage, with a concurrent blast of effort against her restraints.

Storm sagged forward and moaned. The pain in her lacerated wrists was so bad she felt faint. She couldn't even feel her hands, let alone the binding rubber. It was all she could do to keep from flopping onto one exhausted hip, but her instinct for survival restrained her. If she tipped over the board now, she'd never have the energy to get back on. It was all she could do to stay balanced.

"Owwww, help," she keened, and her voice rose and fell with exhaustion. Head turned to one side, she watched the last pinhole of light sink below the surface of the water. A subtle glow from below the surface was all that lit the cave. And only a few cubic feet of air remained.

Chapter Thirty-seven

Storm panted. The oxygen level was dropping in the cave. She set her teeth against the pain and rasped her hands against the cave wall. It was harder and harder to tell where the rubber was. This last swipe hurt enough to take her breath away. She leaned forward and gasped as if she'd been running.

The cave, as it filled, was becoming darker. Storm rested her forehead on the surfboard. Her wrists felt as if they bled; if she used her imagination, she could feel coolness running down the palms of her outwardly turned hands. She rested for a moment and fixated on the sensation across her poor, abused wrists.

And that whining noise must be from the lack of oxygen. Was she just going to drift off? She was so tired, she could probably go to sleep. Would she wake up when she fell off the board? She hoped not.

There was that whining again. If only her one shoulder wasn't so painful. It was because her one hand lay palm up, beside her on the surfboard. Moving that shoulder had hurt like hell.

Wait, she'd done it. Her hand was free. That last swipe against the vicious, sharp lava had cut the leash, and she'd been so numb she hadn't noticed for almost a minute.

The notion of freedom brought improved mental clarity. Not only were her hands prickling with renewed sensation, her shoulders, which had been pulled and strained, felt as if knife blades were imbedded in them. Blades of liberation, though.

Storm jerked upright and clobbered the back of her head against the ceiling of the cave.

The whining was not part of her disorientation. It was an engine, heard as if from underwater. She drew deep breaths and looked around the small space as if she might notice other changes. Maybe Hamlin was outside, looking for her. He had to be frantic by now, didn't he?

"Hamlin," she screamed. "Hamlin!"

A man's muffled voice answered, but she couldn't make out his words. Too much water and rock between them. She couldn't be sure, but it didn't sound like Hamlin. Still, Hamlin would have gone for help. It could be City and County lifeguards on a jet ski or boat. They'd be looking for her, wouldn't they?

"Help! I'm in here."

The whining sound got closer, then dropped to a lower pitch. The man's voice sounded again, but she lost most of the words in a crashing thump and a surge of water. "….dive… entrance…out…"

Storm braced herself on the rocking surfboard. Both her hands were still numb from being bound so tightly, and she shook them to get the blood flowing.

What did he say? Dive? Storm eyed the only place where light still seeped into the darkening cave. It was underwater, below the little holes that had let in the air she so desperately needed. How much had the water risen? How deep was the hole? It had disappeared below the surface of the water before she'd regained consciousness. How long ago had that been?

She had to try. After all, what did she have to lose?

Storm was terrified. She swallowed hard and took deep, methodical breaths while she talked to herself out loud. "Can't be that deep. He got you in here, right? Even if it's five or six feet down, it's nothing. You do that all the time." Right.

Storm floated the surfboard toward the imagined entrance. Her hands were still tingling clubs, and they made clumsy paddles. Her fingers were barely functional, though sensation was beginning to burn through them.

She heard a shout from outside the cave, and the pitch of the engine rose. It got loud, and then faded, as if he'd headed away. Hadn't he heard her?

"Stop!" she shrieked. "Stop! I'm here!"

That was it, she had to go. Slipping from the board into the cold water revived her more, and she took a desperate last gulp of air before she dove.

Storm felt her way down the bumpy rock face. Her numb fingers were just able to grasp protrusions on the wall, enough to pull her deeper into the water. The cave wasn't completely dark, and she knew the faint glow had to come from beneath the surface of the water. There wasn't enough light to see clearly, and all she could make out were light and dark shapes. But none was a beacon of escape.

Storm felt along the wall, pulling herself deeper by grabbing onto jagged knobs of lava. Her lungs were on fire, and her diaphragm began to convulse with the need for air. With a cry of anguish, she let go of the wall and kicked frantically to the surface.

The cave seemed even darker, and when she broke surface, she almost hit her face on the nose of the drifting surfboard. It took up most of the remaining space, and she hung on for a minute while she wheezed for whatever oxygen was left in the diminishing room.

She leaned her face on the board, and tried not to give in to despair. She had to dive again. And keep thinking. If the entrance involved a short tunnel, it wouldn't necessarily let in enough light to be visible from the surface of the water. She'd have to go deep to find it. That must be what the person outside was trying to tell her. But she had to find it this time. There wasn't enough oxygen left in the cave.

Hyperventilating might help, especially in this thin air. She knew free divers who'd died from the practice, but it was a chance she'd have to take. She was going to die if she didn't.

Ten breaths. Ten deep, slow breaths. Storm actually used her fingers, splayed on the surfboard, to count. And she dove again, straight down. When she'd surfaced before, she'd been surprised to find that she'd only been about four feet down, though it had felt much deeper. She didn't grope along the wall this time. Instead, she kicked and stroked as hard as she could, down, down, until her ears popped. Where it was dark, and there was still no bottom that she could see.

She grabbed the wall, crabbing along sideways, head toward the bottom. Around the perimeter, if she had to. No, just along the wall where the light had come in. That was her best chance.

Storm actually surprised herself with these thoughts, glad that her brain still functioned on some level. She had very little time. Already, she'd guess that twenty or thirty seconds had passed. How long until she passed out? Two minutes? Three? Don't think about it.

Her eyes were getting used to the diminished light. She could just make out the bottom, sandy and scattered with black rocks. There was even a little fish, a reef triggerfish, common to anyone who enjoys swimming or diving along Hawai'i's shoreline. In fact, it was a *humuhumu-nukunuku-ā-pua'a*. Storm giggled, which sent a few bubbles to the surface. Oops. The humuhumu with a snout like a pig, her own *pua'a*. Little pig-fish. Uh oh, she was getting silly. That was oxygen deprivation again, wasn't it?

Where'd that fish go? There he was, two feet from her, and heading into the wall. Into the wall. Storm grasped a bulge in the rock and pulled herself toward him. She kicked hard, rounded a corner, and peered ahead, where a halo shimmered.

It was a tunnel, more of a long arch, about three feet wide, but deep. It extended to the sandy bottom. Lots of room, if she could go two or three feet deeper. And if it wasn't too long; she couldn't see the end.

Storm's diaphragm shuddered with need, but there was light ahead, only six or seven feet away. There was the little fish again, nibbling at something on the wall of the tube. Good little pig-fish. Wished she had gills, like he did. Pull with her arms, use 'em like he does his little pectoral fins. Kick, kick. Feeble feet, not nearly as good as a tail fin.

Wished her eyes were letting in more light; she was getting tunnel vision. Black on the sides. Pull with those pectoral fins. Maybe use a dolphin kick. Her vision was fading, but she could still swim. Follow the little *pua'a*. Helpful little fellow, finding that tunnel for her.

Chapter Thirty-eight

"Hey, I've got you. Can you climb on?"

Storm squinted and coughed. Her lungs heaved, and the ocean surged around her, pelting her with droplets and foam. It was too bright, like she'd walked out of the theater in the middle of the day. Startling, too harsh. Cough, cough. The buzzing stink of an engine, too.

What was this guy doing to the back of her bathing suit, anyway? It's not a handle, for crying out loud. She felt like a hooked fish, and flopped an arm in his direction.

His voice cracked with urgency. "Help me out here, there's a set coming."

Storm squinted up at him. "Goober? What're you doing out here? Hey, that hurts." He was crushing her hand in his, trying to pull her arm out of its socket.

"Get on, Storm. Quick. We're going to get pushed onto the rocks." He looked behind. "Hurry!"

Storm scrabbled for the hull of the jet ski, but her fingers still weren't at their best. She started to slide.

"Jesus," Goober muttered, and scrabbled for one arm and whatever else he could grab. The big jet ski tipped while Goober snagged the back tie on Storm's bathing suit. It unfastened like the bow on a gift box, and Storm yelped with surprise.

"Good grief," she sputtered as he hauled her up and left her sprawled face down like a set of saddlebags across the seat behind him.

In this position, she noticed the towering and jagged rock wall that loomed a mere foot from her face. Still not thinking clearly, she reached out in an instinctive attempt to shove the watercraft away from an imminent crash. At that moment Goober gunned the big engines, and Storm seized what was closest—a cleat and a foothold—to keep from flying off the back. Head down, flopping on her stomach like a beached tuna, she held on for a ride she couldn't see, and hoped she'd never experience again.

Goober wheeled the machine sideways and up while Storm held on for dear life with her hands and grappled with her feet for some kind of toehold on the craft's other gunwale. There was something attached to that side by a tight bungee, and she hooked one foot through the cord, though the other leg floundered.

By the howl of the engines and the angle of their climb, Storm could tell that the big Kawasaki was too close to the speeding wave to go directly over. Forget about trying to sit up now. She bounced on her stomach, glad it was empty, and prayed she could hold on while she watched her bathing suit top flop around her straining wrists. The triangular bra cups filled like little sails. If the situation hadn't been so desperate, the ridiculous banner would have cracked her up.

The powerful watercraft roared over three waves before Goober cut the throttle to a mere rocketing speed and reached back to grab Storm's nearest arm. "You can sit up now."

"Right." But she pushed herself up from her face-down position, somehow managing to keep one bathing suit strap hooked to her left wrist. She had to grab Goober's waist to get there, and he scrambled to help her by latching onto her left arm. They both watched the bra sail away.

"Oh, no," Storm shouted above the rumble of the engines.

Goober pulled his wet and faded sweatshirt over his head and handed it back, but he kept his eyes out to sea. "We've got bigger problems."

Storm followed his gaze. They did. Goober had managed to get them out of a partially protected rocky cove just in time to avoid being pounded against a craggy volcanic shelf. But the concept of protected was a relative term. The cove was dangerous with rebounding waves and currents and without any possible landing point. In order to get around the rocks and to an approachable beach, they had to go farther out to sea, into the really big stuff—the roiling stew of huge surf.

"Where are we?"

"Just north of Pupukea."

Storm grabbed hold of Goober with one arm and a handle next to her seat with the other hand. The big machine roared out to sea, and Goober read the incoming swells as if he'd driven the City and County rescue watercraft before. She felt like hugging him with gratitude.

Instead, she hunkered down behind him, out of the wind. A hundred critical questions ran through her mind. When he got beyond the break zone and eased off the throttle, she couldn't hold back. "How'd you know where I was? Who put me there?"

"Let's get out of here first," Goober said, and headed out toward a plain of white, breaking water without answering the questions. Engine noise made it impossible to talk, so Storm waited until he cut back on gas to get his bearings before she tried again.

"So who put me in that cave?" she asked over his shoulder, and readjusted her seat so that her leg fit around the surfboard lashed to the side of the jet ski.

Goober's shoulders seemed to droop a bit. "I'll tell you what I know when we get to shore. We don't have time to sit here. Conditions are getting worse, and I'm afraid we'll run out of gas."

"What?" Storm nearly stood up on the back of the craft.

"Hey, I grabbed what I could. Took me a while to find you, too."

"I know it. Thanks, I appreciate it." He wouldn't look at her; his eyes scanned the shoreline.

"Where'd you get this machine?" she added.

"Stole it from City and County. I've got keys to one of their storage sheds." She could just make out his words over the wind.

"I see." Storm recalled that Sunny had mentioned he assisted Gabe unofficially. "The lifeguard fleet?" That explained the surfboard, which would be used for rescues.

"Yeah, I had to take what was left."

"How'd you get the keys to my house?"

Goober gunned the motor. "We've got to move on." He gave the big machine enough gas to send Storm sliding backward. She grabbed his waist, and noticed that he was covered with goosebumps. A shiver went through her, along with a surge of gratitude for not only Goober's efforts, but his sweatshirt. Though it was soaked, it still provided a layer of insulation.

She looked toward land and shouted into his ear, "You don't think we can get in here?"

Goober shook his head. "It's closed out. We'd better not chance it."

Storm could see for herself. There was no place they could go in without being overcome by following surf, which barreled toward land faster than even the big Kawasaki could travel. There was also a powerful current that carried them parallel to shore, toward Waimea.

"We're near Pipeline. We don't want to get chewed up on those reefs," Goober shouted. He gave the machine more fuel and headed downwind.

Storm huddled behind him and held on tight. She was tired, cold, and scared. Hamlin would be going crazy. The thought of how close she'd come to dying in the cave brought on a renewed fit of trembling.

Goober zoomed along a course parallel to the coastline. His head swiveled as he watched the incoming sea for unexpected swells and currents. From time to time, he stood to better see over the peaks and valleys of the heaving ocean.

Meanwhile, the watercraft climbed and plummeted like a chunk of driftwood in the huge swells, and her stomach rose and fell with it. When they dropped into a trough between waves, Storm would have believed they were a thousand miles from land. It was disorienting, dizzying.

They couldn't even see shore, nearly a half mile away, until they got to the top of a swell. When they did, everything from the sand to a quarter mile out to sea was solid whitewater.

Storm held on and stored up the questions she needed to ask Goober. Whoever had put her in the cave had killed Nahoa, she was certain. And Goober had known where the cave was. He'd suspected that she'd be there.

"Maybe we can get the attention of one of those choppers," Storm shouted over his shoulder.

She felt, rather than heard, Goober grunt a reply over the noisy engines and whipping wind. All she could do was hold tight, her arms around his waist, while parts of his baggy sweatshirt filled with air and parts clung clammily to the rest of her body. She shivered, and tried to see the gauges on the machine.

Then she wished she hadn't. The gas level was in the red, though that included an entire quarter of a tank. Criminy, how fast did these things burn fuel? By the engine noise, she'd bet they weren't exactly the Sierra Club's top pick. Jesus, she had to hope Goober knew what he was doing.

He seemed to. They flew along, sometimes literally airborne, slapping back to the water's surface with jolts she could feel down her whole spine.

"How far away are the 'copters?" she yelled.

He had to turn his head, and the wind whipped his words toward her. "Nearly a mile, I think."

"Do we have enough gas?" And she wished she hadn't asked, because his answer was a shrug that she could only feel. If they ran out of fuel here, they were motes in a vast sea. Their bodies wouldn't even be found.

So Storm settled into the rough ride and concentrated on moving with Goober, leaning when he did, hunching down to lessen the craft's wind resistance. Maybe they'd conserve fuel. She could only hope.

Meanwhile, her stomach lurched with the machine's pounding, screaming flight and sent pangs that she alternately interpreted as hunger and motion sickness. Or maybe it was just stress.

The helicopters loomed closer and Storm could see a basket dangling from the bigger one. A person wearing the brightly colored singlet of a surfer huddled in it.

"Surf may be closing out here, too," Goober shouted over his shoulder. He slowed the machine to a throaty rumble. Storm was glad for a rest from the bone-jarring ride, but she wondered why he'd cut power, because the waves tossed and battered the machine when it wasn't moving forward.

She watched the helicopter rescue and swallowed hard. When a wave bore them high enough to see shore, she asked, "You think they're calling the meet?"

She couldn't see anyone, but she had the feeling she wouldn't be able to see a person in this sea until she was almost on top of him. She wondered if the helicopters could see the two of them.

"Maybe."

That was not good news. "How far are we from the surfers?"

"A few hundred yards or so. You think you could drive this thing?" Goober asked.

"What? Are you nuts?"

She could feel a quiver go through Goober, and she hoped he was just cold.

"Look," he said after a pause. "It'll go faster and use less gas with one person on it. I'm going to surf in." He reached back and unfastened one end of the bungee that held the surfboard to the side of the craft. "It'll be lighter and easier to maneuver without the board, too."

"We're almost out of gas?" Storm yelled to be heard over the roar of the ocean and the wind whipping around them. The Kawasaki sputtered and the surfboard began to slip from its perch.

"Close."

"Oh, God," Storm murmured.

Just as the surfboard splashed into the water, she snagged the leash attached to its tail. "I'm going to surf."

Goober eyed the waves building on the horizon, and she realized he was either contemplating their chances or he was in shock. He looked very young to her right then.

"I've never driven one of these. You've got to take it," she told him.

"I'm a better surfer."

"You're supposed to keep your head dry."

She didn't know what else to say. Never mind that they were both soaked and shivering. If she waited one more second, she'd chicken out. Goober had already rescued her from the cave, he deserved this chance.

She slid into the water and grabbed the board. "Don't argue, we don't have time. Now, get out of here."

Goober stared at her, surprised. Then he tried to smile, but his lips had a bluish tinge and they seemed to stick to his teeth.

"You can ride the whitewater, you know," he said.

"I know." Both of them knew she couldn't. The surf was too big.

Goober paused one more second. "Go see O'Reilly." He kept his eyes on the jet ski's controls.

"I'll see you when we get to shore. We'll both go. And send one of those helicopters after me."

Goober looked up at the chopper with the basket, which was carrying its dangling passenger toward shore. "Right."

Storm turned to fasten the surfboard leash around her ankle. The sweatshirt was heavy and weighed her down in the water, but she was cold and didn't want to take it off. She also didn't want him to see the fear that had to be all over her face. Even her movements felt jerky with it. She felt as if she were twelve again, in waves like the ones that had taken Bert Pi'ilani's life.

The jet ski coughed, and Goober gave it a tiny bit of gas. It moved him about ten feet away, and he disappeared in the heavy seas.

Chapter Thirty-nine

Storm didn't watch him go. Instead, she examined the seas between herself and the strip of beach so far away. Sitting upright on the board and floating atop a wave, she caught a glimpse of a surfer about a hundred yards from where she floated.

That was where she needed to go. She needed to move to stay warm, plus she had to get to the lineup, which was not only where she'd find other people, but where the waves first hit the outer reef and changed to a shape that could be ridden. Goober had left her outside the break zone, but it was also an area where currents could carry her farther out to sea and down the coastline, where her chances of getting help would diminish.

Her wrists burned from their re-immersion in the sea and she shivered from cold. The ordeal in the cave had thoroughly chilled her. Storm began to paddle, partly to generate body heat. She was relieved to note that once she got moving, her arms loosened up and felt stronger. In some ways, it was good to get off the bouncing jet ski and into a medium that was more familiar.

She could no longer see Goober, nor could she hear the machine. She thought about his last look, though, and the admission that he'd broken into her house. Talk to O'Reilly, he'd said. So O'Reilly was behind the break-in? Goober had been living in his guest apartment, so maybe he'd felt a sense of obligation that extended to burglary. Which was stupid, and she'd tell him so later. In fact, she and Sunny would have to have a talk with him about his sense of obligation, or desperation, whichever it was. It was way too easy to become sucked into other people's deceptions, chicaneries, and rationalizations.

Storm found it easier to ponder these issues as she paddled than to think about the challenge that faced her. If she thought about the size of the waves around her, she'd be paralyzed with fear and hopelessness. No, it was better to think about Goober, O'Reilly, and Nahoa. Especially Nahoa, who had taught her some crucial concepts about surfing and the ocean.

She could tell she was getting closer to the break zone. Whenever she heard the roar of a breaking wave ahead of her, and felt the familiar clench of fear that coincided with the noise, she shook her arms out and forced the tension out of her shoulders and neck. By now, her neck was getting tired of its craned position, always trying to peer over the chop around her. From time to time, she sat up and waited for a swell to elevate her so she could see where she was headed.

She wasn't far from the lineup, and she could see at least two heads still bobbing around in the water. If she could see two, there were probably more. Contest participants or not, these were maniac big-wave surfers, the kind who surfed to brush up to a power greater than one's self and who sought to test their own strength against dispassionate brute force. They were kindred souls with other athletic extremists—certain mountain climbers, scuba divers, pilots, and others who wanted to measure their courage, their skill, and their wits against the earth's might.

Nahoa may have fit into this group, but she didn't. And right now, she wanted to get to land so badly it nearly brought tears to her eyes. Yet she couldn't let herself think about her chances, or how cold she was, or even hope like crazy that Goober had been able to get to shore and send help.

She sat up on her board to shake the shivers out of her arms and roll the tension out of her neck. Good grief, there was Gabe Watson twenty yards away. He looked her way, then did a genuine double take. His mouth even dropped open. If Storm hadn't been stiff with cold and terrified, she would have laughed. But she wasn't amused, and he wasn't the kind of person she'd rely on for help. Better that she put some distance between them.

Not far away, a jet ski whined, but she couldn't see it in the troughs between the waves. She hoped it was Goober. At that moment, fear gripped her to the point that she wondered if she'd ever see Hamlin again. She shouted and waved in the direction of the noise, but it was too far away, and the sound of the engine faded without her ever catching sight of the machine.

She couldn't even see Gabe anymore. Instead, she pitched in the chop that covered the approaching swell. The jet ski had likely dropped a surfer onto a wave. Storm sat up and turned seaward to get a read on how big the approaching set might be and whether she was positioned where she wanted to be. Seas like this would move her quite a distance without her knowing, and the ocean could easily shift her into what surfers referred to as The Zone. This was the dreaded area landward of the break zone where there was no escape from the oncoming wave. In a second, she'd be caught in the rip current, too far inside to catch the wave, and not enough time to paddle over it. She'd get worked, pounded by tons and tons of water. Pushed all the way to the bottom.

The wave coming at her right now was a monster, the biggest she'd ever seen. Storm flopped down on her board and dug into the rising water with pumping arms. The wave was still growing, and her shoulders ached with the effort of getting to it. It was fast as a bullet train, and it was imperative that she get over it before the lip started to curl. Rising on its flank was like being on one of those outdoor elevators, where her ears popped twice before getting to the thirtieth floor.

The next second, it passed by her, and she tore down the backside. This plummeting swoop presented its own challenge, because the wind-generated chop threatened to jerk the board out from under her.

Storm extended an arm to slow and turn. She needed to watch the wave's progress toward shore, to get a read on the ocean's rhythm. At the same time, she took deep, even breaths and told herself not to be frightened. They couldn't all be that big. Aim for one wave, just one. But one that was smaller, perhaps nestled between the huge sets. One that she could ride to shore.

But the passing wave did what she'd most feared. It broke across the entire shore, all the way to Kalalua Point, which jutted more than a half mile to her right. The shoreline was closing out. There'd be no swimming around a wave that turned out to be bigger than she wanted. Once she got into the break zone, she'd be committed. There would be no bailing out, no avoiding the mountain that would either bear her on or beneath its thundering race to land.

Storm shuddered. If anyone had ridden that wave, and she couldn't see from where she sat, he'd have needed the slingshot action of a jet ski just to catch that rocket. Which was what tow-in surfing was all about. Storm had heard that the good tow-in surfers could swim five miles in the open ocean and hold their breath for more than two minutes in a roiling brew.

No, she'd have to bide her time, pick her progress. A swell bore her up to view the whitewater left behind by the wave. She was just in time to see a surfboard shoot twenty feet into the air, riderless, its broken leash trailing like fishing filament from a marlin.

The surfer hadn't appeared, and his partner zoomed back and forth, parallel to shore, waiting for the soup to subside enough to roar in on the jet ski. Just to get near where the surfer was last seen. She hoped he'd practiced holding his breath.

The helicopter, having dropped its last passenger on the sand, probably at the medical tent, was on its way to where the surfboard had popped out. Two more helicopters hovered, though they seemed focused on the whitewater, not in the break zone. Another shiver ran through Storm and she frantically waved both arms at the approaching chopper. But as she sank into the trough between swells, she saw the tail rotor pivot toward her. The pilot had turned away.

Storm suppressed a moan of despair. If Goober made it, she told herself, he would go for help. With the next swell, she scoured the whitewater for any sign of the his jet ski. But she only saw the one, pacing like a dog looking for its lost master.

Storm looked away. Right now, you're on your own. Get back to basics. Study the ocean. And most of all, stay calm. Remember Nahoa's advice. Number one was to relax and go with, rather than fight, the power of the water.

She had the feeling she was in a lull between sets of monstrous waves. Several minutes had elapsed where the distances between ups and downs in the cobalt depths hadn't seemed as dramatic. Storm repositioned herself and paddled in a bit closer to shore.

She shivered. Fatigue washed over her, and she noticed her fingers were numb again with cold. The rising wind whipped at her hair. Hawai'i waters are warm compared to many other places, but people still suffer from hypothermia and exposure. It was easy to underestimate the effects of the temperate climate. It was balmy if you were hanging out at Waikiki Beach, but not on a mountain ridge, a lava flow, or in the ocean.

Storm had been in the water for hours. She didn't really know how long, and she pondered this fact with the same urgency that she usually remembered to make her annual dentist appointment. Oh yeah, it's that time again. It was her own reaction that clued her in to the fact that her emotions were no longer commensurate with her circumstances. This was a root canal, not a tooth cleaning. Creeping complacency showed degeneration in her judgment, which could be deadly.

She slipped off the board and ducked her head underwater to slick back her hair. The water, which was probably around 77° Fahrenheit, felt warm compared to the air, which was another sign she was chilled. It was time to go. She needed to sharpen up, pick her ride, and get set to make the drop on a wave bigger than anything she'd ever ridden.

The dip revived her. In fact, fear tightened her throat to the extent that it was hard to draw a deep breath. She slithered back onto the board and moved slowly into the break zone. She looked around for other surfers, but couldn't see any in her vicinity. She remembered how Gabe had dropped in on Sunny. He'd deliberately snaked her. Here, where the waves were bigger, dropping in would more likely happen by accident, for the simple fact that it was hard to see people. But accident or not, impacting another person with a heavy big wave surfboard, with its pointed tip, sharp skegs, and reinforced rails, could be fatal. Big wave boards were called guns for a number of reasons, and one of them was deadly speed.

Storm scanned the water again, but didn't see the telltale flash of colored singlet or board shorts, the splash of someone's arm or leg. One wave steamrolled by, and she tried to observe its form, which way it broke, and how the wind blew its curl. But they were moving fast, and were hard to read. Each wave looked different, and if she picked the wrong one, it could send her up a blind alley to a booming wall of water. Even the right choice was going to be a tough ride.

It happened before Storm intended. One moment, she was craning her neck to observe a wave form on her left. The next, her board was sucked up the face of a wave.

Chapter Forty

The water made the decision for her, and she was committed. No choice but to paddle, hard. Three strokes, and the wind tore at her face. The sucking, roaring current obliterated all other sounds. Wind-borne water blinded her to the point that she had to rely on sensation rather than sight, and that sensation consisted only of speed. Teeth-chattering, flesh-rippling speed.

Aware of a thinning, transparent curl of greenface, Storm remembered Ben's and Nahoa's shouts when she'd gone out with them. "Stand up," they'd yelled. She popped to her feet. Just in time, and she instinctively adjusted her weight toward the tail to avoid pearling, and going over the falls to tumble down the face of a wave. A wave whose size and velocity wouldn't allow her to penetrate its surface. If she fell, she and her board would bounce along the wave's face like stones skipping down a concrete dike. Boards and backs could be snapped like toothpicks when that happened.

The rising wave created its own vortex and, combining with the force of the day's offshore trade winds, whirled stinging droplets of saltwater so that she had to squint and draw only shallow breaths. Her body was like a sail, keeping her aloft before the plunge. Now she understood why big wave surfers used foot straps. The board chattered as if she jammed over cobblestones, wanting to lag behind the wave, while the wind filled the now-accursed sweatshirt.

"No!" she shrieked to the ocean, the wind, the board under her feet. And she bent her knees to right angles while she shifted her feet to drive the board, increase its speed. To her relief, the fins dug in, though the jolting lifted the board entirely out of the water. It was like standing on the bouncing back one of the Big Island quarterhorses she'd grown up with, though she'd never done that at a full gallop.

She'd never felt the effects of momentum so strongly. Her thigh muscles burned. Even her toes ached in their desperate grip on the waxy surface of the board, and she held her arms like an osprey plunging for sustenance. And plunge she did, crouching so low on screaming quadriceps that her fingertips brushed the water gushing by the rocketing slab of fiberglass.

At one point, she sensed rather than saw the wave curling too close above her head, and she managed to scoot up the wave's face to a point where she clung, just ahead of The Zone. The wave broke left, which, with her goofy-footed stance, helped her. Its translucent lip curled just over her shoulder.

She raced toward land, still a quarter mile away, but knew she'd done it, she'd made the drop on a wave that had towered above her. She'd also negotiated the break zone, which was what she'd most feared.

Storm felt like she'd clung to a guardian angel's thunderbolt as it rocketed through the perils of hell. The wave she'd ridden hadn't been as big as the ones the tow-in surfers took, and she'd been fortunate that it had come along. Not only was she not skilled enough, but the board she rode wasn't built for that kind of speed. But she'd never have done it without the pointers Nahoa had given her. Ben and Goober, too. She'd been incredibly lucky.

Her thighs quivered with fatigue and spent adrenaline. Storm relaxed her stance and straightened a bit, just to give her trembling legs a reprieve. It was a mistake. Though the ocean hissed a warning, she was too tired to react.

An eddy of wind twisted the still-curling lip to Storm's left, and folded it over like a book slamming shut. One moment, she was congratulating herself on the biggest ride of her life. The next, she was cartwheeling through whitewater.

Storm's first thought was to protect her head against assault by the catapulted surfboard she'd been riding, but her limbs were helpless, pulled willy-nilly by the boiling soup. Her mind worked, though, and Nahoa's words popped into it. Stay relaxed and curl into a ball. Don't fight. Hopefully, the surfboard was far above her.

It was all she could do not to struggle. Tons of water tumbled her like a leaf in a river. Opening her eyes didn't give her any information; she couldn't tell up from down. She was in the green room, and there was nothing she could do about it until the ocean decided to release her.

Her hip banged against the bottom, and she felt the baggy sweatshirt fill around her head as she somersaulted. When her shoulder bounced painfully off a rock, the sweatshirt billowed like a drag racer's parachute. It may have protected her to this point, but the shirt was extra baggage now. The neck and sleeves were all that held the shirt on; the rest fluttered around her head. Storm shook her arms, tucked her chin, and let the water pull it free.

At the same time, she got her bearings and kicked to the surface, where she gasped for air. Two breaths later, another breaking wave roared toward her. She dived a split second before it got to her. It still flipped her end for end twice before she clawed her way back to daylight.

Oh, shit. Another frothing wall of water barreled toward her. Jesus, this wasn't even the impact zone. She tumbled for longer this time, and for the first time wondered what happened to the leash and board. The board might help her get to shore, even if she plowed through whitewater on her belly. The reassuring jerk on her ankle wasn't there, and when she finally reached the surface, she knew she'd either broken the leash or pulled free.

She couldn't hold her breath any longer. Little red and black spots flickered in her peripheral vision. Her ears rang. Her arms and legs felt like dead weights. Desperate to get out of the foaming boil, Storm flailed to align her body so that she would at least be aimed at shore. Go with the waves, she told herself. Even if she got sucked back, the next one would take her closer. She hoped.

So when the crackling, amplified voice came from above, she didn't even hear it. It had to ask twice before she sputtered and twisted her neck toward the noise.

"Can you grab the basket?"

Storm nearly cried with relief, and swung one arm wildly in the direction of the hovering craft. But wind from the helicopter rotors pushed her arms back into the water, and the basket swung two feet above her head. She wasn't anywhere near it.

She swung again, and missed. The pilot was trying to get lower; she could tell. The sound of the rotors was deafening. They pelted her with water droplets, too.

"C'mon now, you can do it," the voice from above said.

It took three tries. Even when she'd managed to snag it, her arms were so weak and shaky, she wondered if she could pull herself aboard. That took long seconds too, struggling not to backslide into the water. When she flopped into the basket, she lay limp and panting.

A few minutes later, the basket deposited her on the sand and people surrounded her. She couldn't react to them, and felt like she moved in a dream-like state. Exhaustion and relief had depleted her final reserves.

Someone threw a warm blanket around her shoulders. She couldn't yet discern faces, though she wondered if Hamlin might be nearby. She was shaking so hard, it was all she could do to hold onto the blanket.

"How'd you get out there?" someone asked, but dirty looks from two emergency technicians shut him up.

"Let's get her warmed up and checked out." One of them put his arm around her shoulders and led her inside the medical tent, out of the wind and away from the crowd.

"Did Goober tell you to come after me?" Storm asked. Someone had given her hot chocolate in a heavy paper cup. It was the best thing she'd ever tasted.

"Who's Goober?" one of the medical people asked.

"The guy on the jet ski." But Storm could tell by their expressions they didn't know him. "How'd the helicopter find me?"

"A City and County surfboard shot into the air, then washed toward the beach. It wasn't supposed to be out there, plus the leash was broken. So we started looking for a rider."

"Did you see a jet ski?" Storm asked.

"An unauthorized one? No," one person answered, but Storm had everyone's attention.

She told them how Goober had taken one from a City and County storage shed and rescued her from a cave. The rest of their questions were the same ones she wanted to ask Goober. She didn't know any of the answers.

"We've got to find him," she said.

One emergency technician, a woman, frowned at her. "You don't want to hang around a guy who'd leave you in twenty foot surf, especially with that board."

"He didn't have a choice."

Storm could tell from her grunt she didn't agree.

"Those tankers aren't made for big waves," another tech said. "You didn't actually surf that thing, did you?"

Storm nodded. The techs stared. Finally one of them spoke softly. "You're damned lucky, you know that?"

Storm swallowed hard. Her hand unconsciously went to her neck, where she still wore Aunt Maile's little pig charm, which, unlike certain articles of clothing, had stayed with her. She knew she'd been very, very lucky.

Chapter Forty-one

"Could I make a couple of phone calls?" Storm asked.

Someone handed her a phone and she punched in Hamlin's cell number.

His voice was ragged with worry. "Storm, where are you?"

"On the beach, in the medical tent. Where are you?"

"Leaving Sunny's house. Are you all right? What happened?"

"I'm all right. I'll tell you when you get here."

Storm's next call was to Brian Chang. He was out in the field, but she left a message for him, then one for Detectives Ursley and Yamamoto.

When Hamlin burst into the tent, she was having a third cup of hot chocolate and wearing one of the contest's logo T-shirts in a long-sleeved style. *The Intrepid* blazed across her chest in orange. Underneath, except for the emerald-eyed pig, she was nude, which felt a lot better than her clammy bathing suit bottoms and stiff, salt-encrusted hair.

Hamlin hugged her hard, let her go for a few minutes to listen to her story, then grabbed her again. One of the EMTs filled in with the part about the C & C rescue board, which had prompted the helicopter to look for a rider not entered in the contest. No one had seen an old City and County jet ski.

"Ian," Storm muffled into his shoulder, "could we go back to the cottage? I want a hot bath and dry clothes."

Hamlin went after his car, and bundled her in. He wrapped her in a big towel from her beach bag, which he'd been carrying around since she disappeared. "How are you feeling?"

"I'm tired, but I'm okay. Hamlin, I was really frightened, but I was even madder than I was scared. I wish I'd seen who did this to me."

Hamlin's eyes glinted with fury, and he was about to respond when Storm's cell phone rang. She dug it out of the beach bag. "Hi Brian, I'm glad you got my message. It's got to be the same person who killed Nahoa. I think it might be O'Reilly."

"Why do you say that?" Brian asked.

"Goober told me to talk to him."

"Storm, sit tight. Leila, Robbie, and I will be there in a few hours. Meanwhile, I'll get hold of someone in the North Shore Patrol District to come take a report."

Storm hung up and snuggled next to Hamlin. "All I want is a hot bath and to know that Goober is okay."

"I want to find the asshole who did this to you." Though he kept his eyes on the road, she could see the simmering rage in his narrow gaze.

"Me, too." Storm frowned. "Word is going to get out that Goober rescued me, and he's going to be the next target."

"The police will find Goober," Hamlin said. He looked over at her. "Unless he doesn't want to be found."

Storm chewed her lip. "He risked his life to come after me. He's not going to leave town."

"You're sure? He's a kid who avoids authority."

"He'll help."

Hamlin still looked doubtful. "I hope you're right."

"I hope he's safe."

The car's dashboard clock read 5:14. It would be dark in an hour, and Kamehameha Highway was clogged with departing spectators. Storm chewed a hangnail and observed Hamlin hunched over the steering wheel as if he could will the traffic to move faster.

Maybe they needed to think about something else. "What happened with the surf contest? Is everyone else okay?"

Hamlin leaned back, but tapped one hand on the wheel impatiently. "Kimo Hitashi is leading, but one of the Australians is only three points behind," Hamlin said. "Another guy needed fifteen stitches when he wiped out and his surfboard cut his head, and there was a search on for another surfer who had been swamped by a big wave."

Hamlin looked over at her. "Come to think of it, Barstow and a group of lifeguards asked O'Reilly to close down the meet an hour early. They were concerned because the wind was coming up and waves were getting blown out. It took some persuading before O'Reilly agreed."

"How'd Ben do?"

Hamlin shrugged. "He's got a few more points than his partner, the guy with the tattoos. They made the cut for the finals, but they're not in the top three."

"Did Barstow look happy?"

"He looked tense all day. Even the TV announcers picked up on it."

"Maybe he and O'Reilly haven't been seeing eye to eye for a while. Plus, he's got to be worried about Ben."

Which brought her thoughts back to Goober. O'Reilly would know that Goober had rescued her and was being sought by various rescue teams. The boy's peripatetic habits were known to his friends, but how many of them knew that his last residence had been O'Reilly's guest apartment? And what if he went back there for his belongings?

Both Hamlin and Storm, lost in their concerns, were quiet for the rest of the drive. At the cottage, Storm headed directly to the hot shower, and when she got out, two uniformed HPD officers were waiting in the cottage living room.

"We'll file a report with the detectives on your case," one officer told Storm. "They may give you a call later, but they're out on another case."

Storm repeated her account of how she was attacked and put in the cave while the officers recorded her statement.

"Have you found Goober?" she asked when she was finished. "He saved me."

"No, and we're looking," the officer said. "We've got people posted along the shoreline. There's even a Coast Guard helicopter searching."

When the officers left, Storm sank into the sofa. For a few minutes, she looked out of the cozy, brightly lit room, past the lanai, toward the blackness of the pounding ocean. "Hamlin, we've got to look for him."

"You heard the police. They've even got one of the big choppers involved."

Storm sat quietly for a few moments. Hamlin had brought a glass of wine, and she sipped it. She was grateful the authorities were out there, but she and his friends knew more about him. And she couldn't forget how he'd come when she needed help.

She took Hamlin's hand and squeezed it. "Please don't be upset with me, but I can't sit here and wonder where he is."

She picked up the phone on the end table next to the sofa. Sunny's answering machine picked up after four rings. "Sunny, call me back. It's important." She left the same message on Sunny's cell phone.

"Hamlin, I want to drive by O'Reilly's place."

Hamlin shook his head. "What are you going to do?"

"I've got a couple of questions for him. I also want to watch his reaction when he sees me."

"Storm, it's too dangerous."

"I doubt he'll be alone. And we'll call Brian and tell him what we're doing."

"Brian called while you were in the shower. They're on the road, but they ran into an accident on the H-2, around Wahiawa. Traffic's backed up. They'll be here around eight."

"We'll still tell Brian where we're going. He can tell the North Shore police. O'Reilly isn't going to do anything if you're there and we tell him the cops are on the way. But our showing up may keep him from hurting Goober."

"Storm, you've had a hell of a day."

"I'll be okay. You'll be with me. Hamlin, I owe Goober."

Hamlin paced the floor. "We don't go in his house, agreed?"

"Right," Storm said. "We'll talk to him outside."

Traffic from Laniakea to Chun's Reef was lighter than it had been when everyone was trying to get to the surf contest, but there were still more cars on the road than usual. It was seven o'clock and dark. Most people were headed toward them, out for a Saturday night in Haleiwa.

It took Storm and Hamlin about fifteen minutes to reach O'Reilly's neighborhood. Except for a light over the door, the house was dark.

"He's probably at dinner," Hamlin said, and pulled into the drive next to a dark Porsche Boxter. Storm couldn't tell if it was black or navy.

"I'm going to knock, anyway."

"I'm going with you." Hamlin got out of the car. "Looks like he's got an awesome view."

"It's a great house." Storm rapped on the front door, waited a few seconds, then tried the doorbell twice. They were about to leave when they heard soft footsteps approaching the door.

Ben opened it, and stood wordlessly in the dark foyer. Even in shadow, his face looked blotchy. "Storm. It's you," he said. "I'm glad you're here."

He didn't sound glad, and Storm could smell alcohol on his breath from five feet away. She felt a creeping dread. "Is Goober here?" she asked.

Ben shook his head, and when he spoke his voice cracked. "His body washed ashore down past Kalalua Point."

Storm felt as if she'd been punched in the stomach. She sagged against Hamlin, who put his arm around her. "Oh, no," was all she could say.

"When?" Hamlin asked. His voice was shaky.

"Dad just called, but I guess some people walking the shoreline found him about a half hour ago."

"Where's your dad?" Hamlin asked.

"Having dinner with O'Reilly and some of the media people."

"Where did they go?" she asked.

"Where'd they go?" Ben looked down at his bare feet and seemed to ponder the question. "Probably Damien's or Rosie's Diner."

Chapter Forty-two

Miles Hamasaki, Storm's first legal mentor, had always warned that a guy who answered a question with a question was lying. And Uncle Miles had interrogated a lot of individuals in his long, successful career. For a moment, Storm wanted to give Ben the benefit of the doubt. Maybe Barstow hadn't been specific about where they were going for dinner. But Ben would have just said that, wouldn't he? And he wouldn't be acting so strangely.

There was an awkward moment, with Hamlin looking back and forth between the two of them. "Okay," Storm said softly. "Thanks, Ben."

She turned without saying another word and went back to the car, where she slumped into the passenger seat. Hamlin was a half-second behind her.

"What does it mean if he's lying?" He started the car. "He couldn't have put you in the cave. He was surfing."

"He knows something he's not telling us."

"Why would Ben cover up for O'Reilly?" Hamlin backed the car out of the drive and started down the street. "For that matter, why would Goober?"

"Goober was desperate to be in the contest." She jutted her chin toward the Boxter. "And Ben's made a lot of money. He might try not to notice something squirrelly." She sighed.

"But Ben and Nahoa were good friends, right? Goober, too. Who'd put up with that shit, even if it did get you a Porsche?"

"Not just a car, Ian." Storm's voice was sad. "He's making thousands in endorsements and he's a top-ranked competitor on the world pro-surfing circuit. It's the big time."

"I still can't see it." Hamlin squinted into the rearview mirror, as if he could get a read on Ben by looking back at the house. "He's got his whole life to do that."

"He's been on a roller coaster lately, with his parents' divorce in the works. They're playing emotional ping-pong with him."

With that thought, Storm pulled out her phone and punched in a number. "Hello, Stephanie."

"Storm, thank God you're all right."

"I was lucky."

Stephanie's voice trembled. "Did you hear about Goober? It's on the news."

"I just saw Ben. He told me."

"Ben? Where is he?"

"At O'Reilly's house."

"Did you see Marty?" Stephanie was the only person who called him Marty.

"No, Ben was alone."

"Oh." Relief was apparent in Stephanie's voice.

"Just for curiosity, how did you know I was with Goober?"

"One of the EMTs in the medical tent is a friend of mine. She told me that you got picked up by a helicopter, and you were asking about a guy on a jet ski. Some people saw you with Goober earlier." Stephanie paused. "I saw him this morning at Starbucks. Some guys were razzing him about bombing his first wave. Goober has a pretty good sense of humor, but he didn't laugh. Then he said something odd."

"Like what?"

"He said things weren't what they thought. I'm not sure anyone knew what he meant. The rest of the guys got kind of quiet. Part of it was his attitude, you know?"

"What do you mean?"

Stephanie thought for a moment. "He looked sad. Goober's usually kind of happy-go-lucky, but he looked determined.

The way he put his head down and shoved open the door to leave."

"When was this?"

"About nine-thirty this morning."

"Stephanie, do you have any idea where I might find O'Reilly and your ex at this hour? Ben said they'd gone to dinner."

"They eat at Damien's sometimes." Stephanie didn't sound happy about this fact. "They usually come in late, around eight-thirty. They have a few drinks somewhere first and hash out plans for the next day."

"Where do they go for drinks?"

"Pipeline Pub & Grub. Or just to each others' houses."

"Thanks, Stephanie. If you see either of them, call me back, okay?"

"Sure. I'm really glad you're all right."

Storm hung up the phone and frowned. "The more I think about Ben, the stranger I find his behavior. I don't think Ben wished Goober harm, but they weren't that close. Do you think he'd be as upset as he appears to be?"

"You're right." Hamlin kept his eyes on the traffic, which moved slowly but steadily along in a string of red taillights. "He'd be bummed, but drinking alone in the dark is a bit extreme."

"Remember, they quarreled the first day we met them. The day Nahoa got the package with the *lei o manō*."

"You're right. Still, they were peers. Ben might feel the accident could have happened to him."

"Goober drowned because he came after me," Storm whispered. She sank in the seat.

Hamlin reached over and took her hand. "You don't know what happened after he left you."

Storm didn't answer.

"Storm, do you think Ben might have known where you'd been taken, too? And now he feels guilty because he didn't help rescue you?"

It made sense, but Storm didn't feel like it was the whole picture. "Maybe." She still needed to talk to O'Reilly. "We've got to turn around."

"I thought so," he said. "Barstow lives out past Sunset Beach, doesn't he?"

"Yes, and O'Reilly might be there."

She got out her phone and punched in the number to Sunny's mobile again. This time, Sunny answered. There was a lot of noise in the background, but Sunny shouted over it.

"Storm! Thank God! Dede, it's Storm." Storm heard another shriek over the background noise.

"Where are you?" asked Sunny.

"I'm in the car with Hamlin. We're looking for Steve O'Reilly. Where are you?"

"Pipeline Pub & Grub. My God, we just heard about Goober. And Buster DeSilva told us how you'd gone after him. We were so worried." Sunny's voice shrilled with distress. "Where did you go?"

"I'll tell you about it later. Is O'Reilly there?"

"Haven't seen him. Wait a sec." Storm could hear her ask Dede, and Dede shouted to another person. After a minute or so, Sunny came back with a negative. "What are you doing?"

"I need to talk to him. I'll explain later."

"If I see him, I'll call." Sunny paused. "And Storm, be careful."

"Right." Storm hung up thoughtfully. She wished she'd asked Sunny if Goober had told her anything about O'Reilly. Storm pondered calling Sunny back, maybe even asking her to come with them, but the bar was so noisy they were having a hard time communicating. It could wait a few hours.

"At least we won't be talking to O'Reilly alone," Hamlin said. "After this, can we relax and have dinner?"

Storm smiled at him. "You bet. By then, Leila, Brian, and Robbie will be here. They can join us."

"Sounds good."

Storm pushed the button she had programmed for Leila's cell, and Brian picked up. "Leila's driving," he explained. "We just passed Schofield."

"Perfect," Storm said. "Meet us at Kimo's Pizzeria in about an hour."

"Great. We're all starved."

"We are, too. If you get there first, order a pitcher."

They disconnected and Storm tucked the phone back into her sweatshirt pocket. She slouched in the seat and shivered. Her long ordeal in the ocean had thoroughly chilled her, and distress about Goober was nearly overwhelming. She trembled again.

"You all right?" Hamlin asked, and put his arm out. He drew her to him, like teenagers on a date.

She put her head on his shoulder. "I'll be a lot better when we get this over with."

"I bet. You know what you want to ask him?"

"I'm going to start with why Goober broke into my house. I hope he reveals what he was trying to find." She sat quietly for a moment. "I wonder if he found it."

"Maybe he saw Goober talking to you on the beach," Hamlin said.

"That's what I was thinking, too. And then he followed me when I ran after him."

Storm directed Hamlin into the subdivision where Barstow rented his beach house.

When he caught sight of the place, Hamlin whistled. "And I thought O'Reilly's house was nice. There's some money to be made in this business."

"It seems," Storm said dryly. The same modern globes that she'd noted before lined the wide drive. Probably solar energy. Slick, she thought.

"Doesn't look like anyone's home." Hamlin pulled in.

"He had the garage doors down when Stephanie and I were here, too. It's hard to tell if he's in or not."

"So let's find out." Hamlin set the parking brake. "What does a person do with a three-car garage in a vacation home?"

"I don't know. I'd settle for one." Storm's cottage in Honolulu had an open carport, typical of many Hawai'i homes.

They rang the doorbell. After a couple of minutes, when no one answered, Hamlin stepped back to peer through one of the tall windows. "Looks like a study," he said. "The computer's running. It's not even in sleep mode."

"Maybe they just left," Storm said, but she rang again.

"They would have driven right by us."

"You don't think we'd miss them? It's dark."

"Streets are too narrow. Besides, I was watching." Hamlin walked back to the door and rang, then banged loudly.

A moment later, Barstow threw open the door. He was a bit out of breath. "Hello, Storm. What a surprise. Sorry, I was working in the front of the house. Didn't hear you at first."

"This is my associate, Ian Hamlin. Sorry to drop in on you like this—"

"No problem. Come on in." Barstow gestured for them to enter and closed the door. He stuck out his hand to shake Hamlin's. "Nice to meet you." He looked to Storm. "Is this the attorney you wanted me to talk to?"

"Have you had another threat?" It seemed like a week had passed since she'd talked to him about Buster DeSilva.

"He hung around the whole meet today. Whispering to people, cozying up to the media." He turned to Hamlin. "I'd like to discuss this with you. I might need protection."

"We're here about another matter, but I can give you my contact number," Hamlin said.

"We wanted to talk to Steve O'Reilly. Is he around?" Storm asked.

"O'Reilly? He's on the way." He waved for them to follow. "Come on in. I can at least offer you a cocktail. He's always late."

Hamlin and Storm followed him to the front of the house. When they got to the front room, Hamlin's eyes lit up. The wall facing the ocean was entirely in glass, and shaped like a ship's prow. Outside the window, the ocean's dark expanse gave the impression the house was isolated, exclusive in its domain.

Hamlin let his gaze travel from the high cathedral ceiling to the natural bamboo flooring, on which lay a plush Chinese carpet in green and rose hues. He gestured to the natural stone fireplace. "Do you ever use that?"

"Sure, it got cool enough last night. Have a seat." He indicated a cushy leather sofa and walked to a wet bar in the back corner of the room.

Storm thought she heard a thump, and wondered if the surf hit a sea wall out front. It was too dark to see beyond the rail of the lanai outside the huge window. She was about to ask, but Barstow spoke first.

"What would you like to drink? Wine, beer, whiskey… I just opened a nice cabernet."

"That would be fine," Hamlin said.

Storm heard the thump again. It didn't seem as regular as breaking surf, plus the noise seemed to come from the back of the house. "I'll have the same," she said, and looked about for a clue as to where the noise came from. Maybe Barstow had a dog.

Hamlin had apparently noticed it, too. "Is that—"

Barstow held one glass of wine and took a step toward them. Hamlin rose to take it from him, but before Hamlin got to him, Barstow reached behind his back, pulled out a pistol and fired.

Chapter Forty-three

O'Reilly lay on top of a musty-smelling bed in a dark, unused guest room at the back of the house, trussed like a duck in a Chinatown market. At least he wasn't hanging from a hook, he told himself. Not yet, anyway. And he nearly choked on his fury. Who would fucking believe this?

What had Barstow said? It was hard to remember after that awful shock. The sonofabitch had tasered him. Knocked him down flat. Messed up his head, too—memories of the last hour or two were coming back in dribs and drabs. Like someone turning a film projector on and off.

This was unbelievable. Who would have thought the guy was wound so fucking tight? O'Reilly took a deep breath through his nose. But here he was, trying not to panic at the gag Barstow had stuffed in his mouth. His own sock, and some moldy old handkerchief.

Barstow had gone ballistic, then threatened to blackmail him. Blackmail him! O'Reilly snorted and flopped on the mattress, which squeaked with abuse, and banged the headboard against the wall. It gave him a sort of juvenile satisfaction, but shit, he could hardly breathe. Christ, he had to stay calm.

First, Barstow had told him he knew about the cocaine Goober had procured for him. Shit. Then he went on about how he had some local girl's father lined up to go to the local paper and accuse him of statutory rape. What girl, O'Reilly asked himself. The one you thought was a tourist? She wasn't fifteen, she was driving a car. But you didn't ask her age, did you, old buddy?

What had set Barstow off, anyway? More like *which* event had done it. Barstow had been getting more and more eccentric. He'd turned into a fanatic with those protein blender concoctions. Had to have one every morning, his special ritual, with *awa* and some other crazy Hawaiian remedies.

Jesus, maybe he should have seen this coming. They'd been arguing over everything the past few days, from the lineup to whether to call the meet early this afternoon.

O'Reilly sagged into the mattress. He had to think about this whole thing. His first real glimmer of Barstow's instability, though he hadn't seen it as such, was his reaction to Pua's appearance. It wasn't anything O'Reilly couldn't handle. In fact, she'd looked great and he'd found he wanted to talk to her. Apologize, even.

But Barstow had called security, then pelleted O'Reilly with questions. He couldn't let it go, wanted to know all about her, and what O'Reilly's relationship had been with her.

O'Reilly could see now where he'd fucked up, but he'd had no idea Barstow was as bad as this. He was just trying to needle him, show him that they both had faults, get him off his back. So he'd made a comment about how Barstow had manipulated the slate of contestants. Letting him know that he was aware two qualified surfers had been bumped from the contest so that Ben and Goober could compete.

O'Reilly remembered the flickering light behind Barstow's squinting stare and got very still. O'Reilly admitted to himself that in many ways, he'd been a self-involved fuck-wad. But he'd also been working his ass off trying to make the Intrepid a world-class event. He felt like a juggler keeping ten balls and a dozen spinning plates aloft, simultaneously trying to pull money from the air.

He'd done it, too. The contest was a booming success. But he'd lost track of things, too. People, that is.

Goober had tried to warn him, but he'd been too busy to listen. The kid had come back to the house this morning after Barstow left and started spouting some pretty wild stuff. Something about Barstow using a cave and stealing a warrior's *mana* through his teeth.

Teeth? O'Reilly still had no idea what he was talking about. Goober's timing, as usual, sucked. O'Reilly was already ten minutes late leaving the house for an interview with five—count 'em—TV networks. PR was the bedrock of this business.

But he should have paid attention. O'Reilly sucked air through his nose and struggled against the line around his wrists. The headboard banged the wall again. He'd make it up to the kid, send him to college or something. He should have listened.

Chapter Forty-four

It happened in slow motion, yet so fast that Storm felt like she was frozen in a nightmare. She could only yelp in confusion and dread. Oddly, the gun didn't bang. It made a hissing pop, which at first Storm thought was a silencer. Then she saw the two wires shoot out and stick in Hamlin's chest.

Hamlin yelped with pain, bent over, and dropped to the floor. Aghast, Storm recognized the way she'd been brought down earlier in the day. Barstow had a taser, a kind of stun gun. She'd never seen one before, but she'd heard Brian and other members of the police force discuss them.

Though frantic with worry for Hamlin, she knew he hadn't been shot with a bullet and he would recover. She also figured the wires had to stay in contact with him, so her first priority was to pull them out.

"Ian," she shrieked, and dashed toward his twitching form.

Jesus, what was all that blood? He was bleeding—a lot. His face was covered, and it was dripping onto the bamboo floor, brilliant red against the blonde wood.

Barstow took a step toward Storm. "Not another step," he shouted.

"You pea-balled, spineless jellyfish." She kept coming.

Barstow pulled the trigger again and Storm, horrified, watched Hamlin convulse. She didn't see Barstow's free hand swing at her head, but she felt the impact. He'd struck her flat-handed, a blow that knocked her to her knees between the couch and the heavy glass coffee table.

Storm shook her head, dazed. Her eyes watered with shock. Unbelievable. He'd actually hit her. Rage decelerated the tableau to slow motion. He would not get away with this.

Still on her knees, Storm grabbed the big crystal vase on the glass coffee table. She didn't even bother to dump out the water and sunflowers. Like a potted shrub held between her and Barstow, she jumped into a surfer's balanced crouch, aimed, and hurled.

In the split second before the vase connected, Barstow's squinty leer flicked back and forth between Hamlin's prone body and Storm's advancing one. Like a gluttunous rat, he couldn't decide who posed the greater risk. Chauvinist to the end, he chose the male as the bigger threat.

The vase connected with a noise like a cantaloupe on concrete and Barstow crashed to the floor. He also released the gun, which skittered under a rosewood cabinet.

Hamlin moaned, and Storm jerked the probes from his shirt front. "Hamlin, can you hear me?"

She groped in her sweatshirt for her cell phone, and struggled to hold her shaking hand still enough to speed-dial Leila and Brian. She needed cops and an ambulance.

Before she could bring the phone to her ear, the crash of breaking glass brought her to her feet. Someone was breaking into the house.

Afraid it might be an accomplice of Barstow's, perhaps O'Reilly, Storm jumped up and grabbed the vase, which was thankfully still in one piece. She flattened herself against the wall, out of sight of anyone entering the room. If it was more than one person, she didn't have a chance, but she had to protect Hamlin, who was still down and helpless.

"Storm?" He sounded weak and confused.

Loud footsteps, those of several people, clattered down the hall. "Storm!" a woman's voice called. "Are you here? Are you okay?"

Storm leaned against the wall in relief and lowered the vase. "Sunny?"

Ben, Sunny, and Dede raced into the room. "Oh," Ben cried. "It's true." He dropped to his knees, his eyes on his father. He didn't approach him, though. Instead, he looked at Hamlin, who held his hand over a gash on his forehead and struggled to sit up.

Sunny and Dede ran to Storm, then to Hamlin. "Thank God. We were so scared for you we broke the front window to get in."

All three turned their attention to Hamlin. Dede ran to the kitchen, and came back with a wet dish towel and a zip-lock bag of ice.

Storm threw her arms around him. "How are you feeling?"

"Kinda shaky, to be honest." He shook his head. "I'll be okay, though."

Dede peered at him. "You need stitches."

Storm told them about the taser.

"Your head must have hit the edge of the coffee table," Dede said.

"I was helpless. I couldn't avoid it," Hamlin said.

Storm looked at Sunny and Dede. "How'd you know where we were?"

"You said you were going to talk to O'Reilly," Sunny said. "Goober had told me something bad was happening with the surf contest, and he needed to talk to O'Reilly. Then he died. So I called Ben to see if he knew where you'd gone."

"How'd you know I'd talked to Ben?" Storm asked.

"Stephanie called me," Sunny said.

Storm was going to ask for more information, but an electronically-transmitted shouting got all their attention. "Did you leave a phone off the hook?" Sunny asked.

"It's coming from the couch," Dede said. "And it's calling your name."

"Hold on," Storm shouted. She grappled under a cushion for the mobile phone she'd dropped when she heard the glass break.

"Storm, what's going on?" Brian Chang yelled. Storm could hear Leila in the background, asking what was happening.

Storm told him where she was and what she knew. She also asked for an ambulance.

"We're on the way," Brian said.

Chapter Forty-five

"Is he dead?" Ben's voice was sad. Except for his splayed limbs, Barstow looked like a funeral corpse, piled with sunflowers.

Dede felt his neck for a pulse. "No, he's alive." She saw the taser filaments on the floor and pulled the gun from under the cabinet. "One of us had better watch him until the police get here." She peered at the gun. "I wonder if we could use this on him."

Sunny looked at Ben. "Tell Storm what you told me."

Ben sighed heavily. "I saw the bowl."

Storm frowned at him. "What bowl?"

"The artifact. A calabash, you know, with the teeth. Dad said it was very rare, that only a few private collectors had them anymore."

"What did he tell you about them?"

"That the winner of a battle took the teeth of the losing warrior to gain his power and spirit. His *mana*."

"Your dad has one of these bowls?"

"Yes." Ben whispered his next words. "And I think he's making one of his own."

"Holy Mother of God," Storm breathed, and sank down next to Hamlin.

Sunny and Dede stared at Ben. "You didn't tell us that," Sunny said.

Ben just looked at the floor, deflated. "I wasn't supposed to see it. That's when I decided he was losing it."

No one spoke for several moments. Storm wondered if Sunny and Dede knew about Ken Matsumoto's and Nahoa's missing teeth. She didn't want to be the one to tell them. It was just too awful.

"What's that noise?" Sunny asked. "Something thumped."

"I heard that before," Storm said.

"Me, too." Hamlin struggled to his feet. "It's upstairs."

Ben and Dede stayed to watch Barstow, but Sunny, Storm, and Hamlin found the staircase, a wide, modern affair up which all three of them barged. It didn't take them long to find the room where O'Reilly was tied. When they opened the door, they found that he'd slid off the bed and was attempting to roll across the floor.

Sunny pulled a Swiss Army knife out of the pocket in her cargo shorts and cut the gag off him, then sawed through the nylon line around his arms and ankles.

"Are you okay?" she asked him.

"Yeah." His bloodshot eyes showed white around the blue-gray irises. They darted from Sunny's face, to Hamlin's, and to Storm's.

"Where's Barstow?" he gasped.

"Storm knocked him out." Sunny gestured toward Storm, who stared at the man with a mixture of mistrust and astonishment.

From the guy's behavior, it looked like Barstow had turned on him, too. But how much had he known about Barstow's activities? Had he actually confronted the man? Or had he somehow stopped fitting into Barstow's sick and deluded plans?

O'Reilly's eyes dropped to the ground. His hair stood up in clumps, his wrists bled from the nylon line that had bound them, and his elbows and knees were abraded from his struggle across the carpeted floor. The frayed khaki shorts he wore were stained and he smelled of urine.

He took a staggering step and shook his head from side to side. "He's crazy, you know."

"Probably," Sunny said. She took his arm and led him out the door to the top of the stairs. "Can you walk okay? We've called an ambulance."

Storm and Hamlin followed, ready to catch him if he stumbled. Hamlin still held ice to his oozing forehead. The paper towel that was wrapped around the zip-lock bag was bloody. They were halfway down the staircase when the police pounded on the front door. It sounded as if a battalion had arrived. Piercing blue lights flashed through the broken window.

"Storm, Hamlin," a man's voice shouted. Storm recognized Brian Chang's voice.

"We're okay," Hamlin yelled back, and opened the door.

Five or six officers burst in, all wearing Kevlar vests. They put away their drawn weapons when they saw the calm but bedraggled welcoming committee. Detectives Yamamoto and Ursley followed the wave of armed police, with Brian close behind.

EMTs were the next group to enter, with a gurney and equipment. Some of them went directly inside while two approached O'Reilly, who sagged against the wall. Sadness and defeat permeated his demeanor.

"Where's Goober?" he asked, and when no one answered, he grew paler. Detective Yamamoto and the EMTs led him outside to a waiting ambulance.

Hamlin, Sunny, and Storm followed Detective Ursley and Brian into the house. "Dede and Ben are watching Barstow," Hamlin explained to Brian.

Brian watched Ursley direct her officers to keep their eyes on the still-unconscious Barstow while the emergency techs loaded him onto the gurney, then put his hand on Hamlin's shoulder. "Let's have someone look at that gash."

"It's not that bad," Hamlin said. "Head wounds just bleed a lot." He lifted the bag of ice for a moment.

"Ugh. He can't see it, can he, Storm?" Brian said.

"You need stitches," Storm said.

Ursley looked over at Storm and Hamlin. "Get on over to Kahuku Emergency Room. We'll talk to you after."

Leila and Robbie had ventured in now that the danger had passed. Leila hugged Storm. "It was so scary when you dropped the phone."

"We could hear everything that was happening," Robbie said.

"We finally figured out you were okay." Leila looked grim. "But we also knew someone was hurt."

A hush had fallen and Storm and Leila turned to watch Ben enter the kitchen. With Ursley behind him, he knelt to rummage in a cabinet. First, he extracted a commercial-sized blender and set it on the counter. Then he got out a box labeled with a popular protein additive.

"Dad had some herbs. He's always been spiritual," Ben said. "He thought he could win mom back, you know."

Storm's heart squeezed. The boy still wanted to look up to his dad and defend his actions. No wonder it had taken him a while to recognize that he'd gone overboard.

Ben leaned down, dug further back into the cupboard, and came up with a nondescript, brown corrugated box, about a cubic foot in size. He put it on the counter, then turned away. "It's in there. I…I think he was using it for his special drinks."

Detective Ursley, who wore gloves, opened it. No one spoke. Even Brian Chang, who was out of his territory and stood by to support his colleagues, froze with part-fascination, part-dread. His eyes slid to Storm's. He nodded gently, a move only she and Leila saw.

Leila moved away with her hand on Robbie's shoulder, so that he went with her.

Storm hesitated a moment, just long enough to see Ursley pull out a wooden bowl.

White inlays shone around the upper rim. Those would be human molars.

Storm turned her back. It had been years since she'd seen one of these, but she didn't need to see another. Especially if she knew the tooth donors. No wonder the Bishop Museum no longer left them on display.

Hamlin made a low, sad noise, and pivoted away, too.

Suddenly, Brian was beside them. "Time to get that head looked at." He nodded toward Ursley, as if to remind Hamlin it was time to obey her directive. "We'll meet you at the medical center."

"Give me your keys. It's my turn to drive," Storm said. She was mildly surprised when Hamlin handed them over without protest.

Storm and Hamlin spent about ten minutes in the waiting room before an ER physician appeared to lead them into an examining room. Just as they stood up to follow, Detective Yamamoto approached them.

"I'd like to ask you some questions when you're done," he said.

"You might as well come in," Hamlin said to him. "I'd like the distraction."

Everyone looked to the doctor, who shrugged. "It's up to you."

Hamlin, Yamamoto, and Storm all winced when the doctor began to inject around the wound on Hamlin's forehead with Lidocaine.

"Ouch," Hamlin said. "That stings." He looked at Yamamoto. "Talk to me."

"Tell me why you went to see Barstow," the detective said.

Storm let Hamlin do most of the talking, though the detective wanted to hear her version of her experience in the cave. Now that she knew Goober hadn't survived, the telling was even more disturbing, especially when she got to the part where Goober had taken the jet ski.

She choked up. "I thought he had a better chance than I did. Now I think he knew it didn't have enough gas. And I had the only surfboard."

Yamamoto's expression was sympathetic. "You thought Goober robbed your house?"

Storm twisted her hands together. "His words were, 'Talk to O'Reilly.' So I thought O'Reilly made him break into the cottage."

She looked miserable. "But now I think he was telling me who I needed to see to put the story together."

"That jibes with what I've been hearing." Yamamoto looked grim. "But it was probably Barstow who made him do it. It looks like Barstow offered him a spot in the lineup for doing certain jobs." The detective glanced at his notes. "It was Barstow who pushed to shorten today's meet, which coincided with the spreading rumor that you'd been rescued from the water and were in the medical tent."

Yamamoto continued. "O'Reilly saw Goober give you something. But he didn't know what it was. Nor did he know that you'd followed Goober off the beach."

"Have you talked to any of the other surfers?" Storm asked.

Yamamoto nodded. "Seems like the day Matsumoto disappeared, Barstow and he had a big confrontation in the water. From what I hear, Matsumoto was kind of a rich kid with a big ego. He made a big deal of accusing Barstow of snaking him."

"What?" Hamlin asked.

"Dropping in on his wave," Storm explained. "Among surfers, it's considered stealing."

She remembered how Gabe had snaked Sunny. That day, it had been a direct threat. She frowned. "That was a week before Nahoa died. Were Barstow and O'Reilly in the islands?"

"Barstow was, though he'd told O'Reilly he was in California, working on a real estate deal. Ben told us he'd met his father for lunch, but Ben wasn't to let anyone know he was in town." Yamamoto shook his head. "Ben's almost an adult, but it was still painful for him. The father kept chipping away at the relationship with the mother, but still wanted her back. And he wanted his son's respect."

"He was insecure," Storm said.

"Seems that way. The way he played the kid."

Storm stared down at the worn linoleum floor. An idea had flitted through her mind, and she struggled to regain it. She looked up suddenly. "Ken Matsumoto died of a head wound, right?"

"He had some water in his lungs, but the head wound would have been fatal. He had a V-shaped wound, consistent with the nose of a surfboard. We're looking for the board."

"Talk to Moʻo Lanipuni. He may recognize the board, or its shaper."

"Thanks, I will."

"Did you talk to Gabe Watson?"

Yamamoto snorted. "Another big ego. He said Matsumoto was buying his way onto the lineups of some of the meets. Specifically, the Sunset Triple Pro."

Storm wasn't finished with her hunch, though. "Did Nahoa die as a result of a head injury?"

"No, water in his lungs showed that he drowned." Yamamoto was on her train of thought. "You're thinking about the taser, right? Unfortunately, he'd been in the water too long for the ME to tell if he'd been zapped."

"I was afraid of that," she said. She watched Hamlin rub the area where the barbs had stuck. They'd left red welts on his skin.

"Can you prove Barstow killed Matsumoto and Nahoa?" she asked.

"We're working on it. We've got the teeth, but I hope Barstow will brag or want to justify his actions. A lot of people knew about that cave." Yamamoto tapped his pen on his notebook. "It's too bad Goober's not here to share what he knew."

The detective asked a couple more questions, then left Hamlin and Storm about the time the ER doc handed Hamlin a prescription for painkillers. They thanked the doctor and made their way into the ER waiting room.

O'Reilly sat in one of the molded plastic chairs, his head in his hands. Someone had given him a faded T-shirt and some rubber slippers. He looked up at them. "Do you have a minute? Please?"

"Let's go outside," Hamlin said. "I could use some fresh air."

"Me too," O'Reilly said. His skin was still pasty. Bruise-hued skin underscored his eyes.

Out in the nearly deserted parking lot, O'Reilly folded his arms across his chest. Storm looked up at the sky, which was brilliant with stars. The cloud cover had dissipated to a few wisps, which tumbled across the indigo expanse like scraps of lace. For a few minutes, no one spoke.

O'Reilly broke the silence. "What's that term surfers use when you're held deep underwater and everything is the same color? You can't even tell up from down?"

"The green room," Storm said.

"Yeah." O'Reilly sighed. "That's where I've been. I wanted to say how sorry I am."

Storm gazed at him. The man looked like he'd been to hell and back. "I've been there," she said softly.

"Me too," Hamlin said.

"Goober tried to tell me, but I got carried away with the idea of success and greed." They had to strain to hear O'Reilly speak. "He was a good kid. I guess you know that."

"He was," Storm said. "I think he got sucked into it too, for a while."

O'Reilly nodded. "Maybe. But he figured it out."

"So did you," Storm said.

"Not soon enough." O'Reilly finally met their eyes. "I was too wrapped up in my own issues." He scuffed his slippers against the blacktop.

"I feel responsible for Goober, too," Storm said.

O'Reilly looked up at the stars and shivered a little. For a few minutes no one spoke.

"You said you'd been there before. Does it get any better?" O'Reilly's voice was soft and low.

Storm grimaced and hoped he couldn't see her face in the dark. She remembered her dream, and how she had felt responsible for Bert Pi'ilani's death. Why had she survived when he hadn't? How was she going to deal with Goober's death, now?

"I'm not sure," she said. "But you find a way to live with it."

She looked over at Hamlin, whose eyes were dark pools in the starlight. He knew, too. He'd survived his brother.

O'Reilly nodded. Storm thought she heard him sniff.

"You want a ride?" Hamlin asked.

He looked up as if Hamlin's question had startled him from thoughts a hundred miles away.

"The moon's bright tonight," he said. "I'll walk. I can use the exercise." He gave them a twisted smile, though his eyes stayed sad.

"You sure? You're a ways from your house."

"I'll be okay." He shrugged. "I need to think. Some people jog farther than I'm going."

Storm and Hamlin walked to the car. "You think he'll be all right?" Hamlin asked when they got out of earshot.

"Yeah, I do," Storm said. O'Reilly was learning some tough lessons, but she had a hunch he was also going to find a core of strength when he faced them.

"He's growing up."

And so am I, she thought.

Glossary

'āina—land, earth

'aumakua—family totem

ama—arm of an outrigger canoe

awa—*Piper methysticum,* shrub known in some Pacific regions as Kava. Used as a drink at special ceremonies, also for medicinal purposes.

hali'a—nostalgia

hanohano—honor

haole—originally meant stranger, but has evolved to mean white person.

ho'oponopono—to correct, to put in order or put to rights, mental cleansing, family conferences in which relationships are set right

huhū—angry, irritated

kai—ocean

kaki mochi—salty crackers, a local snack

kapu—taboo, forbidden

keiki—child

keiki hānau o ka ʻāina—native son, literally a "child the land gave birth to"

kolohe—mischievous, naughty

kōnane—ancient game resembling checkers, used to teach strategic thinking to warriors

kuleana—concern, business, responsibility

kumu—teacher

lōlō—crazy

lomilomi—to massage, or to crush

lua—ancient Hawaiian martial art, extensive study in the art of life and death

luaʻai—series of bone breaking techniques in the art of lua

makai—toward the ocean, as opposed to mauka, or toward the mountains

make—dead

malihini—newcomer, stranger

manju—popular island pastry, usually filled with coconut, sweet beans, or fruit

nori—seaweed used to make sushi

pau—over, done with

popo—Chinese for grandfather

pūpule—crazy, reckless, wild

ʻuku—body louse (plural?)

ule—penis

References

Readers who wish to learn more about surfing in Hawai'i may enjoy the following:

The Big Drop: Classic Big Wave Surfing Stories, edited by John Long and Hai-Van K. Sponholz, Falcon Publishing Inc., Helena, Montana, 1999.

Surfing Hawaii, Leonard and Lorca Lueras, Periplus Editions (HK) Ltd., Singapore, 2000.

Surf Rage, by Nat Young, Nymboida Press, 8 Bay Street, Angourie, NSW, 2462 Australia, 2000.

For more information on the Eddie Aikau Big Wave Invitational, which last took place at Waimea Bay on December 15, 2004, visit http://www.quiksilver.com/eddie_aikau_04 .

For information on tow-in surfing, including links and great photos, go to http://www.towsurfer.com/index.asp .

To receive a free catalog of Poisoned Pen Press titles, please contact us in one of the following ways:

Phone: 1-800-421-3976
Facsimile: 1-480-949-1707
E-mail: info@poisonedpenpress.com
Website: www.poisonedpenpress.com

Poisoned Pen Press
6962 E. First Ave. Ste. 103
Scottsdale, AZ 85251